Run To Me

Cynthia Eden

This book is a work of fiction. Any similarities to real people, places, or events are not intentional and are purely the result of coincidence. The characters, places, and events in this story are fictional.

Published by Cynthia Eden.

Proof-reading by: J. R. T. Editing

CHAPTER ONE

"You are the most beautiful woman in the room."

Willow couldn't help but tense as the rich, masculine voice seemed to wrap right around her. She'd heard him approaching, of course, and she'd known that he was closing in on her. She could feel him right behind her, not touching her, but now barely a whisper away.

She lifted the champagne flute to her lips and took a slow sip. The sweet liquid bubbled on her tongue, and she rather liked that feeling. What she didn't like…

Willow turned to face the man who'd just complimented her. Tall and absolutely gorgeous, Jennings "Jay" Maverick seemed to dominate the ballroom. He wore a black tux that emphasized his golden tan, and his dark, blond hair wasn't tousled for once. Instead, he'd shoved it back in a style that just emphasized his high cheekbones and the rough cut of his jaw.

More men in tuxes were behind him—dancing and flirting with women in gorgeous gowns. People who seemed to not have any cares at all. People who laughed and drank and had normal lives.

People who were not like her. "I don't want to be here," Willow whispered. She put her hand on his tux, right above his heart. "*Why* am I here?" He'd bought her a dress, some little piece of black silk that felt like heaven against her skin—she wouldn't lie about that—but the dress didn't seem to be her style.

Not that Willow had any idea what her style was.

Hell, she wasn't even sure that *Willow* was her real name. She didn't know a thing about her past or her life. But every instinct she had screamed that she'd never been the type for these fancy ballrooms. She didn't fit in with these people, and part of her just wanted to vanish.

But Jay's hand rose and his fingers—long and strong—curled around her hand. He was tall, over six feet, and he leaned toward her, his pose almost protective.

Not that she needed protecting. She was stronger than everyone in that room. Mostly because they were *normal* humans. And she…wasn't.

I don't know what I am.

"You are the most beautiful woman here," he said again, his voice a sensual rasp. His eyes—a deep, dark brown—held hers. There was gold in the depths of his gaze. Gold that could burn with his anger. But he wasn't angry right then. She wasn't quite sure what he was. "You're beautiful, Willow. So you don't need to stand in the corner, away from everyone. You don't need to hide a thing about yourself from the people here."

Oh, he was so wrong. This was his world. Rich and powerful. Because Jay was apparently *the* man of the hour. A tech billionaire who could have anyone or anything he wanted with a snap of his fingers. But…

He can't have me.

"The people here would freak out," Willow told him, her voice soft, "if they knew the truth about me."

The truth—that she was a lab experiment gone wrong. Part of the top secret Project Lazarus. A dead woman walking, literally.

She pulled her hand away from his. "How much longer do we need to stay? Haven't I been on display long enough?" Granted, she *had* been standing in the corner, but she'd entered the ballroom on Jay's arm. She'd walked into the building with him courtesy of an actual red carpet. Dozens of cameras had flashed at their entrance. She'd been seen by everyone, and Willow knew that was the point. Jay was using her to attract attention. Or rather, to attract specific attention.

Jay was hunting a very dangerous predator, and he was using her as bait in his hunt.

A muscle flexed along his jaw. "No, you haven't been on display long enough." His voice had roughened. Behind him, the band began to play a new song. A slow, sensual song. "Let's dance," Jay demanded.

Dance? Willow knew horror must have shown on her face. But it was too late to stop him because Jay had pulled her away from the wall. Eyes were instantly on them as he made his way to the dance floor, taking her with him.

Wherever Jay went, gazes followed. Women flirted. Men vied for his attention. Money truly did talk.

And, of course, the fact that Jay was sexy as hell just made him more of a media obsession.

He took her right to the middle of the dance floor. Pulled her close. Put one hand at the base of her spine, touching her skin because there *was* no back to the dress he'd picked out. His other hand cradled her palm, holding her carefully.

His head lowered toward her, and Willow turned her face to his ear, hissing, "I can't dance," even as she felt a flood of heat stain her cheeks. This was going to be another humiliation for her. Another in a long line.

She had no memories of her past. No idea who she'd been before she woke in some godforsaken North Carolina lab. She'd been put in Project Lazarus, and Willow had lost her life. When she'd escaped that facility, she'd made the mistake of trusting the wrong man—a killer. If Jay hadn't helped her, if he hadn't gotten her to a safe place…

"Fuck me, baby," Jay rasped. "I'm sorry. I didn't think…Look, all you have to do is just hold on to me."

*He didn't think…*Hadn't realized that while she might know how to kill a man in a hundred different ways, she didn't know how to dance. Didn't know how to laugh and flirt and act like she was a normal woman.

He pulled her even closer. The couples around them were moving in sync, doing *much* more advanced dancing. Were those couples waltzing or something? She didn't know. Willow just wrapped her arm around Jay's neck and buried her hot face against his tux.

She wanted this night to end.

"One foot," Jay murmured, and now his mouth was near her ear. He'd curled his body into hers, and she felt almost protected. "Then the other. Just move with me. Sway. That's all you have to do. Close your eyes and listen to the music."

Her eyes closed.

His hand tightened on hers. "I've got you."

The safety of his arms was a lie. She was smart enough to know that. She couldn't trust

Jay. Jay *was* Project Lazarus. He'd been the guy to help bankroll the operation. And now he was there, with her, because he was trying to atone. The guy didn't get it. You *couldn't* atone for some things in this world.

But she kept her eyes closed. She listened to the music. And she found her body moving in a slow, natural rhythm with his. They seemed to flow together as they moved across the dance floor. Murmurs teased her ears, whispers that she hadn't been intended to overhear, but Willow's senses didn't work like an average human's.

"Who is she?"

"Jay's newest lover isn't what I expected. He usually goes for a more cultured sort."

"I'd fuck her."

At that last, rough pronouncement, Willow stiffened. "I'd like to leave now." Her head lifted. "I've been on display for long enough." She'd done her part. Now she was getting out of there. And if Jay didn't like it, too bad.

But instead of another argument, he gave a grim nod. Then he took her arm and tucked it into the crook of his elbow. He didn't look to the left or the right as he led her out of the ballroom. Her heart was about to jump right out of her chest, and her high heels clicked over the gleaming floor. They were just at the wide, double doors when—

"Leaving so soon?" A tall, handsome man with dark, coffee skin had stepped into their path. West Harper. Jay's best-friend. His head of security. And his only family. West raised one brow. "I think the party is just getting started."

Jay shook his head. "Willow's done." His voice didn't carry past their little group. "And if one more man looks at her like he can't wait to get her naked, I'm going to lose my shit."

Willow blinked. "Um, what?"

Jay turned his face toward her. The gold in his eyes was definitely burning. "Lose. My. Shit." Each word was growled. "They are practically drooling, and I'm about to kick some asses."

West clapped a hand on Jay's shoulder. "Seriously, *when* is the last time you kicked ass? Remind me again?"

Jay bared his teeth at the other man. "Don't push me right now. It's been one hell of a night."

She actually thought West was the only guy who *could* push him. Jay didn't let anyone get close to him—well, no one but West—and she knew that was because those two had known each other for so long.

It must be nice to have a past with someone else. Actually, it must be nice to *have* a past at all.

"Stay at the party as long as you want," Jay muttered. "I'm taking Willow home. You and I can talk tomorrow."

A waiter came by with a tray full of champagne flutes. West snagged one, and then *he* was snagged by a gorgeous lady in red.

"Let's go, Willow." Jay's voice was still clipped as they marched toward the elevator. Since she was more than ready to get out of that place, she kept a quick pace with him.

Several people tried to stop Jay as they closed in on the elevator. People were trying to push ideas and apps at him, but Jay just shook his head. "Not now. Call my office."

An attendant held the elevator for him, and the same attendant made sure that only Willow and Jay got on the elevator.

"You need anything, Mr. Maverick?" The attendant's gaze was wide, more than a little star struck. Apparently, being a tech billionaire was better than being a movie star. She'd been told a few of those had been in the ballroom. She hadn't particularly cared to find out their identities.

"Make sure my car is waiting downstairs." Jay's hand reached out and shook the attendant's. Willow saw the younger guy quickly pocket the money Jay had slipped him in that casual touch.

"Absolutely." The attendant's smile was huge. "You have a great night, Mr. Maverick."

The elevator doors slid closed. Right before they did, Willow was pretty sure she saw a woman in a glittering, blue grown snapping a pic with her phone.

And then…

Silence.

Such a blessed relief. "I don't like being in crowds." She stood with her shoulders against the back of the elevator. The walls were covered with mirrors, and her own reflection stared back at her. "I'm sorry if I was a-a disappointment tonight—"

"You could *never* be that." And he caught her hand. At his touch, a little, electric spark seemed to shoot through her body. That always happened when he touched her. She became too aware, too sensitive.

Turned on.

He moved closer, putting his body in front of hers. They'd been on the top floor, so the elevator ride would take a little time, she knew that. Time in which she'd be alone with Jay.

His gaze held hers. "Every man there wanted to fuck you."

Now Willow winced. "Not exactly what I wanted to hear."

"My damn fault." Now his gaze dropped to her body. "The dress…"

"*You* bought it."

"And you make it look like a fantasy."

That was, well, rather nice.

Jay shook his head. "You'll be unforgettable. To the men and the women. That was the point." He let go of her hand. Took a step back.

Straightened his shoulders. "Your picture will be in the press. On the Internet. You'll go worldwide, baby. Somewhere out there, someone will recognize your face."

That was good and bad. "How much longer do I have to be bait?"

Now he flinched. "It's not just about you being bait." His voice was guttural. "It's about finding your past. It's about—"

"It's about you wanting to hunt down Wyman Wright." *Wyman Wright.* Just saying the name made her tense. Wyman Wright was the man who'd set the wheels in motion for Project Lazarus. The man who'd chosen the test subjects, the man who'd turned them into monsters.

Wyman Wright was also the man who'd seemed to vanish—quite literally—off the face of the earth. Only Jay thought he could coax Wyman out of hiding. Jay thought that Wyman would come after Willow.

And that's why I'm bait.

The elevator dinged. They'd reached the ground floor.

The doors started to slide open.

Jay reached out his hand and pressed a button on the elevator control panel. Immediately, the doors closed. The elevator didn't move.

But Willow's heart raced a little faster.

"I want to make things right." His face had tensed, and his gaze seemed to burn.

And there it was again. His guilt. Always between them. "I'm not some pet project." Her words came out angry, crisp. "Not some mistake you just get to wipe away." But...*wasn't* she a mistake? Her chest ached, and she lifted her hand, pressing her palm against her racing heart.

"You're not a mistake." His gaze burned. "You could never be that."

He moved toward her once more. Very, very close. And his hands rose to curl around her shoulders. She stiffened because that electric awareness was there again, and Willow tried to retreat, but there was nowhere to go. Her back was pressed to the mirror behind her.

Emotions swirled inside of her. Dark and twisting. Sometimes, *she* was twisted, too. She could do things, such bad things. She could slip into a person's mind and turn fears into reality. She'd...hurt people.

And Willow knew she'd hurt others in the future. *That* was who she was.

"You shouldn't touch me," she reminded him, her voice hushed. "You know touching me is dangerous."

Because if she touched her prey, it gave her power. The power to slip right into her prey's mind—

"Do I look afraid?"

She blinked. No, he didn't look afraid. He looked—

"Ever wonder what it would be like if we kissed, Willow?"

Her lips parted in surprise. Heat stained her cheeks because she felt as if he'd just gotten into her mind. Yes, she wondered. She fantasized, even though she knew it was wrong. He wouldn't want to be with someone like her. He felt guilty, that was all.

"Because I do," Jay continued in his dark, rumbling voice. "I wonder about it, oh, a thousand times a day. I think you wonder, I think you feel the need, too. This…desire. This craving."

"It's not natural." Her voice was so low.

But the narrowing of his eyes told her that he'd heard her words. "Why do you say that?"

Because nothing about her was natural. She'd come back from the dead. She *was* a monster. Maybe she was evil. She didn't know. Willow didn't answer his question. She stood there, feeling the heat of his body press to hers, inhaling his crisp, masculine scent.

And she fought her need.

"Do you want me, Willow?"

Her lashes lowered, concealing her gaze. She needed him to back away. Her emotions were all over the place and… "You're the man who financed Project Lazarus." She made her voice flat. Willow eased out a low breath, schooled her expression, and forced herself to meet his stare once more. "How do you think I feel about you?"

Jay flinched. His hands immediately fell away from her shoulders. "Right. My mistake." He backed up.

She missed his warmth.

Her hands fisted at her sides because Willow *almost* reached out to him. She couldn't do that, though. Touching—her touch—was too deadly.

He turned toward the control panel, giving her his back. "Let's go home." Suddenly, he sounded weary. Weary beyond belief. "Don't forget, when the doors open and we head outside, cameras will be flashing." He glanced over his shoulder. "So just try to pretend that you don't hate me."

The doors opened. He offered his arm to her.

She looped her arm with his. *I don't hate you.* She didn't. Her high heels clicked on the gleaming, marble floor. Attendants rushed to open the lobby's double doors for them, and then the cold night air was whipping against them. Jay bent protectively toward her as cameras flashed. Voices shouted. Questions rained down on them.

She and Jay were on the red carpet. A long, thick, red carpet that led through the throng of reporters. She could see the limo waiting up ahead. Less than ten feet away now. She could make it to the vehicle. No problem. The circus was almost over. Willow pasted a smile on her face.

"Kiss her!" A voice shouted.

Her gaze jerked toward that voice. She found a man in a big, thick, gray coat grinning at her. He had a whole film crew with him.

"Let's get a video," the guy called. "Viewers will *love* this shit!"

Her attention snapped back to Jay. He'd paused on the carpet, making her stop, too.

But he shook his head. "She isn't for your viewers." He smiled at Willow, and it was such a tender, warm smile.

More cameras flashed.

"She's only for me," he added.

Her chest ached again. *If only he meant those words.*

Then they were walking once more. She was smiling, only the smile felt easier now. Almost real. Jay was warm and strong beside her. His body moved protectively with hers. For just a moment, she could almost imagine what it would be like to *really* be his date. To be the focus of his intense attention.

To kiss him.

To make love with him.

The driver was holding open the back door to the limo.

She bent, preparing to go in first but…

Willow glanced back.

Jay had turned to respond to a reporter. He was answering some question about a new security feature he was adding for his users, and she heard…

A sharp crack. The thunder of gunfire.

The questions stopped. The screams began.

And Willow found herself in Jay's arms. She didn't remember lunging toward him. Didn't remember grabbing him, but his arms were around her, and he was staring down at her in absolute horror.

She tried to smile. He'd said that she needed to smile for the cameras. The cameras were flashing. People were screaming, but cameras were still on her and Jay. Still watching.

"Baby, baby, you're bleeding." Jay's voice was shaking. Emotion blazed in his eyes as he held her tightly. He surged toward the limo, shoving them into the back of the vehicle. "*Get the fucking car moving! Get us to the nearest ER!*"

She distantly heard a door slam. Had the limo driver done that? He shouldn't be walking around outside. Someone was shooting out there.

"*Willow.*"

Jay's voice snapped her attention up to his face even as she felt the limo lurch forward. Tires squealed.

"Baby, you're bleeding badly."

She realized he was pressing down on her chest. Odd, she didn't feel his touch. Or any pain.

She barely seemed to feel anything at all. "Sh-shot…"

"Yeah, you were shot." For an instant, she could have sworn that he looked afraid. "But I'm going to get you to a hospital. You're going to be all right."

She wasn't so sure of that.

"Can't…hospital…" Her words were softer. Talking was an effort. But she couldn't go to a hospital. The doctors would realize how different she was. "H-home…" He just had to take her home. "Heal…" Jay knew she'd heal. He understood about her differences.

"Look at me." His voice was a fierce demand. *"Look at me, Willow."*

Her lashes lifted. She hadn't realized her eyes had closed.

"I think the bullet…God, there is so much damn blood! I think it nicked your heart. Or got an artery or—shit, I'm not a doctor, I don't know! I just—it's bad. Very bad and you—"

Her lashes closed again. She couldn't make them stay open.

And she also couldn't hear Jay. Not any longer. That was strange. Her senses were so strong. She should be able to hear him.

But…

There was just nothing.

***

"Willow?" Jay pressed his hands down harder on her chest. He could feel her blood on his fingers. *Willow's blood.*

She didn't react. Didn't flinch. Didn't move.

Didn't breathe?

His right hand flew up and pressed to her throat. The limo was bouncing and flying down the road, weaving and jerking to the left, then to the right. His fingers shook as he searched for her pulse.

A pulse she didn't have.

No. Fuck, *no.*

This shouldn't have happened. The goal had been to attract attention. To get eyes on Willow. *Not* to get her hurt.

The limo screeched to a stop. He heard the slam of a door. Jay knew the limo driver was rushing back to help him.

Jay's fingers were still on Willow's throat.

The door opened. The interior lights immediately came on, illuminating everything with a soft, warm glow. Illuminating Willow's beautiful face. Her small nose, her delicate jaw. The heavy, dark mass of her hair.

The blood on her neck. Blood that had come from his fingers.

"We're at the hospital," the driver managed to choke out between quick pants of breath. "Let's get her inside, let's—"

"We don't need the hospital." He had to play this scene carefully. When she'd been hit, he'd freaked the fuck out for a moment. He'd just seen her blood. He'd felt her go limp. And he'd lost his mind. Jay cleared his throat. He moved to Willow's side, and he pulled her into his lap.

Her head sagged limply against him.

Swallowing, he wrapped his arms around her. Willow's black dress hid most of the blood.

"Sir?" Now the driver sounded worried.

He should be worried.

Jay pressed a kiss to Willow's head. He swallowed once more to clear the lump in his throat. "The wound wasn't nearly as bad as I feared." He glanced at the driver. The man gaped at him. Jay gave a brisk nod. "She's just resting now. Willow has requested that we go home, and that my personal physician, Dr. Elizabeth Parker, attend to her."

The driver didn't move. "She…she isn't moving, sir."

No, she wasn't. He held her tighter. "She's resting. Now, hurry, get us home."

The driver still hesitated.

"Home," Jay snapped. "Cops and reporters are going to chase me down, and I want Willow safe and taken care of before I have to face them." He jerked his head. "The hospital is the first place they'll look. I won't have Willow subjected to that hell, not after—not after some bastard shot at

her." He could still hear the thunder of gunfire in his head. "Get us home. She'll be safe there, and I can take care of her at our house."

The driver slammed the door shut. Either the fellow had decided to listen to his boss—or he'd just decided that Jay was insane and that his employer was cradling a dead woman. Either way, didn't really matter. What mattered was that the limo was soon moving again.

Jay's eyes squeezed closed as he held Willow. "You'll come back to me." His body began to rock just a bit as he held her. "That's what you do. The Lazarus subjects always come back." The subjects were supposed to be able to survive anything, except a bullet to the brain. They died, but they came back. Just like the original Lazarus. They were the dead, rising.

She just had to rise.

"You'll come back," Jay said again. He pressed another kiss to her temple. "You'd fucking better."

CHAPTER TWO

She was sleeping beauty. An honest to God fairytale. Only as he stared at Willow's still form, Jay felt as if he were trapped in a nightmare, not a dream.

Jay sat in the chair in the corner of his bedroom. He leaned forward, his hands clasped between his legs, his eyes on the figure of the woman who lay in his bed.

He'd stripped her. He hadn't wanted her to stay in that blood-stained dress. He'd cleaned the blood from her body. He'd tried to not freak the hell out. He'd failed.

"The bullet is out," Dr. Elizabeth Parker said as she straightened, eyeing her patient. "It's just a matter of time. She's going to come back." She glanced over at Jay. "I can stay with her. You should go get cleaned up." She motioned toward him. "You've got blood on your tux."

And on his hands. Willow's blood.

"She's healing already," Elizabeth added, voice reassuring. "She'll wake up soon."

He swallowed. "I don't like this shit."

Elizabeth exhaled slowly. "No, I don't either." Her lips pressed together. She was a beautiful woman, smart, kind…and his former lover. They'd stayed friends after their break-up, and now they were both entwined in the madness that was Lazarus.

"Do you wish you'd never created the formula?" Jay asked her.

Because it had been Elizabeth's brilliant brain that came up with the serum. The secret formula that could bring back the dead. She'd created the preservation process for the bodies, she'd worked for years to get her formula just perfect. And then Wyman Wright—asshole and sonofabitch extraordinaire—had stolen her serum. He'd used it on people without their permission. He'd tried to create his own freaking army.

Elizabeth's dark gaze turned pensive, but instead of answering him, she asked, "Do *you* wish you'd never funded the project?"

Because *he'd* been the one to pump money into Lazarus. He'd been Wyman's biggest backer. Jay worked plenty of covert deals with the U.S. government, but Lazarus had been different. He'd understood why Elizabeth wanted the formula to work. My God, if death could be stopped…

But Jay hadn't realized the full costs.

His gaze slid back to the woman on the bed. *Willow*. His heart ached. "I can't find her past. She doesn't have any memories. No flashes of anything at all. I've looked and looked, and it's as if she never existed before she woke up in that North Carolina lab." Now he rose and stalked toward the bed, as if he were pulled to Willow. His gaze lingered on her face. Her eyes were closed, and he wanted her to wake up. To come back. To open her incredible blue eyes. "What if she has a lover out there, someone searching for her?" A bastard who was going insane because he'd lost her. Jay wanted to reach out and touch Willow. Because he wanted it so badly, his hands clenched into fists.

"Someone obviously knows who she is," Elizabeth murmured.

His gaze immediately snapped to her.

"The shooter," she said bluntly as she tucked a thick lock of dark hair behind her ear. "Whoever tried to take her out tonight—that guy knows exactly who Willow is."

His spine straightened. "West is still at the scene."

"West *and* Sawyer," Elizabeth added. Her face softened a little when she said the second name.

Sawyer Cage. Her lover and the first Lazarus test subject. Elizabeth had walked through hell to get Sawyer back, and Jay had helped her. After all, he'd paved that road to hell, hadn't he? "With Sawyer's super senses, he should be able to hunt down the shooter." The words were gritted out because fury rode Jay so hard. If he could get his hands on the man who'd shot Willow...

"He's definitely better equipped than the cops." Elizabeth reached over and put her fingers on Willow's throat. "She's coming back. I feel her pulse."

Jay tensed.

"I, um, I think I'll leave you two alone. I'll go call and see what Sawyer's found. And you know, you've got cops at your door. You might want to think about *handling* them soon."

He'd handle them after he took care of Willow. He had power in D.C. Power and pull, and the cops could wait a little longer on him.

She eased from the room, and the door clicked closed behind her. As soon as he heard that soft sound, Jay's shoulders sagged. He released a deep breath, and he sat on the edge of the bed. His hand reached for Willow's. Caught hers. Held it tightly. "Open your eyes." He realized he sounded close to begging. Screw it. She'd been *dead.* He needed her eyes to open. He needed her back with him.

He'd never been so fucking scared in his whole life. Not even when he'd been an eleven-year-old kid, tossed onto the street with no shoes, torn clothes, and not a damn thing else in the world to call his own.

He felt her hand jerk in his grasp. A quick, light flinch. "Baby…" He leaned toward her.

Her eyes opened. She stared straight at him, and then she screamed. Her scream pierced Jay straight to his soul. "Willow, Willow, it's okay, you're safe, you're—"

She jerked upright in bed and screamed again.

The door flew open behind him. He heard it thud into the wall. "What's happening?" Elizabeth cried out.

Willow had jumped from the bed. She stood on the far side of the room, her back pressed to the wall, her gaze darting between him and Elizabeth.

Slowly, Jay rose. "Willow." He said her name deliberately. Tenderly. Carefully. "You were hurt when we left the ball tonight." He reached for the covers. Jay held them in his arms as he began to make his way toward her. "But you're okay now. Everything is okay."

She blinked. Once. Twice. And then her eyes widened as recognition finally flared in her gaze.

His heart was beating so damn fast. Jay was sure the thing was about to jump out of his chest. For a minute there, Willow hadn't remembered him. He knew she hadn't.

Fucking hell. *I did this to her.*

"J-Jay…?"

He nodded. Still advanced slowly. When he was close enough, he lifted the covers and wrapped them around her naked body. She shuddered and her breath panted out.

"I was…shot…"

Something else that was his fault. He'd taken her out in public and put her on display. He'd used her as bait. Why the hell hadn't he considered that she could get hurt? "Yes."

Elizabeth cleared her throat. "Willow, are you okay? I know coming back can be a bit unsettling…" Her voice trailed away.

Willow clutched the covers. "Coming back," she repeated. She looked down at Jay's hands. "That's…my blood, isn't it?" Her gaze rose. The blue was so bright. "I died?"

"Yes."

Her shoulders hunched.

Fuck. "Elizabeth, give us a minute, okay?"

She retreated without a word. The door shut once more.

And Jay pulled Willow into his arms. She stiffened, but a moment later, her body softened against his. He held her, cradling her, wanting to take away all of her fear and pain.

"I…died?" Willow asked him again, but there was a hitch in her voice. Fear. He didn't want her to be afraid.

"You came back." He eased away a few inches so that he could slide his hand under her chin, tipping her head up and staring into her eyes. "You came back, Willow. Everything is okay."

A tear slipped from her eye. One, then another.

A guttural growl tore from him. Her tears were killing him. *Killing* him. "Don't, baby, don't." Jay pressed a kiss to her cheek. He kissed her tears away.

And her body stiffened.

Shit. He'd overstepped. He hadn't meant—Jay immediately lifted his head. "Willow—"

"Kiss me."

Those were the last words he'd expected to hear her say. Stunned, he just stared at her.

Another tear slid down her cheek.

His chest burned. "Baby…"

She stood on her toes and wrapped her arms around his neck. The bed covers dropped a bit, but then got caught between their bodies. "Kiss me," she whispered again.

Since there was pretty much no damn thing that he wouldn't do for her—and since he wasn't a fool—Jay's mouth took hers. The kiss was light at first. A brush of his lips against hers. She'd just *died,* for shit's sake. He didn't want to rush or scare her.

But her lips parted beneath his. His tongue slid into her mouth. He tasted her. And he was lost. The kiss deepened as he tasted her. Savored her. He pulled her even closer, and his cock shoved hard toward her. *Willow*. She moaned, a soft sound in the back of her throat, and his desire surged even higher. Her hands were digging into his shoulders, she was pressing her body to his, and all he wanted was to taste every single inch of her. Right then and right there.

She'd been shot. She'd died. But she was warm and alive in his arms. His Willow was back.

A fist pounded against the door. "Jay!" A man's voice barked. "Jay, Elizabeth told me you asked for some time, but I need your ass out here, *now*."

That was West. A pissed West.

Fair enough, West had just pissed Jay off, too.

Because Willow was pulling away. Slipping from his arms even as she grabbed the covers and wrapped them around her body. She stared at Jay with wide eyes, and her gorgeous lips were red and plump and wet from his kiss.

"Willow…" Jay began.

Willow, I want to kiss every fucking inch of you.

Willow, I want to sink into you and make you scream as you come.

She blinked. Her cheeks flushed. Her breathing hitched, and she quickly glanced away.

Jay's gaze narrowed. The Lazarus subjects had psychic bonuses, he knew that. Had Willow just picked up on his thoughts?

"Jay!" West pounded on the door again. "The cops are demanding to see you! Your damn money can only buy you so much time. Get your ass out here!"

He hadn't even realized West was at his house, not until the guy had interrupted at the absolute wrong time. He'd thought the fellow was still at the scene of the shooting. Jay spun on his heel and marched for the door. He opened it, but just enough to stick his head out. He didn't want West seeing Willow right then. "Give me a minute," he snapped.

But West threw his hand up against the wood of the door before Jay could shove it closed again. "Not happening," West fired back. "The cops have played it cool as long as they could. They're demanding to see you." His voice was low. "Man, the stories are already spreading, okay? Reporters are saying online that you freaked out, and you've holed up with your dead lover's body. This shit isn't good."

He hated the press somedays—no, he hated the tabloids that liked to rip his life to shreds. "She *isn't* dead."

"Of course, not. She's Lazarus." West's dark gaze held his. "So get her out here for the cops to see before they start tearing your house apart in their search for a corpse."

Oh, hell, no. "They wouldn't dare."

West just sighed. He'd ditched his tux coat and rolled up his sleeves. "Man, you think because you've got more money than God that people will do *everything* you want?"

He didn't have more money than—

"Shit doesn't work that way. You fled from the scene of a shooting. You took what people *think* is a dead woman to your bedroom. You've got to talk to the authorities, now, before this gets worse."

Jay rolled back his shoulders. "Fine."

West's lips twitched, but then the faint smile vanished. "We didn't find anyone at the scene."

Jay clenched his teeth.

"Sawyer searched, I searched, but we couldn't find a trail."

Dammit. West was former Delta Force and Sawyer—the ex-Navy SEAL had enhanced senses. If those two couldn't find the shooter… "That's not good."

"No, it's not." West inclined his head. "Bring out Willow before the cops bust in." He turned on his heel and strode down the hallway.

Jay shut the door, and his hand lingered against the wooden frame.

"Is that my blood?"

He looked at his hand. Then he glanced back at her. She stood near the bed, the covers shielding her body. "Yes." He headed for the bathroom. Ditched his tux coat, tossing it into the corner, and then he yanked on the faucet.

"I…don't remember much after the shooting."

She'd followed him into the bathroom. She stood beside him, her reflection right next to his in the mirror.

"Tell me what happened?"

He turned off the water. Dried his hands. Never took his gaze off their reflection. "We got in the limo. The driver raced us here. You woke up." His words were bit off.

Willow shook her head. "You're glossing over things."

Yes, he was. Jay swallowed. "Fine." Now he turned toward her. Their bodies were barely a breath apart. "I held you in my arms. I couldn't stop the blood. You died *in my arms.* The driver had gotten us to the hospital—we went there first—but I knew there wasn't a damn thing those doctors could do for you. So I ordered the driver to bring us here."

A furrow appeared between her brows. "After I died, what did you do with me?"

"I told you, I got the driver to bring you here—"

She shook her head. "My…my body, I mean, what did you—"

"I fucking held you," he growled. "And I told you to hurry that sweet ass up and come back to me." His lips tightened. "You scared the ever-loving hell out of me, *but you came back."*

Her eyes were wide. Deep. And for the life of him, Jay could not read the expression on her beautiful face. Did she hate him? Did she fear him? Did she just want to get away from him?

He strode out of the bathroom. Headed for the bedroom door. "I'll take care of the cops. You just stay here and rest. Everything is going to be okay."

She didn't stop him, and he didn't glance back. He'd discovered that when he looked into Willow's eyes too much, too long, Jay could have sworn that the woman started to steal his soul.

***

I died. I died, and I came back.

Willow wrapped one of Jay's thick, white robes around her body. She was shivering, and she couldn't seem to stop the chills that raked through her. She'd died.

Where had she gone when she died? Heaven? Hell? She couldn't remember, but a tight ball of fear was heavy in her stomach. The dead weren't supposed to come back. She wasn't supposed to come back.

But she had.

Because she was some kind of freak. A monster that had been created in a lab. A creature of real nightmares.

Only Jay had kissed her. He'd wanted her, she knew it. His desire had been real. Desire for a woman, not a monster.

Voices were raised downstairs. Shouting. She had enhanced hearing so it wasn't any struggle to make out the words. A *normal* human would have been able to hear those angry words.

She opened up the door to Jay's bedroom.

"We need the body, Mr. Maverick. Just give us the body!" A man's voice, slightly high, nasally.

"There is no body." Jay. She'd recognize his deep voice anyplace. "My friend is resting upstairs. As you can imagine, the night has been quite intense for her. Someone *shot* at my companion, and you should all be out there looking for the bastard. Not in here, harassing me."

A beat of silence, then… "We saw the blood, Mr. Maverick," the same nasally voice responded. "You can't keep a dead woman's body in your home."

She crept toward the staircase. Peered over the big balcony and railing. Jay was in the middle of the room below, his hands on his hips. Blood stained his clothes. Her blood. His hair was tousled, his expression—well, it was pissed. West stood at Jay's side, and he looked just as angry.

Dr. Elizabeth Parker was there, too, sitting on the couch, and Sawyer Cage was positioned right next to her. A slightly protective position. Made sense because Sawyer *was* protective when it came to Elizabeth. She was his lover, after all.

No, the way Sawyer looked at Elizabeth…*she's his everything*. And Willow was jealous of that. Perhaps not jealous, but, envious.

It would be nice to have someone care about her so much.

"Don't make us search your house." The nasally voice again. Willow's eyes narrowed. The speaker was a man in a long, brown coat. Tall and built along sturdy lines, the fellow sported dark red hair, and he was carrying a gun. Willow could just make out the bulk of the holster and weapon under his arm.

Three uniformed cops were there, too. Looking very, very uncomfortable. A woman with blonde hair, an African American cop who had a gaze that kept sweeping the room, and a young, short fellow with curly, black hair. He was sweating and rocking forward onto the balls of his feet.

"Don't think I remember seeing a search warrant, Detective Haskin." Jay flashed the fellow in the trench coat a broad grin. "Maybe come back when you have one, hmm?"

The detective's face flashed red. "You know what that swarm of reporters are saying out there? You've gone batshit crazy, you're keeping your dead lover's body in your bed, you're—"

"I'm not dead." The words slipped out from Willow.

And suddenly, all eyes were on her.

The sweating cop had even pulled his weapon, aiming it up at her.

West immediately grabbed the weapon from the fellow. "Don't aim that shit at her."

Willow released a slow breath. Her gaze darted toward Jay. His grin was gone. "I'm not dead," she said again, and Willow knew she was directing those words at Jay. She just didn't know why. *I want him to keep seeing me as a woman. Not a freak.* "Jay brought me here because I truly was fine. I didn't need a trip to the hospital."

"Uh, miss?" The detective scratched his chin. "I'm going to need you to come down the stairs."

Jay tensed, but he didn't argue.

Willow began walking down the stairs, far too conscious of the robe around her body and Jay's stare—a stare that never left her. Her fingers trailed over the wooden banister as she descended the spiral staircase, and when she reached the last step, Jay was there. He rushed toward her. Pulled her close.

"You should be resting."

Were his tender words just for the audience watching them? Probably.

But he wrapped his arm around her shoulder and pulled her against his body. He was warm and solid, and the knot of fear in her belly seemed to ease.

"She doesn't look like she was shot," this came from the female officer. Her narrowed gaze swept over Willow.

Willow forced a smile. "I'm fine."

The detective crossed his arms over his chest. "There's an awful lot of blood on Mr. Maverick's clothes for you to be *fine*."

"The bullet grazed me. Nothing more." Did she sound brisk? In control? Or panicked?

The detective's attention shifted to Jay. "You left the scene of a crime."

Jay pulled Willow even closer to his body. "Someone was shooting at my friend. I had to leave. What did you want me to do? Stay there and keep letting her be a target?"

No…no, he was wrong. "Jay…" Willow began.

He gave her shoulder a squeeze. "Leaving was my only option. I needed to protect Willow."

But she hadn't needed protecting. "Jay—"

"You need to find the man who shot at her." Jay's voice was colder, harder. "Sweep the streets. Pull every single bit of surveillance video you have of that area. I want you to find the sonofabitch who tried to kill Willow before—"

"The shot wasn't aimed at me." There, she'd finally gotten her words out. Finally made Jay *listen.*

His head whipped toward her. "What?"

"The shot was intended for you, not me. I jumped in front of you because I knew—" She broke off, not saying more. *I knew I could survive.* He couldn't have.

Jay blinked. Once. Twice. And then anger flashed on his face. No, not anger. Rage. His hold tightened. "You took a bullet meant for me?"

His words were low, obviously intended just for her, but she knew Sawyer could hear him, too. Super soldier senses and all.

"Willow...*don't.*" Jay shook his head. "Don't ever fucking risk yourself that way again."

But it hadn't been a risk. She'd come back.

Jay's eyes blazed.

She cleared her throat and began to pull from his arms. For a moment, she wasn't sure he'd let her go. His hold tightened. "*When we're alone...*" Jay's voice rumbled.

Willow shivered. She wondered just what *would* happen when they were alone.

But they weren't alone right then. She had an audience, and she needed to come up with a story for the detective and his officers.

"Miss?" The detective's head cocked to the right. What had Jay called him? Haskin? "How did you know the shot was aimed at Mr.

Maverick? How could you tell that? Did you see the shooter? See him aiming? See—"

"I could hear the shot coming." An absolute truth. She'd heard the whistle of the bullet as it flew through the air.

Detective Haskin blinked owlishly. "Come again?"

Jay cleared his throat. "You've seen for yourself that Willow isn't dead. Now, really, don't you have a criminal to apprehend—"

"You *heard* the shot, ma'am? Is that what you're saying?" The detective stalked toward her.

"Everyone there heard the thunder of the gunfire. That's why everyone was ducking for cover." West had stepped forward, moving closer to Jay and Willow. "I think what Willow meant was that she'd seen the glint of the weapon, right, Willow?"

That wasn't what she'd meant.

And Detective Haskin didn't look convinced by West's explanation, either. "Big difference between seeing and hearing, and she's saying that Maverick here was the intended target. Think I deserve to hear more information..." His gaze swept over her. "From Maverick's, um, companion. Or friend. Or whatever she prefers to be called—"

Her shoulders snapped up. Her hesitation vanished. "I'm his bodyguard."

Jay swore. Softly, but very inventively.

"I use the cover of his companion." She gave the detective a hard smile. "But my job is to keep Jay safe. And I did that tonight. I spotted the weapon, the glint…" Her gaze cut to West. She was going to be more careful now. She'd just been shaken before, but she had this. She could lie. Every day was a lie for her. "I rushed to Jay and got him out of the shooter's range. Then coming back here, that was *my* idea. Not his. I wanted Jay to be safe. Someone out there was gunning for him, and it was my job to protect my client."

The detective laughed. "Nice story. I'm really supposed to buy that *you* are the bodyguard?"

Now he was just being insulting. "Come at me."

His laughter died.

Once more, Jay swore.

"I can prove I'm *exactly* what I say." She motioned to the detective. He didn't move. So she wiggled her fingers toward the cops. "Try to take me down." *I dare you.* "You'll see that I have plenty of training. I can handle any threat, anytime. Tonight, I was surveying the scene. Looking for danger. I saw the danger, and I reacted." Willow thought she sounded cool, calm, and in charge.

And no one had to know that her heart was about to surge right out of her chest.

The detective sauntered toward her. A faint smirk twisted his lips.

"Don't," Jay snapped at the guy. "Don't even *think* it."

The detective had stilled, less than two feet away from her. His chin jerked up, and based on the sudden stiffness of his body, she knew Haskin was going to heed Jay's warning. But if he heeded the warning, the detective wouldn't believe her.

So Willow lunged forward. In a blink, she'd taken the detective's weapon. Turned the gun on him.

"Christ, Willow," West barked. "You don't do that shit."

Jay had gone statue-still beside her.

She could feel Elizabeth and Sawyer watching her. The uniformed cops had frozen, too.

The detective's wide stare jumped from the gun to her. "How—"

"What do you fear, Detective Haskin?" Willow heard herself ask him.

"*Willow.*" Jay's hands closed around her shoulders. His touch was warm, strong. "That's enough of a demonstration for tonight."

She rather thought she'd just been getting started. But, well… "Here's your gun." She flipped it around and offered the weapon to the detective. He snatched up the weapon, his cheeks burning red.

"Willow is my bodyguard." Jay didn't release her. "She stays with me, twenty-four seven. But that isn't information for the press, got it? So when she says that the shooter was aiming at me, we believe her." Not a question.

Sweat trickled down Haskin's temple. "You got some enemies, Maverick?"

Jay's sigh was loud and long. "Yeah, yeah, I do."

"Then you should start making a list of them."

***

After question after question—what seemed like a million questions—the cops left. Finally. The silence in the house stretched and stretched.

Everyone was in the den. A fire crackled in the fireplace. Willow had changed into jeans and a white sweater. She stood in the middle of the room and squared her shoulders. "I'm sorry I messed up."

Jay downed a whiskey. She was pretty sure that might have been his second. Maybe his third. "You got *shot*. You don't do that shit again, understand?"

Sawyer Cage stood. His dark blue gaze swept around the room before he raked a hand through his black hair. "I think we should call it a night." He nodded to Elizabeth. "Everyone is about to crash. We can check in and regroup tomorrow."

Elizabeth hesitated as she focused on Willow. "Are you sure you're okay?"

Willow opened her mouth to reply—

"She just came back from the dead," Jay announced. "Why wouldn't she be fine?" He slammed down his empty glass. Then he marched toward Willow. His body was too tense, and his face was locked into angry lines. "Don't do that shit again. Don't you ever risk yourself for me."

It hadn't been a risk. The Lazarus subjects could come back from death, provided they didn't take a bullet to the brain. Because she was a walking zombie now and she—

"I am not worth it." Jay was right in front of her. His eyes gleamed. "No bullets. No blood. Promise me."

She wasn't going to make any promise.

"Definitely time to call it a night." West appeared behind Jay. He slapped a hand on Jay's shoulder. "You know you can't handle your whiskey for shit."

Jay turned his head and met West's stare. "She died. In my arms."

West sucked in a sharp breath. "Oh, man, hell, I'm so sorry. It made you remember our sis—"

"I never forget her." Jay shrugged away from his hold. "It's two a.m. Definitely time to call it a night." He nodded toward Elizabeth. "Thanks for your help, Beth. As always, you're a lifesaver." His lips twisted. "We'll pick up this mess again tomorrow. See just who came gunning for me. Maybe it's Wyman. Maybe it's one of the other dozen bastards who want my head on a platter. Either way, we're done for the night." He motioned toward the door. "Limo is still out there. The driver can take you all home."

Everyone filed out. Everyone but Willow.

And West. His stare lingered on Jay, and there was no missing his worry. "You all right?"

"Just another sin to add to my soul." Jay's voice was mocking. "Get some sleep, man. We'll talk tomorrow."

Reluctantly, West filed out. Jay turned away from Willow. He headed toward the fire. Stared at the flames.

Willow found that she couldn't move. She felt absolutely rooted to the spot. And her gaze was on Jay's broad back.

"Why did you do it?"

His voice was so rough and hard.

"Why the hell did you take a bullet...*for me?*"

CHAPTER THREE

She didn't answer his question. Jay stared into the flames, rage tight in every cell of his body. "Wasn't it bad enough that I was using you as bait?" He couldn't look her in the eyes. Just couldn't do it. "But you risked yourself for me, too?"

The floor creaked beneath her footsteps. She was coming closer. Her scent—lavender, the woman liked lavender body lotion and he'd freaking bought her a truckload of the stuff, literally—swept over him. His eyes squeezed shut. "You dying wasn't part of the deal. We were supposed to lure Wyman Wright out into the open. You weren't supposed to be hurt."

"I don't stay dead. We both know that." Her voice was soft, confused. "Why are you reacting this way? I saved you. You should be grateful."

Grateful? Something inside of Jay just snapped. He spun around and found her close enough to touch. So he did. His hands flew out and wrapped around her slender shoulders. He pulled her against him, hating that he was being rough but unable to hold back his fury. Fury at her. At himself. "Your blood was all over me. I saw you die. I wasn't grateful. I was fucking in hell."

Her eyes were wide. Stunned. "But…but I came back."

His hold tightened. "You think watching you die is easy? That shit ripped me open." He was still raw. "Never again."

"Jay—"

"Promise me." He'd asked for that promise before. Now he demanded it. "You never do that again. Swear it."

But she shook her head. "I won't."

What?

"You're not being reasonable. This isn't like you." She pulled out of his arms. Stood staring at him, her expression confused. "You're the logical one. I mean, I understand Sawyer. He's like me. The darker emotions live in us. They thrive inside because of what was done *to* us. But you…" Her words trailed away as she shook her head.

Jay's mocking laughter escaped him. "Oh, sweetheart, you think the super soldiers cornered the market on *dark* emotions? Trust me, I can be plenty dark." He spun on his heel, turning away from her. "Go to bed, Willow. You've been through hell tonight." Because of him.

But she didn't walk away. The scent of lavender lingered in the air. "You're mad at me?"

His hands clenched into fists. "Mad doesn't cover it. Try pissed off. Enraged. So shit-faced furious I can barely breathe."

"Why?" Her hand was on his shoulder. "I saved your life!" Now she sounded angry, too.

He didn't turn back to look at her. Her touch seemed to burn right through him. "I don't want you hurting because of me." Not ever. Jay pulled in a deep breath. He was trying so hard to make things up to her, but he was failing at every turn.

"Would it have been better to let you die?" Her voice rose a bit. "Because that sounds like a terrible plan to me. We both know I'm the indestructible one. We both know—"

"You should go to bed, Willow." His voice was guttural.

She didn't stop touching him. "Why aren't you looking at me?"

Because he was fighting to keep his control in place. Fear and fury had merged inside of him. His emotions were never in full check when she was near. And he kept thinking about their kiss. About the way she'd gone wild when he'd tasted her.

When he'd touched her, even though her blood had been on his hands.

Jay glanced down at his hands. Saw his clenched fists. The cops had taken his clothes. Bagged them as evidence. He'd even had to give them Willow's ball gown. Now Jay wore jeans. A t-shirt. And the thin t-shirt was no barrier to him. He swore he could feel her touch right against his skin. "Stop."

"Stop what?" She'd inched even closer. "Why won't you look at me?"

"You should stop touching me."

She sucked in a sharp breath. "I'm sorry." Her hand jerked back.

He finally turned toward her. Saw that she'd paled. Her eyes were—what the hell? Was Willow about to *cry?* He reached for her, but she immediately backed up.

"I forgot," Willow said. A tear leaked down her cheek. "I forgot, but you didn't. You don't ever forget, do you?"

He had no clue what she was talking about.

Willow lifted her hands and stared down at her fingers. "I touch and I make people afraid. Make those terrible fears that lurk inside seem to turn into reality. I wonder what it was like before. When I could touch someone and nothing would happen? When I could just be normal?"

"I'm not fucking afraid when you touch me." His voice was low. Angry.

Her gaze flew up to his. "But you told me to stop touching you."

Not because he'd been afraid. "Because I want you."

She shivered.

"You understand that, Willow? I want you. And it's not some easy, controlled attraction. I crave you. When you touch me, my control nearly shatters. You're not ready for what I want. Hell, you made it clear last night that you didn't want me—"

"Not true."

He blinked at her denial. In the elevator, she'd been the one to stop him. Because she couldn't ever get past what he'd done with Lazarus.

"I kissed you before, didn't I?" Red tinged her cheeks.

She had kissed him, but—"You'd just woken up from the dead." His jaw hardened. "Your emotions were out of control. You weren't yourself."

"Hard to be yourself when you don't really know who that is." Her weak smile nearly broke his heart. "Am I the monster? The killer?"

"Willow…"

"The damsel in distress? The fighter? The lover? The traitor? All of the above and everything in between?"

His back teeth were clenched so hard that his jaw ached. "You're a woman, Willow. A beautiful, smart, strong woman."

Her gaze slid from his.

Fuck me. "We've been over this. I'm the one who pumped the money into Lazarus. You said it yourself." He waved toward the door. "Go upstairs. Go to bed, Willow. You don't want to be close to me right now." He was trying to warn her, while he still could. His need for Willow was far too strong.

She turned away from him and slowly made her way to the door. Before leaving, though, she paused. "I know what you did. All your secrets."

No, she only thought that she knew them all.

"And, Jay, I don't want you fucking me because you feel sorry for me."

He laughed. Actually just burst into laughter.

Willow spun back toward him, her blue eyes flaring wide. "Are you laughing at me?"

"Oh, sweetheart, you have that so wrong." He shook his head, but Jay's smile lingered. "Let's be clear. I want to fuck you because you're the sexiest woman I've ever met. You star in every single dream I have. I look at you, and I ache." He exhaled and rolled back his shoulders. "*Sorry* isn't what I feel for you. You can stop worrying about that."

He saw the surprise appear on her face. Her expression softened. Her breath hitched. She took a step toward him.

If she touches me again, I won't be able to stop. "Go upstairs." Now his smile was gone. "Because you're still riding an adrenaline high. I don't want you doing something that you'll regret or something that you want to take back." His gaze didn't leave her face. "Because if I ever do have you, once won't cut it for me. Fair warning."

She didn't move. Neither did he. The tension seemed to stretch between them. All he wanted was to take her into his arms. To take *her.* And because he wanted that so badly—"Good night, Willow." His voice was almost tender, a supreme struggle. "I'll be here in the morning when you wake up."

"You always say that," she murmured. "Such a strange thing." Her hand pushed back her hair. "I don't know why that makes me feel safe."

Even during the early days when he'd been trying to figure out if she was the enemy or if she could be trusted, he'd always left her with those words.

Good night, Willow. I'll be here in the morning when you wake up.

"When I woke up in the lab, I was strapped to the exam table. Naked. I screamed because men and women in white coats were all around me."

Jay was rooted to the spot.

"I begged for them to let me go. I begged for someone to help me. But no one did. I woke up alone every single morning in that lab."

He hated her pain. *I did this. Of course, she'll never want to be with me. I'm her monster. I'm the one she hates.*

Willow's gaze swept over the room. Then came back to linger on him. "I'm glad you're close when I wake up now."

What?

Willow swallowed. "Good night."

She walked away, and Jay knew he was going to need another whiskey.

***

The attack had been caught on camera. And the video was released everywhere, playing all across the Internet, on every celebrity news show in the world.

After all, Jay Maverick was a major public figure.

A fucking big deal.

"And in my way," Wyman Wright muttered as he stared at the computer screen. He could see Jay Maverick's face so clearly on the screen. The guy had scooped up the unidentified woman, his "companion" as the news dubbed her. Jay held her so tightly, and the fear on the fellow's face was plain to see.

Wyman knew the identity of Jay's mysterious companion. *She's my Willow.*

Willow had been shot. Her blood had spilled on the ground.

Wyman wondered if she'd died in the limo. He didn't know because the car had raced from the scene. Jay had taken her away.

For the moment.

But Wyman would get her back. And he'd make Jay Maverick *pay* for what he'd done.

***

Doing the right thing was freaking hard.

Jay stared into the flames. Willow had gone to bed over an hour ago. He'd wanted nothing more than to follow her upstairs. But he hadn't.

He'd been the gentleman. Even though he could still taste her. She'd been so sweet.

His eyes squeezed shut. Maybe he'd try a cold shower before bed. Maybe he'd get his ass in check that way. The whiskey hadn't helped so he sure needed to try something else.

But then a faint sound reached him. A cry?

Instantly, he was out the room and running up the stairs. The sound came again, a whimper, and he knew it was Willow. She was the only other person in the house. It had to be her, and she sounded as if she were in pain.

Maybe she hadn't healed completely from the gunshot. There was so much about the Lazarus subjects that no one understood.

"Willow?" He knocked on her door.

Another soft cry was his only answer.

He twisted the door knob. Locked. Dammit. He pounded on the door. "Willow?"

A whimper.

Screw this. He kicked in the door. It flew back, banging against the wall. Jay raced across the room. Willow was still in bed, tangled in the covers, her hair tousled. Her head moved back and forth across the pillows, and those soft cries continued to slip from her.

She was afraid. Terrified. And dreaming.

He reached out to her, his fingers curling around her shoulder. "Baby, wake up—"

At his touch, she screamed. A long, piercing cry, and her eyes flew wide open. For an instant, she stared at him with zero recognition on her face.

And then her hand flew up. She touched his chest.

The room vanished. It was as if he'd blinked, and Jay found himself somewhere else. *Someplace* else.

Back in the limo. He was sitting on the leather seat. Willow was in his arms. Her blood was on his hands. Her eyes were closed. She wasn't moving. Wasn't breathing. "Don't!" The shout broke from him. "Don't do it!" But she was…she was dead. He shook her, again and again, even as fear clawed through him. This couldn't be happening. He couldn't lose someone again, couldn't hold her while she died, and he was helpless to do a damn thing. "Willow!"

And just like that...

The scene faded. The limo was gone, and he was back in his home, standing beside the bed. Only Willow wasn't in the bed any longer. Jay shook his head even as his breath sawed in and out of his lungs. Willow was across the room, her arms wrapped around her stomach as she rocked her body back and forth.

"S-sorry, so s-sorry..."

He looked down at his body. Back up at her.

"Didn't mean..." Her voice trembled. "I...had a bad dream. I didn't know...where I was...*sorry*."

"Willow..." He moved around the bed, stepped toward her.

But she stiffened. "You don't want to touch me."

He sure as all hell did.

"I can control it." She gave a quick nod. "I can, I promise, I can. But I wasn't myself. I didn't know what was happening, I—"

"You had a nightmare." His heart still raced too fast. "That's normal, Willow. Everyone has nightmares." His hand reached out, and he turned on the nearby lamp. A soft pool of light spilled onto her.

Willow flinched. A tear slid down her cheek. "I made you fear."

"Yes, I was worried when I heard you cry out—"

"I made you *see* what you feared."

And he tensed. "Is that why you're pressed against the wall? Because you woke up from a bad dream, and you accidentally used your power on me?"

"I made you *fear*. You won't touch me again. Won't let me touch you. You—"

He closed the distance between them. Caught her hand. Put it over his chest. She tried to jerk back, but he tightened his hold. The woman had super strength, if she really wanted to break away, Jay knew she could.

But she didn't.

Her breath hitched. "Jay…?"

"Do you know what I saw?" But he didn't wait for her to answer. "You. I saw you, in the limo, dying." *Dead.* "That's what I fear. And it's not a secret. I fear hurting you. I fear not being able to help you. That shit has happened to me before, you see. West and I…we had a foster sister once. Emeline. Sweetest little girl you've ever seen. But one day while West and I were in school, our foster dad—the sonofabitch got angry with her. He pushed her, and Emeline, she was so fucking little. She fell when he pushed her. Hit her head. Only the bastard thought she was okay. Just a little bump." His voice roughened as he kept her hand against his heart. "When I came in from school, I knew something was wrong with her. West and I—we got her. We took her out of that house. The SOB tried to stop us, but West hit him." West had been fifteen, and more than a match for the prick. He and West could have taken the guy any day. But Emeline… "She was eight. And I was carrying her. Running down the road because there wasn't a phone anywhere, and we had to get her to the hospital. I was carrying her, holding her, when she stopped breathing."

When she'd died, he'd fallen to the ground. He and West had begged her to wake up. They'd tried CPR, they'd just learned it in their health class at school, and they'd thought they could get her to come back.

Emeline hadn't come back.

But Willow had. He swallowed and tried to keep his voice gentle. "You were afraid, and you just acted instinctively. It's okay."

Another tear leaked down her cheek. "No, it's not."

She was breaking his heart. "It's late, baby. Come back to bed. Get some sleep."

Her breath hitched. "And you'll be here in the morning? Just like you say?"

"Of course." *I'll be where you are.* "Where else would I be?"

She shuffled back to the bed. Slid under the covers. He stood there, watching her, feeling absolutely helpless. After a moment, he turned off the light, plunging the room into darkness before he turned for the door.

"I like the light." Her soft voice stopped him.

He looked back, straining to see her in the darkness. "I can turn the lamp back on."

"Just…will you open the blinds? Let the moonlight in."

And he wondered if she really liked the light or if she liked to see outside. To know that she wasn't a prisoner any longer.

Another sin on his soul. *He'd* been the one to design the rooms—the *cells* that Wyman Wright had used with the Lazarus subjects. Rooms that had allowed the researchers to see inside, to watch the subjects at all times. Like they were lab rats. Without a word, Jay pulled open the blinds, letting the moonlight trickle into the room. "Better?"

"Thank you." Her voice was so soft.

He gave a grim nod and headed for the door.

"Stay?"

Jay froze.

"Just for a little while? I can't remember the dream. I never can, but I think it would be better if I wasn't alone."

He glanced around the room. Saw the chair against the wall. "I'll sit here—"

"Would you…could you…"

Jay's head cocked as he padded toward her. "What do you need?" *I'll give you everything.*

"Could you just maybe stay beside me a moment? I was always alone in the lab. And I just—never mind. Forget it."

He'd never forget. Jay slid into the bed with her. He reached for her and pulled Willow into his arms. She stiffened for a moment.

"You don't have to touch me," Willow whispered. "I know you're worried about what I'll do—"

"I'm not worried about a damn thing. You just close your eyes and relax." His hand stroked along her side. "You won't be alone. And you won't be in the dark." Not ever again on his watch.

And the tension slowly left her body. He kept gently caressing her, holding her, and he felt the moment when she eased into sleep once more. Jay knew he could get up then. He could slip from the room.

But Willow would be alone when he left. What if she had another bad dream?

Besides, he liked holding her. Liked it too much, truth be told, but his eager dick could just settle the hell down. This wasn't about sex. This was about her. About what Willow needed.

He stared up at the ceiling. She felt good against him. Right.

As if she fit him.

***

Willow came awake slowly. She stretched her body, arching, and her eyes opened as—

As she touched someone. Someone in the bed with her.

In the bed with her.

Willow's head jerked to the right. Her gaze fell on Jay. A still sleeping Jay. A Jay with his hair tousled and his long lashes against his cheeks. A Jay who wasn't wearing a shirt and who had the covers shoved down near his waist, revealing the muscled expanse of his chest. For a man who spent a whole lot of hours typing on a keyboard, the guy was *built*. Rippling muscles, washboard abs, and—

"You're in bed with me." The words blurted from her.

And she remembered last night. Waking up. Touching him. Sending his worst fear slamming into his head.

She whipped into a sitting position, hauling the covers with her and clutching them to her chest.

Jay's eyes opened. She expected him to stare at her in horror. She'd messed with his mind last night. Then he'd stayed with her? Oh, God, she pretty much remembered begging the guy to stay. Because she'd been afraid. And like all of the darker emotions, fear hit the Lazarus subjects too hard. It had slithered through her, chilling her, weakening her and—

"Morning, beautiful." He smiled at her. A killer grin that made her hold the covers a bit tighter.

"You..." Okay, she sounded like she was squeaking. Willow cleared her throat. "You stayed."

His smile dimmed. "Of course, you asked me to."

He'd stayed. She lifted the covers and realized that she was still wearing her t-shirt and jogging shorts. She'd changed into them right before climbing into bed. "We didn't have sex."

"No." Laughter lurked in the one word. "But if that's an offer..."

Willow jumped out of the bed. She pulled the covers with her, and when she did, she saw that he was still in his jeans. "*Why* did you stay?"

He sat up in bed. "Because you asked me to." The same words he'd just said. His head cocked as he studied her. "Soon enough, you'll realize, that's all you'll ever have to do."

Her gaze was on his jeans. On the very *prominent* front of his jeans.

Jay laughed. "Yeah, that happens in the mornings."

Normal reaction. Nothing to do with her. A guy thing. An unfortunate guy thing, but—

"I've wanted you for a while, but I'll never do anything *you* don't want." He rose from the bed, stretching himself. "Think I'll go take a cold shower. Meant to have one last night, but couldn't bring myself to leave you that long."

And that was it. He walked past her and headed for the door. Her hand flew out, but she stopped herself, not touching him, vividly recalling everything that she'd done and he'd said the night before. "I'm sorry."

At the bedroom door, he glanced back at her.

"About Emeline. I'm so sorry you lost her."

His expression hardened. "Thank you."

She wanted to say something that would comfort him. But she didn't know how to comfort. She only knew how to make someone's fears worse. How to drive a person to the brink of sanity. So she didn't speak again, and Jay walked away. The door shut softly behind him.

When he was gone, Willow let out the breath that she'd been holding. She found herself returning to the bed. Her fingers reached out and touched the pillow he'd used.

He'd stayed with her.

That mattered, didn't it?

She was pretty sure it did.

I'll be here in the morning when you wake up.

CHAPTER FOUR

"I'm not going to keep a low profile," Willow announced that night as she marched into Jay's study. She found him dressed in a suit, looking drop dead sexy with his hair pushed back, and his collar turned up. "You aren't leaving me at home tonight."

Jay sighed. West stood at his side, and the guy smothered a laugh. "Told you. No way you're leaving without her."

"Willow." Jay gave her a smile. She found it fake. "You were shot last night—"

"But you were the one being shot *at,*" she interrupted him curtly. "Not me. And if you're going out because you think you can attract the shooter's attention again, if you think *you're* going to be the bait, then you're taking me with you."

His jaw hardened. "I'm going to the opening of a club. And I'm only doing it because I need the media to see that I don't hide from anyone. If the person gunning for me wants *me,* then he'll need to get his ass out there and come for me.

Sawyer and Flynn will be there, they'll both be looking for the shooter. Searching for anyone who doesn't belong. We'll have the super soldier aspect more than covered."

Her eyes narrowed. He was saying he didn't need her. Bull. "Sawyer and Flynn are great." Flynn Haddox was another super soldier who'd been put inside Project Lazarus. The first time she'd met him, well, that little meet and greet hadn't gone so well. Mostly because she'd been told he was the enemy. That he wanted her dead.

The man who'd told her that particular lie? Bryce King? He'd turned out to be an absolute psychopath who wanted to use her for his own agenda.

A liar she couldn't trust.

She had a tendency to put her trust in the wrong places. No, in the wrong people. And that was why she couldn't, wouldn't, allow herself to trust Jay. "They're great," she added with a nod, "but they aren't me." She marched toward him, aware that the sleek, red dress she'd put on felt way too tight against her skin. Body-hugging to the extreme, but it was the look she'd need for this particular club.

Jay's gaze dropped to the dress. To her body. He swore.

"The media is in a frenzy." A quick glance online had shown her that. "Someone at the police department leaked the news about me being your bodyguard. If you go out and I'm not with you tonight, what do you think that will do? Won't they just start up with the stories again about me being hurt? Dead?" Willow didn't give him a chance to answer. "But if I show up at your side, those stories will stop."

West scratched the back of his neck. "She has a point."

"You aren't helping," Jay immediately groused at him.

West just laughed as he lifted his hands, palms out, toward him. "My mistake." But he winked at Willow. West was also dressed in a suit. One that fit his muscled body perfectly. Jay and West both always looked like, well, money.

Because they were.

Absolutely rich.

While she had nothing. Jay had bought her everything she had in her closet upstairs. All that she had. It was time she started paying him back. "I want the job for real."

Jay lifted one brow. His right index finger began to tap against his leg. "What job?"

She'd thought about this all day. Now Willow smiled at him. "The job of your bodyguard."

He stopped tapping his finger.

West let out a laugh, but quickly smothered it when Jay glared at him.

"It's *not* funny," Willow announced, just so they were all clear. "You both know I'm more than capable of doing the job."

"Oh, I wasn't laughing at the idea, Willow. I promise, I wasn't." West's voice was gentle. "I was laughing because I know Jay isn't going to be able to find a way out of this one." He straightened his shoulders and his voice sharpened as he added, "Jay, as your head of security, I think you absolutely need a twenty-four, seven bodyguard. In light of the attempt made on your life last night, this is another security measure that I feel is necessary for your safety—"

"Screw off, West," Jay growled at him. "You've already got five new bodyguards on me. I know they're going to be tailing me tonight."

West shrugged. "Yes, but they're just, well, not Willow."

Her chest warmed. "I'm the best. I can stay at your side and no one will—"

"Everyone already thinks you two are sleeping together," West tossed out.

Willow's lips parted. Her cheeks heated. They *had* slept together. They just hadn't actually had sex.

"The story is everywhere online. 'Tech guru falls for hot bodyguard.'" West strolled around the room. "It was your face that gave things away, buddy. After the shot was fired. Reporters were snapping pics, hell, anyone with a phone was taking pics, and apparently, your expression was quite revealing."

"Screw. Off," Jay ordered again.

West just laughed.

She wasn't sure what West meant about Jay's expression. She'd been bleeding all over him, so she figured the guy must have looked horrified as hell.

"It's settled." West clapped his hands together. "Willow will stay at your side because she can keep your ass safe, *and* we can continue trying to draw out Wyman. Not much has changed, except," now his gaze sharpened, "another one of Jay's enemies has come out from the woodwork."

"Give us a minute alone," Jay said. His face was locked in angry lines. "Now."

West shrugged. "The cars are waiting. I'll be in the lead vehicle. You take the second one. Don't linger here too long. You two can have a private talk in the limo."

He gave a salute and strolled out.

Jay put his hands on his hips as he focused all of his attention on Willow. "You took a bullet last night." He stalked toward her. "*Maybe* you should just sit this one out. Did you consider that? That instead of getting right back into the line of fire you should, oh, I don't know, take the damn night off?" His eyes glittered.

She tilted back her head as she stared at him. "You're not taking the night off."

"I'm—shit, no, I'm just going to a club, okay? Blowing off some steam."

That was total crap. "You're trying to find the shooter. You figure that if someone wants you dead bad enough to take a shot at you, then that person might be tailing you. You're luring him to the club because you'll have your men there—and I'm betting you've already talked to the club's owner, haven't you? You got him to make sure all the cameras were working, that his crew was monitoring the scene for you."

His lashes flickered. "I have been talking to Benjamin Larson. And do you really think he wants you to just sashay your sweet ass into his new club?"

The name made her flinch. *Benjamin Larson.* "You're going...to-to the crime boss's club?"

"Push opens tonight. Since I helped finance the place, I figured I should show up. *I'm* half-owner." He rolled back his shoulders. "Part of my whole *atoning* bit, if you must know. After you made Larson see his personal hell at Sin, I figured I owed him."

Sin. Another club owned by Benjamin Larson. A club in which she and Benjamin had experienced a rather unfortunate encounter.

Her cheeks had gone cold. "I had to do that. I was trying to help. Trying to stop Bryce from killing people."

"I know that." Jay shrugged. "Doesn't mean Benjamin is particularly forgiving of what you did to him."

She exhaled. "Doesn't matter. I'm going. I'm your new bodyguard, whether you like it or not." Why was he fighting this?

He stepped even closer to her, his body nearly brushing against hers. "Fine, but don't you dare get shot. Don't you bleed. Don't you *hurt.* Not for me, do you understand?"

His voice had been low and rough, and it seemed to sink right past her skin.

"Not for me," he said again.

He was going to let her take the job. Willow didn't let her joy show, instead, she notched up her chin. "We should probably discuss my fee," Willow announced crisply, not responding to the words he'd said.

"Fuck me." His eyes squeezed closed. "I'll pay you anything you want."

Considering he had limitless resources, Willow figured she'd better come up with a nice, fat number for him.

"Just don't get hurt." His eyes opened. For an instant, she felt absolutely burned by the heat of his stare. "Because if your blood is on my hands again, you'll see that Lazarus subjects aren't the only ones who can lose control."

***

Jay could feel the eyes on him. The stares. The cameras. The people calling out to him—it was like a swirl of energy as he exited the limo and strode toward the entrance to Push.

Push…Benjamin Larson's new club. *The* place to be in D.C. The guy tied to far too many criminals wanted to be seen as legit, and since Jay owed the guy…he was making this appearance at the big, grand opening event.

His new bodyguards—the guards that West had hired—trailed around him and Willow. And Willow, damn, but she looked *hot*. He didn't even remember buying that dress. It fit her like a second skin, and with her dark hair and olive skin…

Sweet hell.

The neckline plunged, revealing the perfect swell of her breasts. He kept trying to keep his eyes off her breasts. Kept trying to play the role he'd been given.

But he just wanted to grab her and take Willow far, far away from that scene. From all of the eyes, all of the cameras.

"Hey, sexy bodyguard!" A male voice shouted. "Give us a few minutes!"

Jay's head turned to the left. He recognized the reporter from one of the online tabloids—a place that was always profiling celebrities—loving to catch singers and actors and the rich and famous in spots of scandal. Jay's arm curled around Willow's side, and he pulled her against him. "Ignore them all. We'll be inside soon," he spoke the low words against her ear, and she shivered.

From the cold? Because of all the attention she was getting?

Or because of something else?

"A shooter fired into a crowd yesterday." Her voice was a soft breath of sound. "Shouldn't everyone be worried?"

Yeah, they damn well should be. But cops were everywhere. Private security was hidden in the crowd. This time, they were on guard. "You sensing anything?"

She gave a negative shake of her head.

Some of the tension eased from his shoulders as they strode into Push. VIPs only for opening night—the club would open to everyone else the next day. So when they went inside, the place was filled with money. You could practically smell it dripping in the place. Women with perfectly styled hair and dresses that displayed their bodies to tempting degrees mingled with men in suits who stood with studied casualness. Waiters and waitresses poured out the champagne in mass quantities, while a well-known pop star sang on stage.

"What the hell is *she* doing here?"

Jay stiffened when he heard that low, gruff voice. He also grabbed a champagne flute from a waitress and drained that shit fast. Then he faced the speaker, his host for the night.

Benjamin Larson.

"Place is killer." Jay saluted the guy with his empty champagne glass. "Congratulations."

Benjamin growled. He was also in a suit, but the guy didn't carry himself with the easy grace and wealth of the others in Push. Instead, the fellow looked like trouble. Jay wondered how he managed that feat. An interesting talent.

"The club isn't the one who's killer." Benjamin's hard stare was on Willow. "Seriously, what the fuck is she doing here?"

Willow took a step toward the other man.

"Stop right there." Benjamin pointed at her. "You might be sexy as all hell, but you are never getting touching close to me again." He bared his teeth in a cold smile. "I like to keep my nightmares in my head, thank you very much."

Jay saw Willow's cheeks flame. "I was *helping* – "

"Right. Yeah, I get that I was in your way and you were trying to save the day back then and all that jazz." Now he waved his hand vaguely. "But

I don't care about saving the day. And I tend to hold very, very long grudges."

"Enough." Jay moved in front of Willow. "She's with me. I own half this club, so she's staying. And I don't give a shit if you have a problem with that or not." He kept a congenial smile on his face for the folks who were watching. "You wanted to be seen as legit? I'm your ticket to that. So try being *nice* to my companion."

Benjamin just smirked. "Don't you mean your bodyguard?"

Willow's fingers pressed to Jay's back.

Benjamin's smirk vanished. "Careful there. Or she'll have you seeing hell, too."

Did he look worried? "Been there, done that. Without her touch. I see hell plenty well enough on my own."

But Benjamin just laughed. "What would a pampered SOB like you know about hell?"

A sister dying in my arms. Me, sleeping on the streets. No shoes, no food. Rain pouring down. A hunger that never ends. "Go mingle with the patrons. We'll be upstairs." The better to watch everyone else. To peer into the crowd and see if any faces stuck out at him.

Benjamin offered his hand to Jay. Jay just stared at it.

"For the people watching." Benjamin's hand didn't move. "Got to let them know what good buddies we are."

Jay took the guy's hand. Squeezed it a bit harder than necessary. "For future reference, Willow is always welcome wherever I am."

Benjamin studied him a moment, then said, "Poor bastard," before pulling his hand away and laughing as he left.

Jay watched him a moment. "I think that man may have a few issues." A *lot* of issues. "Maybe he should see a shrink. I know a good one." He glanced over his shoulder at Willow. "Let's go upstairs."

Her cheeks were still red. Benjamin had hurt her feelings. Or he'd embarrassed her. Maybe he'd done both. "I should have slugged the bastard." Next time, he would. Screw the eyes watching them. He caught Willow's hand in his and escorted her toward the stairs. "Let's get out of the crowd." Because all of the men there were staring at Willow with lust in their eyes. And Willow—how much of that did she pick up on?

The Lazarus subjects had psychic powers. She could pick up on fears. She could *make* fears a reality. Could she read minds, too? Pick up on the lust of others? On the darkness people kept bottled inside? Willow wasn't exactly the forthcoming sort when it came to sharing her paranormal gifts.

Two bouncers were blocking the stairs, but when they saw Jay approaching, they immediately took down the velvet rope and waved him upstairs. The carpet on the stairs was thick, lush, and it swallowed his steps. In moments, he and Willow were in the VIP room. The boss's room. They were staring through the one-way glass at the men and women downstairs. Watching as they drank, flirted, danced, and left every inhibition they had at the door.

Push. Benjamin thought he was clever with the name. *You can't push your way inside.*

Push yourself to the limits.

Push past the fear.

Push all your desires to the surface.

The guy had told him all that shit. Then said the club had to be called Push.

Jay slid his fingers along Willow's inner wrist as he gazed down at the crowd.

"Why are you still touching me?"

A few faces looked familiar. A little too familiar. Especially the pretty redhead down there. He winced as he kept his gaze on the woman he knew too well. "Because I like to touch you. You feel like silk." He let her go. "But if you don't want me to hold you, then I won't."

"Benjamin Larson hates me."

"Yeah, well, most people think he's a dick, so don't exactly lose sleep over that." The redhead was glaring up at the VIP area. She'd obviously seen him climb the stairs. He leaned closer to the glass as he spied another familiar figure. A rival who just hadn't been able to beat Jay to the punch on the last big launch. They'd been working on similar tech products for Uncle Sam, but Jay had gotten the job done faster, better, and for half the cost.

"Your heart rate has increased." Her voice was tense. "Is something wrong?"

"Just saw a few familiar faces in the crowd." He pulled out his phone and fired off a quick text to West. "Some folks who might not be particularly pleased with me."

"People who want you dead?"

He shrugged. "People who don't exactly like me."

"Do you…lose sleep over that?"

Jay blinked. He put the phone back in his pocket and glanced at Willow. "Business can be hard. I make decisions that impact a lot of people. They're not easy decisions. When my products work, it usually means someone else's don't. And my success can mean another company becomes obsolete. That's jobs lost. People's lives changed. So, yeah, I lose some sleep." He motioned toward the well-stocked bar that waited to the left, taking up the entire wall. "Why don't you grab a drink? I want to see what West and the others learn downstairs."

She didn't head for the bar. "You see…business associates. Those are the familiar people in the crowd below?"

He raked a hand through his hair. "I also see an ex-lover who didn't exactly like our end."

"What?" Her eyes went wide. Then narrowed.

"Things got tense." Serious understatement. That was why he'd mentioned Reva Gray first in his text to West. She could be the bigger problem. "Reva wanted more."

"More…what?"

This wasn't going to win him any points with Willow. But he'd rather just tell her the truth and be done. "We were involved for sex. At least, that's what I thought. No strings, not for either of us."

Willow blinked. Once. Twice. Her expression seemed to go absolutely cold.

"Come on, Willow. People hook up all the time. It's no big deal. I'm sure you've had—"

He stopped. Too fucking late.

Willow glanced away from him. "I have no idea."

Shit, shit, *shit*. "I am such an asshole."

"I think that you are." She gave a brisk nod. "Apparently, that Reva down there does, too. You know what? I believe I will have that drink."

She marched toward the bar and he looked around, wondering if there was a hole he could crawl into. Unfortunately, Jay didn't see one, so he straightened his shoulders and headed after her. "I'm sorry."

She held up a bottle of vodka. "Is this good?"

"Yeah, great. But, listen, I just didn't think when I—"

"You constantly think. We all do. And you—well, especially you. I don't believe your mind ever stops spinning." Her cool stare raked over him. "I'm not so sure your brain works quite like everyone else's. I tried to look inside, to see more than your fears, but I couldn't." She poured vodka into a nearby glass. A *lot* of vodka and chugged it right down.

"Baby, hold up, that's too much—go slow with—"

She slammed down the glass and angrily confronted him. "I go slow with everything." Her eyes gleamed at him. "I go slow because I don't know what the hell I'm doing. You remember all of your lovers. What—dozens of them? Women who didn't matter? Women like me that you just hooked up with and walked away—"

"They are nothing like you." They needed to be clear on this point.

She flinched.

Fucking hell. Why could he not say the right thing to her?

"I'm going downstairs. I'm not the one who can get hurt. *You* stay here." Her words were rapid fire. "I'll find the bastard who shot me and deal with him myself." She tried to march around him.

Jay caught her shoulders, held her tight. "They are *nothing* like you," he gritted out, "because I never wanted anyone the way I want *you*."

Her breath heaved out. "What?"

"They are nothing like you because you are strong—and, no, I'm not talking about your super strength. I'm talking about the core of steel inside of you. You've been through hell, but you're still standing. Because you were strong *before* Lazarus. You're strong where it matters most. In your heart, baby, and in your soul." He sounded like a freaking greeting card, but it was true. She had to stop seeing herself as some kind of freak. She wasn't.

To him, Willow was perfect.

"And I don't just walk away from lovers. I'm not some user. I don't screw every woman I meet. I happen to be pretty picky about relationships. Reva was a friend first. We thought we'd make good lovers. Didn't work that way."

Her lashes covered her eyes. "You think…you believe we'd be good lovers, too. You and I—"

"It's *not* the same thing."

"But what if you're wrong about that, too?"

The way he was on fire for her? Hell, no, he wasn't wrong. If they got together, they'd burn the bed down.

"What if you're wrong, and then you walk away. What happens to me?"

"Willow…"

But she'd pulled away from him. "I'm going downstairs."

"I'm coming with you—"

"No." She pointed at her chest. "I'm the bodyguard, remember? I'm going back down, I'll do a scan, and I'll see who I can find." Her gaze darted around the room. "This area is safe enough. I'm assuming that's bullet proof glass?"

"Yes," he hissed. "But Willow, we need—"

"I think I need more vodka," she muttered as she headed for the door. "And I definitely need some distance from you."

Hell.

Because of those last words, he didn't follow her. He stood there, with his hands clenched at his sides, and he watched her storm away from him. Beautiful Willow. Strong Willow. *Hurting* Willow. He'd done that. With careless words.

The one person he wanted to treasure, and he kept screwing up.

He yanked out his phone. Texted both West and Sawyer Cage. *Willow is heading to the lower level. Keep eyes on her. Anything happens to Willow…*

His fingers paused because a wild, dark thought ran through his head. *If anything happens to Willow, I'll fucking lose my mind.*

Jay swallowed. And he didn't send that particular message to his friends. Instead, he just texted…

Anything happens to Willow, and I'll kick your asses.

***

Fury twisted inside of Willow. Fury and…jealousy? She'd never felt jealousy before, so she wasn't one hundred percent sure what she was dealing with but…

But the image of Jay, kissing that redhead—*Reva.* The image of him holding her, having sex with her…

The fury burned hotter.

She stomped down the stairs. Her gaze swept over the bar. Two men came toward her, smiling, but she moved past them without a word. Her senses were amped up. She was looking for danger. Looking for the shooter. Wanting to get this job finished and get the hell out of that place.

She'd thought that Jay felt something for her. Something real. Perhaps something more than guilt. But she'd forgotten that he'd had a life before her.

And whatever life she'd had, it was long gone. Along with her memories. Along with any family she'd had. Any lovers who'd been with her. Casual lovers. Serious lovers. All were gone.

The scent of perfume—a mix of rose and jasmine—became stronger. Her head turned toward that scent and Willow found herself watching as Reva slid through the crowd. Reva's eyes—a pure emerald green—were on Willow.

Reva was absolutely stunning. Perfect features, heart-shaped face, red hair long and styled to flow over her shoulders. She wore a green dress, one that matched her eyes, and her lips had been painted a bright red.

Men were practically falling at the woman's feet. A faint smile curved Reva's bow-shaped lips.

A gorgeous woman, and Willow decided that she might hate Reva.

Then Reva stopped right in front of Willow. Reva's green gaze swept over Willow, iced a bit. "So you're the new one." Her voice held a crisp accent.

"I don't think you understand…"

Reva met her stare. "I saw the way he looked at you. The way he touched you." She still smiled, but the smile never reached her eyes. "I get that he's feeding the bodyguard story to the reporters, but who is going to buy that line? He's screwing you, and he likes to have you close."

Now she gave a little, tinkling laugh. "Like you're strong enough to be anyone's bodyguard."

The woman was just insulting. "You have no idea."

Reva's smile vanished. She stepped right up to Willow. "No, *you're* the one with no idea. No idea who it is that you're truly fucking." Her voice was low, and the crisp accent had faded into a ragged rasp. "He's dangerous. You can't trust him."

Willow's heart was racing, and she put her hands behind her back. *The better to avoid the temptation to make this woman fear.*

"You want to know the *real* Jay Maverick?" Reva pointed to the left. "Let's get out of this crowd, and I'll tell you his secrets. Then you'll realize the man you've taken into your bed is little more than a monster."

Without another word, Reva turned on her very high heel and stalked through the crowd, heading to the left. Moving toward the ladies' rest room.

Willow gazed after her a moment, then she looked up, her stare going to the second floor. To the VIP area. Her eyes narrowed as she peered up at that darkened glass. Jay was watching.

Little more than a monster.

Her shoulders straightened, and she headed after Reva.

***

"Oh, shit," Jay muttered. Then he surged away from the glass.

CHAPTER FIVE

"No one else is in here." Reva stood with her arms over her chest. They were in some kind of waiting area—like a lounge. Filled with black, leather sofas and chairs. And all of the walls were covered with mirrors. Reva had locked the door right after Willow entered. "Just you and me."

Willow crossed her arms over her chest. "You had sex with Jay."

Spots of color appeared on Reva's cheeks. "Is that what he told you? That we fucked? My, my…and here I didn't think he was the type to kiss and tell." Now she sauntered toward Willow. "Did he tell you all the times? All the places? All the—"

Willow held up her hand. "Don't come any closer to me."

Reva smiled again. The smile that didn't reach her eyes. "Are you afraid of me, bodyguard?"

I'm afraid if you get closer, I'll give into the growing urge to make you see some fears. And that wasn't right. But the twisting fury and yes, *had to be jealousy,* inside of Willow was growing worse with every moment that passed.

"You shouldn't be afraid of me. It's Jay you should fear. You might think he's charming and sophisticated. You might think he can give you the world." Reva shook her head. "But he won't. He'll give you a good time in bed, a *very* good time, but that's it. He'll use you, and when he's done, he'll toss you away."

Willow straightened her spine. "Is this what you wanted to tell me? That you think Jay is going to have sex with me and then walk away?"

"The only lover he stayed with for long…that was Elizabeth. Dr. Elizabeth Parker. And I think he just stayed with her because he liked her mind, not her body."

Shock had rolled through Willow. This…how had she not known *this?* "Jay and Elizabeth were lovers?"

Elizabeth Parker was involved with Sawyer Cage. They were planning to get married. But…

Elizabeth was also the doctor who'd first created the Lazarus serum.

Elizabeth and Jay.

Why hadn't they told her?

"Didn't know that? Oh, right, you've probably met her, haven't you? Jay still keeps her around. Says they are just *friends,* if you believe that lie."

Willow's temples were pounding. "You hate him."

"I hate that he pretends to be something he's not."

"You said that he was a monster."

"He grew up dirt poor, did you know that? On the streets? And it did something to him. Made him savage. Wild. Jay will do *anything* to get what he wants. I've seen him destroy competitors, wreck companies, break lives, and never hesitate."

Someone pounded on the door.

"Go away!" Reva snapped. "We're busy in here!"

"It's the frickin' bathroom," a woman's disgruntled voice snarled back.

But Willow heard the sound of her footsteps stomp away.

"He'll sweep you into his world." Reva's eyes were chips of green fire. "And then when he's done, he'll leave you and never look back."

Willow studied her. Tried to see past the other woman's rage. "You don't hate him. You...love him?"

"No." Reva backed up. "Of course, I don't love him! But I put in the time. Do you understand? Do you know how much money that man is worth? He's—"

"You're mad because you want his money or him?" She was trying to understand.

"I want *both!*" Reva snarled.

"This is a waste of time." Willow kept her voice brisk. "You said that you were going to reveal his secrets, but you didn't tell me anything of the sort. I knew he grew up hard. I knew the two of you were involved." She *hadn't* known about Elizabeth, though. "Unless you're the one trying to kill him, we're done."

And there it was—Willow heard the furious and wild beat of Reva's heart accelerate.

"Never!" Reva cried out. "I wouldn't do that! He's no good to me dead. I wouldn't—"

"I believe you." Because Reva wanted Jay back in her life. She didn't want him in the grave. "Now we're done." One suspect eliminated. She headed for the door.

But Reva grabbed her hand. "We're just getting started."

"You shouldn't have done that," Willow whispered as she stared down at Reva's hand. But it was too late now. Some people projected their emotions so strongly—they all but screamed them. Reva was one of those people. Her emotions bubbled and burned as they erupted from her. When Reva touched her, Willow didn't even have to pull up her powers.

She was immediately hit with Reva's fears. They slammed into her mind, tumbling straight at her, over and over again. A sharp cry broke from Willow because she hadn't expected Reva's worst fear to pierce so deeply.

***

"It's the ladies' room, man," West argued as he stood in front of Jay, blocking the way. "And it's Reva. The woman can't hurt Willow, and you know it."

"There are all kinds of ways to hurt in this world, and *you* know that." The words erupted in a hard snarl.

West's brows shot up. "Does that mean that *you* hurt Willow?"

Yes, he just had, dammit. "I'm going in—"

Then he heard Willow's cry. Sharp. Pain-filled. Jay shoved West out of his way and grabbed for the door. When it didn't open, he kicked the thing in. "Willow!"

She was on her knees. Reva was touching her shoulders. At his cry, Reva spun toward him. Her eyes widened when she saw his face. "I didn't do anything to her!" Reva yelled even as her hand flew over Willow's hunched form. "I swear it! I only grabbed her wrist to stop her from leaving and your girlfriend freaked the hell out! She's psycho!"

"Stop. Touching. Her." But Jay didn't wait for Reva to let Willow go. He bounded across the room and scooped Willow into his arms.

"Some bodyguard," Reva muttered. "More like a drama queen. She—"

"She doesn't want to be on the streets again." Willow's voice was low and flat, totally devoid of emotion. "She thought the streets would be better than home, they hurt her so much there. Over and over, but when she got on the streets, she didn't have any money. She has to have money. Because when you don't have money, you're vulnerable. They'll make you do things. They'll make you—"

"*Shut the hell up!*" Reva's enraged shriek.

The little room went dead silent.

West stepped inside, and he pushed the broken door shut behind him.

Reva stood there, her body shaking and her face stark white. She lifted a trembling finger and pointed at Willow. "How do you know?"

Because that was Reva's worst fear. Jay knew it. He hadn't needed Willow to tell him. Reva had always feared others would find out about her darkest truths. The pain she tried to hide.

"Let me go," Willow whispered to Jay.

He didn't want to let her go. He wanted to keep right on holding her, but she was pushing against his arms. So he lowered Willow to her feet, and he stayed close to her.

"*You* told her!" Reva charged, and then she was racing toward Jay. Her hand flew out and she slapped him with all of her might. "You sonofabitch! How *could* you?"

He hadn't told Willow a damn thing, but he wasn't going to admit that to Reva. If he did, then Reva would know Willow's secret. That couldn't happen. Reva would sell any story for the right amount of money. And there would be a whole lot of money offered if the truth about Willow made it into the public eye.

Reva drew back her hand to hit him again, but West caught her wrist. "Easy..."

She jerked away from him. "Don't you 'easy' me, West Harper! You knew, too, didn't you? What, were you both laughing at me? Making fun of me? Oh, there goes Reva...pretending she's so high class. Pretending she's something she's not, pretending—"

"We all pretend sometimes, Reva." Jay kept his voice gentle. "Nothing wrong with that." His gaze remained on her. "And there's nothing wrong with having a rough start, with overcoming it. With making something of yourself when you've been through a nightmare. If anything, it's a success to be proud of. Not something to hide."

Reva's eyes glittered with tears. "I should have known. You research everyone. Anyone who gets close to you. But...I changed my name, got a new life, *paid* for that life, so I thought I was safe, I thought—"

"You are safe. No one outside of this room ever needs to know about your past."

Her furious glare flew to Willow. "You told your lover, your current screw. You'll tell the next one! You'll tell—"

"He didn't tell me," Willow cut in.

Shit. Jay opened his mouth, trying to get a ready lie in place.

"She's on my payroll," West threw out before Jay could speak. "And has top clearance. She has access to my files and while we're trying to figure out who is after Jay, *I* filled her in about you. There's no one else on the team who ever needs to know."

Some of the tension left Reva's shoulders. She blinked her eyes a few times and then focused on Jay. "You knew all along?"

He had.

"It…didn't matter?"

No, it hadn't mattered. He didn't care about her past.

But Reva was already shaking her head. "Maybe it did matter. Maybe that's why you didn't stay, maybe it's the reason you walked away."

Jay stepped forward and caught her hands. Held her tight. "I walked away because you wanted what I couldn't give."

"Commitment. Marriage." A fine tension held her body in its grip.

Sadly, he shook his head. "No, Reva, you wanted my money. You loved it, and not me."

Her lips parted, but she didn't speak.

"You want security, and there's nothing wrong with that. But I want more. I want a woman who'd love me the same if I didn't have a dollar to my name. Because you see, Reva, once, I didn't. I had nothing. So I'd never judge you, and I wouldn't want you to judge me. But I'll be damned if I spend my life with someone who *doesn't* love me. So I walked away. And I'm going to keep walking."

A tear rolled down her cheek. "Until you find someone who loves you?"

He wasn't so sure that would happen. Not at the rate he kept screwing up.

But Reva was peering around his body. "She's not the one." Her voice was raspy. "She's not going to love you, Jay."

No, Willow probably wasn't. "I think you should go home, Reva."

She backed away from him. Her hands swiped over her cheeks, and it was like a veil swept over her features. Not a veil, but maybe a mask. She always tried to hide her real self. "Why?" Reva demanded. "The night is young. Maybe you're off my list now, but it doesn't mean I'm done." She turned on her heel. Marched out with the grace of a queen. No one spoke until she was gone.

West inclined his head toward Jay. "I think it's time for us to get our asses out of the ladies' room."

Leave it to West. Jay's lips quirked as some of the tension finally broke. "Right. Well, I guess we can mark Reva off *our* list, too."

"Yeah." West exhaled. "And I'll go find Sawyer. See if he's turned up anything. So far, this night feels like a bust." Then West was exiting, too.

Jay squared his shoulders and turned back to Willow. There were dark shadows under her eyes, and she was gazing at him in confusion. He lifted his hand toward her. "Hate to say it, sweetheart, but there's gonna be even more stories about us circulating tomorrow. I'm sure plenty of folks saw me kick in the bathroom door." And he was also sure that Benjamin had made sure no one followed them inside. But it was time to leave.

She crept closer, but didn't take his hand. "I didn't mean to see her fears. She's just a really strong projector."

He nodded and kept his hand extended to her.

"I didn't make her see those fears, though." Her words came quickly. "I didn't do that."

"I know." Again, his tone was soft.

Willow licked her lips. "She's not what I thought. On the inside. I never expected—"

"The world is all about pretending. People are never who you think when you first glance at them." A lesson he'd learned early on. "Perfect lives don't exist. Neither do perfect people. We all fuck up, and we just try to do our best to move forward."

Her hand rose and her silken fingers finally touched his. "You didn't tell her about me. About what I can do."

"Because that's your secret. Reva would have gone to the first reporter she could have found, and then you'd have been shredded." Shredded, dissected, sent to a new lab when the government found out what she could do.

Subject her to that nightmare again? Only over his dead body.

"You protected me."

Now he laughed as he tucked her hand into the crook of his arm. "Sweetheart, you don't have to sound so stunned." He escorted her out of the bathroom as if they'd just exited a limo, and, sure enough, he saw the line of bouncers who'd appeared to keep the crowd back. He'd owe Benjamin again. He also heard all of the whispers. Most were too low for him to make out clearly, but Willow tilted her head, as if she could understand them perfectly.

Which, of course, she could.

"They think you've gone crazy for me." Her head turned and her wide eyes met his. "That you're obsessed."

They weren't completely wrong. "I want you to smile."

Her lashes flickered.

"Every eye in this place is on us. Just smile at me."

She smiled, but he could tell the curve of her lips took effort. He much preferred Willow's real smiles to her fake ones. The real smiles didn't come nearly often enough. He'd work on that.

"Want to dance with me?" Jay asked her.

Her smile faltered. They were walking through the crowd. It seemed like they were finally starting to lose everyone's attention. "A bodyguard doesn't dance."

"Unfortunate. I had so much fun dancing with you the other night." *Last night.* It had been last night. Right before a shooter had tried to wreck Jay's life. "We can go back up to the VIP area."

She glanced toward the stairs.

"But I think we should leave," Jay continued briskly. "We came, everyone saw that I wasn't hiding, and we attracted plenty of attention. If the shooter is here, you would have sensed him."

"I haven't."

Right. "So he's not here. Let's get the hell out of this place."

Willow immediately turned for the front door.

"No, this way." He nodded toward the back of the club. "I told the driver to pick us up in the back. Mostly because my front departure routine didn't work so well last time." He steered her past more bouncers and into an employees' only section of the club. A moment later, though, both West and Sawyer appeared.

"No sign of a shooter," Sawyer's voice was clipped. "West had me check out your competitor, Micah Long. The guy isn't carrying any weapons, and he was more interested in screwing the two women he'd brought here than anything else."

Sounded like Micah. The guy always proclaimed that variety was the spice of life.

"The shooter could be running," West offered as he seemed to consider the situation. "The guy missed you last night, and now he knows the world is after him. If he's smart, he's keeping a low profile. He's gonna try to vanish as fast as he can."

That was certainly one option.

"Or…" Sawyer cleared his throat. "The fellow is just laying low. Waiting for his chance to strike again. Maybe he's waiting for the perfect moment to come at you. Could be plotting how to kill you right now." Jay could only sigh. "Sawyer, seriously, can you ever try sugar coating things?" How did Elizabeth live with the guy?

Sawyer simply shrugged. "Why waste time with that sugary shit?"

Sounded like something a former Navy SEAL would say.

But then Sawyer's gaze cut to Willow. He frowned. "Everything okay?"

No, not really.

"Hey…" Sawyer's voice sharpened. It was just their little group in that backroom. The bouncers hadn't passed the threshold of the door. Jay had no idea where Flynn Haddox was lurking. "Any luck with John Smith?" Sawyer was suddenly asking. "That super soldier we met up in the mountains before Christmas? Is he going to talk with—"

"*Not* now," Jay cut in sharply as his gaze jerked toward Willow. Dammit. That little adventure into the mountains was something he hadn't wanted to talk about with Willow. Not yet, anyway. They'd get to the matter of John Smith much later. Like when Willow didn't look as if she were about to shatter.

"Who's John Smith?" Willow immediately asked.

"Someone we'll discuss later." Right then, he just wanted to get the hell out of Push. He reached for Willow's elbow.

But she shook her head. "No more secrets. Secrets like the fact that you used to be involved with Sawyer's lover, Elizabeth."

Sawyer blinked. His gaze went cold. Hard.

Crap. "That is ancient history, Willow." History he was sure Reva had unearthed. "Beth and I are friends, nothing more."

"You didn't tell me. You kept it secret." Color stained her cheeks. "I don't like secrets."

He didn't either, but, sometimes, secrets were necessary.

Willow's head swung toward Sawyer. "Don't you mind? Don't you...don't you hate that they were together?"

"Makes me want to drive my fist into his face some days," was Sawyer's drawling reply. "But then I remember, Elizabeth is with me. She chose *me.* Then I get to leave his face exactly as it is."

Um, okay. Jay glared at the guy. "Not helping much."

Willow rubbed her forehead. "Everything is jumbled. Confused." Her eyes squeezed shut. "Anger. Jealousy."

Wait—Willow was jealous? Because of Elizabeth? Reva? She didn't need to be.

Then her eyes opened. "Who is John Smith?"

Back to that. Fine. So it looked like they were having this little talk right then and there. "He's another Lazarus subject I managed to track down. You know I'm looking for the others."

She gave a jerky nod.

"I found him right before Christmas." *Tread carefully.* "Turns out, he was in the same North Carolina lab that you were. He remembered hearing the guards talk about you."

Willow took a step back. "I don't know him."

"John said he never actually saw you." So she probably didn't have memories of the guy. Which was why he hadn't pushed too hard for them to meet yet. "But he overheard the guards and doctors talking about you."

"You were the control subject," West murmured.

Really, why was everyone oversharing right then? He tossed a glare at his brother.

West just shrugged. "Man, I get that you're trying to protect her, but sometimes, a person needs to hear the truth." He paced forward. "John Smith was experimented on in that lab, killed again and again, just so he could be brought back. From what we can tell, you were isolated, never allowed contact with him or with anyone else at the facility. You were the controlled comparison. I'm guessing they wanted to see how far they could push John." West inclined his head toward Sawyer. "And all the others. See how far they could be pushed before—"

"They broke?" Willow finished.

West didn't speak.

So Jay did. "We know some of the test subjects can't handle the surge of darker emotions. They go…" Now he was the one to stop, letting his words flounder.

"They go crazy." Once more, Sawyer wasn't sugar coating. "Absolutely fucking psychotic. And that's why we're hunting them. We have to figure out who's sane and who is a threat that has to be eliminated."

Willow's hands twisted in front of her. She stared down at them. "Which category am I in?"

"Willow." Jay's voice had turned rough.

She glanced up at him. "Or are you all still trying to figure that part out?"

Enough. Jay positioned himself right in front of her. He held her gaze as he said, clearly and flatly, "There is nothing else I need to figure out about you. You aren't a threat. You aren't psychotic."

"If you were," West pointed out from behind him, "don't you think Jay would still have you locked up in one of those hi-tech cells he created for the Lazarus subjects?"

Jay's eyes squeezed shut. *Not helping, West. Not helping at all.* "We're leaving." Enough talk. Enough fucking drama. His eyes opened. Willow was staring at him with her wide eyes, and so much emotion burned in her blue stare. The problem was that he couldn't quite decode what she was feeling.

"I'll check the exterior perimeter." Sawyer gave him a nod. "Flynn is still in the club, making sure no signs of trouble are in there." Then Sawyer was heading out the back. A few moments later, he gave a low whistle, and Jay knew they were good to go.

They filed outside. The limo was waiting. A new driver was there, one of the guards West had handpicked. Willow stilled, and her gaze swept the dark alley. A light drizzle of rain had begun to fall on them.

"All clear," she whispered.

The shooter wasn't going to make another appearance. Maybe he had run. *But we'll find you, eventually.*

Jay and Willow slid into the car. Before the door shut, West leaned inside. "I'll have guards tail you. I'm going to do a little more recon. Want to check in with the cops, see if they turned up anything new."

"Watch your back," Jay warned him.

West just smiled. "Don't I always?"

The door slammed shut. A few moments later, the limo was rolling away from the club. When they swept around the corner, Jay glanced through the tinted windows. A throng of bodies surrounded the entrance to Push. His latest investment seemed to be a definite success.

The silence continued in the limo as they drove away from the center of the city. His home was just outside of D.C. Jay liked his privacy, and the estate certainly gave him that. He had several houses, all scattered around the U.S. After growing up without a home at all, he knew he'd overcompensated. But so the hell what?

His gaze swept toward Willow. She was staring out of the window. She looked so beautiful sitting there. Her soft profile. The long tumble of her hair. Her silken skin.

"Why are you watching me?"

His lips twisted. "Because you're absolutely beautiful." An honest answer.

Her head turned. Her gaze met his. "I'm not as beautiful as Reva."

As far as he was concerned, she was a thousand times more gorgeous. "I guess that depends on who you ask."

Willow blinked.

He didn't move closer to her, though he sure wanted to do so. "I happen to think no other woman on earth can compare to you."

Her lips pressed together. More silence. Then... "Lines like that come easy to you, don't they? You can charm anyone you want."

Anger hummed within him. "You think I'm feeding you a line?"

"I don't know." Her response was soft.

His eyes narrowed. "Why don't you just look into my head and find out if I'm telling you the truth?"

Her stare jerked away from his. She stared out the window once more. "I see fears—"

"Is that really all you see?" Jay pushed.

But she'd pressed her lips together once more.

"Now who is keeping secrets?" he murmured.

The limo drove through the darkness. He didn't push her again because Jay knew Willow was already on the edge. He could practically see the fine tension in her body.

"I didn't like the way I felt when I was around Reva." She gave her confession in a hushed voice.

He waited.

"Angry, furious, and I-I kept seeing you two together in my head. She was saying that you wouldn't stay with me, and it shouldn't have mattered. We *aren't* lovers. I shouldn't have cared at all. But I could feel the darkness inside of me. It was getting stronger. Worse."

"Baby, you aren't the only one who has a darkness inside. Everyone does."

She licked her lips. "We *aren't* lovers."

"No." Unfortunately, they—

Her stare came back to him. "But I think I'd like for us to be."

CHAPTER SIX

She'd said it. Actually let those words and the secret desire escape her. But now Jay had gone completely still. He stared at her with his deep, dark eyes, and she could see every detail of his face perfectly. His hard jaw had locked. The skin near his eyes had tightened. His breathing came a little faster. He—

"Be careful what you say, Willow. Some things can't be taken back."

"I don't want to take this back." She still felt jealous. *Jealous.* She was angry. She was scared. Adrenaline pounded through her body, but Willow was sure of one thing. "I want you."

He cursed. "Fucking hell."

Willow blinked as she felt a knot tie in the bottom of her stomach. *Fucking hell.* Not exactly the impassioned response she'd hoped to get. Didn't he still want her? "You changed your mind?"

He gave a rough laugh. "Changed my mind? About you? Oh, yeah, that shit won't ever happen. As long as I can breathe, I'll want you."

But he made no move to close the distance between them. "Wondering about the sudden turnaround, that's all. Because you told me to keep my hands *off*– "

"I want to know what it's like. You remember your lovers. The way they made you feel. The pleasure you had." Jealousy burned again. "But I have none of that. It was all taken from me. Every single moment. I want to get it back. I want to see what it feels like, I want to know more than just fear and pain and rage. I want pleasure, too."

"So anybody would do?" His voice deepened. "A body in the dark? Is that all you need?"

She shook her head. "No." Didn't he get it? "I want *you*."

Now he moved forward. Not a fast lunge toward her. But slowly, carefully, as if he thought she might run away. They were trapped in the back of the limo, where exactly could she go? Besides, Willow wasn't interested in running from him. Not then.

His hand lifted and the back of his fingers stroked over her cheek. "Once won't be enough."

His touch seemed to sink right through her.

"I'll want you again and again."

He couldn't know that. Once might be plenty. Once–

"And I'll make sure you feel the same way." His hand slid down to her chin. He tilted her head up, and then his lips pressed to her mouth. A soft kiss at first. As if he were sampling her, getting to know her taste. Her lips parted for him, though, because she wanted more. She wanted the wild rush of passion. The quick release of pleasure.

His tongue slid into her mouth. A moan escaped her, and her hands rose to curl around his shoulders. Her nails sank into his suit. The kiss started as a tender touch, but with every second that passed, it grew stronger. Rougher. Hotter.

She wanted his clothes out of her way. She wanted to see what it was like to touch him all over. To feel a lover, skin to skin. All of her memories were gone, and Willow felt as if she'd been robbed. Everything had been taken from her. Every. Single. Thing.

It was time for her to take back her life. To start living just like everyone else.

Even if she wasn't *exactly* like everyone else.

She shoved at his suit coat, wanting it out of the way.

But Jay gave a ragged laugh. "Sweetheart, my first time with you *won't* be a rushed fuck in the back of a limo."

Why not? The image was hot.

"I'm going to take my time with you." He was kissing a white-hot trail down her neck. She arched up against him as her heart pounded faster. His left hand had slid down her body. It rested on her stomach, and she wanted his fingers to *move.* She wanted him to touch her breasts. To touch her—all over. That was what lovers did, right? They touched. They pleasured.

"Jay!" A demand hummed in her voice.

"When we get home, I'm going to make love to you all night long."

"I don't want to wait." Her ragged words.

He'd moved his hand. His fingers slid inside the plunging neckline of her dress, and he teased her nipple. She bit her lip because she hadn't expected the shock of quick pleasure.

And she wanted more.

"You don't want to wait? Then how about I give you a taste right now." His hands moved to her legs. He grabbed the material of her dress and pushed it up. Not fast. Not hard. But slowly, sensuously.

Willow realized she was holding her breath. A lick of fear shot through her because this was new. As far as she was concerned, this was her first time with a lover. And she was hesitating. Her gaze darted to the privacy screen that separated them from the driver.

"I can stop right now." His hands were on her thighs. His voice was low and gentle.

She didn't want him to stop.

"The driver can't hear us. Can't see us. It's only you and me. But I can stop right now, if that is what you want."

She wanted more pleasure. She just wanted what everyone else had. Was that so wrong? "Don't stop." A bare whisper.

His fingers trailed up her inner thighs. *So sensitive.* How had she not realized that particular area of her body was so sensitive? Now she wasn't holding her breath, Willow was releasing it in a quick rush because his fingers had slipped up her thighs—all the way up until he was touching the crotch of her panties.

And Jay had moved. He'd slid off the seat. Positioned himself between her splayed legs. His gaze wasn't on her face. He was staring at her body, and she was so incredibly exposed for him because he'd shoved up her skirt.

"These have to go." He pulled on her panties. Harder than she'd expected. The soft lace tore.

The sound turned her on even more.

"Willow, Willow…sweet Willow." His fingers caressed her sex. Stroked her. Made her bite her lip. Made her hips surge against him. "I won't ever be able to go back now."

She wasn't sure what that meant. Didn't really care then because he'd just lowered his head. "Jay?"

He licked her. Licked her and pushed his fingers inside of her, and her own hands flew out to grab onto the seat. Her eyes squeezed closed as her head tipped back. This was so intimate—*of course, it was intimate.* But she hadn't expected this. His mouth on her. It was like they'd skipped a thousand steps and gone right to the finish line. It was like—

She came. An absolute explosion of pleasure rocked through her whole body, and Willow clamped down even harder on her lower lip because she didn't want to scream out her pleasure. It wasn't some short burst of release. It went on and on, seeming to fill every single cell of her body.

Her breath heaved in and out. Her heartbeat drummed in a double-time rhythm. This was sex? This was pleasure? *OhmyGod.* How had she forgotten it?

His fingers strummed over her clit.

A ripple of pleasure surged through her as he pressed a final kiss to her. Then he was sliding back. Pulling down her dress. Covering her legs.

And…going back to his seat?

What?

Her breath panted out more. Her nails were digging into the expensive leather of the seat. He sat across from her, his hands between his knees, his stare focused on her. Completely on her. His face was tight, hard. She'd never quite seen him look that way before.

Dangerous.

Jay usually had a quick smile. He usually seemed to be surrounded by a cloud of energy and zest. But right then, a different intensity clung to him. Almost a predatory intensity.

"You…" Okay, her voice was definitely husky. She tried clearing her throat. "You didn't…"

"I told you our first time wasn't going to be in a car." He even sounded different. Jay's voice was downright guttural. She realized that he held her panties in his right hand. As she watched, he shoved them into the pocket of his coat. "I'll have you in my home. It will just be you and me, and you won't have to bite your lip. You can scream as loudly as you want."

Oh, wow. She swallowed. Made herself take her nails *out* of the leather.

"You are so fucking beautiful. And you taste like the sweetest sin."

She could feel her cheeks burning.

"The first time won't be slow." Again, he was guttural. She rather liked the roughness of his voice. It sent a shiver over her. "I can't do slow with you. Not after I had my mouth on you."

Inside, she felt another pulse of pleasure. Just from his words.

"The first time will be rough. Hard. Wild. We'll do slow later, if that's what you want."

"I don't know what I want." Should she be embarrassed to make that confession? With him, right then, Willow found there wasn't room for embarrassment. It was just him. Just her. And what they were doing together, what they were saying, didn't feel wrong. "I have no idea what I like."

His body tensed. "Baby…" He exhaled slowly. "Are you trying to break me?"

She wasn't sure what that meant. Of course, she didn't want to break Jay.

"We'll find out what you like," Jay promised her as the limo slowed. "We'll find out every single thing that you enjoy. What makes you moan. What makes you come faster. What drives you absolutely wild. And we'll do those things over and over again."

Yes, please.

The limo stopped. She heard the driver exiting. Before he could reach the door, Jay had already opened it. He surged outside. "I've got her." There was a hard, almost possessive edge to his words.

But Jay wasn't the possessive sort, was he? He offered her his hand as she climbed from the limo. She took it, not hesitating, and a tremor of excitement spiraled through her. She couldn't look away from Jay. Couldn't focus on anything *but* him. Jay was all she could see.

Her heartbeat pounded so fast.

Dimly, she heard him giving instructions to the driver. To the guards who were at the gate.

But then she and Jay were heading up the stone steps. Moments later, they were in the house. She heard the quick beep of the alarm resetting behind them. She stood in the foyer, nervously shifting from her left foot to her right on the marble flooring. She waited—

Jay pulled her into his arms. His mouth crashed onto hers. And, no, there was nothing soft or gentle or hesitant about his kiss now. He kissed her like a desperate man. Like he was starving. Or wild. For her. Her mouth opened for him, and she met him eagerly. She'd had a taste of pleasure, and Willow wanted more. She wanted him.

Her hands shoved against his fancy suit jacket, and it hit the floor. Then she was grabbing for his shirt front. Buttons popped and flew, but Jay just laughed. He shrugged out of the shirt, and then he was backing her up, pushing her against the nearest wall. Caging her there with his body while his hands flattened on the wall, positioned on either side of her head. His mouth went to her throat. Kissing. Licking. Biting with the lightest edge of his teeth.

Her breath hissed out. Oh, yes, she liked that. "You said…we'd go fast. Wild." That was what she wanted. Because her body seemed to be burning inside, a white-hot, sensual fire. She wanted to go wild. Wanted to lose all control. To just be—

With him.

He scooped her into his arms. The move was so unexpected that she gave a little cry of surprise. In the next instant, he was kissing her again. Carrying her, kissing her, and Willow wrapped her arms around his neck. Sometimes she forgot just how strong Jay was. He might not be a super soldier, but the man was built. And he carried her as if she weighed nothing.

She loved the way he kissed her. Did all men kiss with such skill? Did they all know just how to use their tongues and their lips?

Or was it just Jay? Just Jay who made her feel so out of control? Who made her want and want and *want?*

He lowered her onto a bed. His bed.

Then he backed away, staring down at her. "Now," Jay growled, "we have our first time."

She still had on her dress. She should take it off, right? Willow figured she should. She eased out of the bed. Stood before him. With trembling fingers, she reached for the zipper in the back.

"Let me."

A shiver rolled over her, but she turned around, giving him her back. His fingers trailed along her skin, and her eyes closed. The hiss of the zipper filled her ears. The dress fell down, puddling at her feet. His knuckles stroked down her spine, making her quiver. She turned toward him. "Jay—"

He tumbled her onto the bed. His hands were caressing her, his mouth was kissing her—all over. Her legs were spread and his hips pushed between them. He still wore his pants, but she could feel the hard press of his erection through the fabric. He was fully aroused. Long, hard, and thick, and she wanted him inside her.

His mouth closed over her breast. He sucked, licked, marked her with the faint edge of his teeth as her back bowed off the bed. Desire surged through her. She was wet and ready for him, and Willow didn't want to wait. He'd said they wouldn't wait. Fast. Hard. Wild. "I need..."

He was kissing his way to her other breast.

Her hips arched again, and her sex surged up against him, riding the hard length of his cock even through his clothes. Her nails raked over his back when he licked her nipple. "Jay!"

He pulled back. Jerked open his pants. Leaned over the edge of the bed and reached into the nightstand. A moment later, he had a small packet in his hand. *Condom.* She hadn't even thought about that, she'd been so intent on having sex for the first time—

Only it might not be my first time. I could've had other lovers. I don't know them. I don't—

"Willow." His voice pulled her gaze up to him. "Are you with me?"

She blinked. Focused on him. Sexy Jay. His hair was tousled, and she vaguely remembered sinking her fingers into it when they'd been kissing. He leaned toward her. Kissed her again. Kissed her with soft passion, then harder need. Kissed her until she was moaning and, yes, *with him*. Only him. Because he was what mattered. Not her past. The past she'd lost. Not her future—a future she might not have.

Just her present. Just Jay.

His erection pushed against her. The head slid against the entrance to her body. Her breath caught in her throat when his fingers twined with hers. He pushed their hands back, moving them so they were on either side of her head.

"Willow." Her name again. Only it sounded like a caress when he said it. "You are perfect."

Jay surged into her. There was no pain. Nothing but pleasure. Nothing but a wildness that ignited inside of her. And she knew he felt the same wildness, too. Her legs rose and locked around him as Jay thrust in and out of her. Again and again. He was heavy, so thick, stretching her, and she absolutely loved it. They moved in perfect time. He thrust deep and hard, and she met him eagerly, even as she felt tension coil within her. Pleasure was close. Her release barreling down on her. She could tell it was coming, and she raced toward it, needing that wild burst of pleasure. Needing him.

"That's it, Willow, hell, yes." He released her right hand. His hand snaked between their bodies. Found her clit. Touched her just right. Exactly in the way she needed. In the way that made her scream with pleasure.

And he was with her. He surged deep inside of her and growled her name as he came. Pleasure exploded through her, and he kissed her. The climax swept over her whole body, *through* her, and Willow never wanted the moment to end. She wanted to hold Jay close. To keep this moment forever.

Never, *ever* forget it.

As she'd forgotten everything else.

***

He'd loved her once. Treated her like a fucking princess. Put her on a pedestal. Spread the world at her feet. Then…

Willow had been gone. Lost to him. A moment in time that he couldn't take back. Rage had torn through him. The pain had been the worst he'd ever felt. He'd thought he could carry on, could *go* on, but Willow had haunted him.

A dead woman, his ghost to always carry.

Only Willow isn't dead. He'd searched for her, for so long. But it had been as if she'd disappeared. Willow had always been good at disappearing. He hadn't given up, though. He'd never give up on his Willow.

Then he'd seen her. With that prick of a billionaire asshole Jay Maverick. *His* Willow. Alive. Laughing. Dancing in a ballroom. She'd looked right at him, and she'd stared at him as if she didn't even know who he was.

Maverick thought he could take her. That he could lure Willow to him with his money and his fame. But what Maverick didn't get—the guy was going to crash and burn. The bullet he'd fired had missed its mark, and for a moment, he'd felt terror claw through him when he'd seen Willow fall.

Not again.

But she was okay. Alive. She'd even headed to a club with fucking Maverick. His bodyguard? Is that how they'd gotten together? Like the news stories said? He doubted that story. But Willow had always been deceptively dangerous. Such a beautiful face, to hide a devious killer. Willow had such deadly skills. Those skills had drawn him to her in the beginning. Willow looked like the best sin in the world, and she could attack a man as easily as she could kiss him.

Was it any wonder he'd fallen for her?

She'd said that she loved him. Once.

Then why did you leave, Willow?

She wouldn't leave again. And she wouldn't stare at him as if she had no clue who he was. He'd mattered to her before. He'd matter to her again. When Maverick's dead body was at her feet, she'd understand.

Willow had always belonged to him. She would *always* belong to him.

He wasn't going to let her go again.

He stared at the house, studying it through his night vision binoculars. Not a house, not really. A freaking mansion. Who needed a place that big?

Guards were at the front gate. Like they were supposed to be a challenge. No, he was more worried about the security system. Maverick might be a dick, but the guy knew his systems. He'd designed plenty of high-tech shit for Uncle Sam over the years. Hell, *he'd* even used Maverick's tech on a few missions that wouldn't be found in any books.

Maybe that was the key. Maybe he shouldn't try to sneak inside of Maverick's place. Maybe he should just get an invitation to go inside. He could walk right up to the bastard. Smile. And kill him.

Yeah, that sounded like a fabulous plan to him.

Willow, I have missed you.

CHAPTER SEVEN

"You shouldn't be here," Willow said the words quickly, even as she took a step back. Shadows surrounded her, a thick darkness, but she knew she wasn't alone.

He's here. He found me. Hadn't he once said he'd always find her?

"You left...where did you go, Willow?" His voice was low, a rough rasp in the darkness.

She shook her head. He shouldn't have found her. She'd been promised that he wouldn't find her. "Leave me alone."

"Never." A low, tender whisper. "You belong to me. I belong to you..."

She didn't belong to anyone but herself.

"He can't protect you." A slight edge of anger slid into the words. "He can't keep you from me."

"I don't need protecting." She took a step back, her feet sliding over the thread-bare carpet. Her hands were loose at her sides, her body tense. "And we're done. Do you understand? We are—"

He surged toward her, a fast burst of fury and strength. *"We're done when I say we are."*

***

"Stop!" Willow cried out as she jerked upright. Her heart thundered in her chest, and a light sheen of sweat covered her body.

"Willow?" Jay's voice. Light flooded on beside her, and she realized he'd just turned on a lamp. The light pushed back the darkness.

He was waiting in the dark. He uses the dark to his advantage. Always has.

She sucked in a deep breath.

"Baby?" Jay was beside her in the bed. His chest was bare, his hair tousled even more than normal, and the covers pooled near his waist. "What's wrong?"

"I—" She floundered. Stared at him. Then her gaze whipped around the room, almost as if she were searching for a threat. She could practically *feel* the threat, but no one was there. *You left…where did you go, Willow*? She grabbed the covers and pulled them up to her chest. "I think I had a bad dream."

Beside her, Jay stiffened. "You don't have bad dreams."

No, she didn't. Not bad dreams. Not good dreams. Not since she'd woken in that lab. Or at least, she didn't usually remember the dreams when she woke up. Things were changing now.

"Willow." Jay seemed hesitant. "Was it a dream or a memory?"

She shook her head. Nothing had been clear in the dream. She hadn't seen the man's face. She'd just felt him. His strength. His anger.

And she'd been afraid.

Willow jumped from the bed, pulling the covers with her. Suddenly, she felt far too exposed. "I need a shower." Sweat still clung to her body. For a bit there, she hadn't even realized she was dreaming. "It seemed so real," she mumbled. Her feet padded across the floor as she headed for the bathroom.

"Willow."

His low voice stopped her.

"Do you want to tell me about it?"

She wanted to pretend it hadn't happened. Not at all. "Shower first." Because she wanted to wash away the fear. It clung to her skin like the sweat. She hesitated. "Join me?" Willow realized that she didn't want to be alone. Not then.

He nodded and started to climb from the bed.

His phone rang. The phone she'd forgotten all about during the, um, activities of the night before. The phone was on the nightstand, and it vibrated, lighting up.

His private line. Calling this late? "Must be important," she said, forcing her lips to smile.

"Maybe we'll take a raincheck." She hurried into the bathroom and shut the door behind her. For a moment, she just stood there, trying to catch her breath.

Her gaze slid to the mirror. She stared at her reflection.

She hadn't been a virgin. Jay wasn't her first lover.

You belong to me. I belong to you...

The low voice from her dream—memory?—swept through her mind once more, and Willow shivered.

***

There was no damn way he'd take a raincheck on joining Willow in the shower. Did he look like a dumbass? Jay grabbed his phone, not even checking the screen. His gaze was locked on the bathroom door. Willow hadn't turned on the water yet. He'd join her before she could.

His finger swiped over the screen. Only a handful of people had this particular number, and whoever this caller was—"Not now," he bit off. "Unless there is a fire, a shooting, or a death, you call me back—"

"There will be a death."

Jay stilled. "Who the hell is this?" Now he did look at the screen.

Unknown caller.

What kind of bullshit was that? What—

"You put her at risk. This is *your fault.*" The voice was low, gruff, but familiar. Jay just couldn't quite place it.

"Who the hell is this?" Jay barked once more.

"Did you ever think that she was hidden for a reason?"

Willow. The sonofabitch is talking about Willow. And suddenly, that oddly familiar voice… "Wyman?" He could hardly believe it. "Wyman Wright?"

Silence.

Every muscle in Jay's body locked down. "You sound amazingly alive for a dead man." Only Jay had known the guy hadn't died. Wyman had just made himself vanish. The fellow was one powerful player in the U.S. and abroad. Wyman had been trying to make his own freaking army of super soldiers, and he hadn't even cared how he got his test subjects.

Sawyer Cage was killed and put into the program. Wyman didn't have a conscience. The guy was a psychopath. He was also the man Jay had wanted to lure into the open, and his plan had worked. Absolutely freaking perfectly.

Wyman had just made his first mistake.

"She was supposed to be dead." Wyman's response came slowly. "But you messed that up."

Jay leapt out of the bed. "Willow isn't dead. She won't *be* dead. You'll never get your hands on her again."

A sharp inhale. "I'm not the threat to her."

"Bullshit. You and your freaking torture labs nearly destroyed all of the test subjects. But it's done, you hear me? You're done. You won't hurt Willow again. You won't hurt any of them. Because I'm going to destroy you and your operatives. You're not the only one with power and connections. I'm—"

"*You're* the threat to her."

The hell he was. "You're done, Wyman," Jay repeated flatly.

The call ended.

Jay could hear the roar of water in the bathroom. Willow had gotten into the shower. He dialed quickly, putting the phone to his ear. West answered on the second ring.

"Jay," West sounded slightly annoyed, "do you have any idea what I'm—"

"Wyman just called. And I've got the sonofabitch's location. You know I can trace every fucking call I get." No one could match his tech, not even Uncle Sam. Hell, he'd *given* Uncle Sam the best products the government had. Jay's voice was low as he continued, "I'm texting the info to your team. If we can get the bastard tonight, if we can track him to his hole..."

"Oh, hell, yes." Now West didn't sound annoyed at all.

"I'll text Sawyer and Flynn, too. They'll want to be in on the hunt," Jay added.

"What about you?" West wanted to know. "This shit has been your baby from the word go. Don't you want to be there for the takedown?"

His gaze was on the closed bathroom door.

You're the threat to her.

He didn't like the way Wyman was so focused on Willow. "I'm staying with her. Wyman is too intent on Willow. If I go, she'll want to be there, too."

A pause. "Don't you think she deserves to be there?"

Not if things went south. "Not if this is a set up. Maybe he wants me to bring her to him. He would have known I could trace the call." Jay shook his head. "Willow stays back on this one. I stay with her."

"Hate to say it, but, yeah, I actually agree with you on this."

Jay's lips twisted. "Watch your ass, man."

"Always."

Jay sent out a flurry of texts, making sure his brother had plenty of back-up ready. He wasn't about to risk West's safety. West was his *only* family. Not blood, but something that went one hell of a lot deeper.

Then he put his phone down. He stalked toward the bathroom. A quick twist of the door knob, and he was inside. Steam drifted lazily in the room. The bathroom was massive, just like every other room in the house. The shower could easily hold six or more people—*not* that he'd ever had that many folks in his shower.

He was more the one-on-one type.

Willow stood beneath the spray of water. Her head was bowed and her hands pressed to the marble walls. The water slid down her body as—

Wait. Was she crying? "Willow?" Jay stepped forward. He could have sworn that he'd seen her shoulders quiver.

At his call, she stiffened. But she didn't immediately turn toward him. The water kept crashing down on her.

Had she heard his phone call? Sure, with her enhanced senses, she probably had, and he'd need to explain but—

Willow turned toward him. Water glistened on her beautiful face. He couldn't tell if she'd been crying or if all of the water just came from the shower. He stared at her a moment, trying to decide if he should force a smile, if he should act like everything was perfectly fine.

Or maybe he should tell her about Wyman. About the team closing in. It was her life and—

Willow lifted her hand toward him.

And he just reacted. He stalked toward her. Caught her hand in his and stepped into the shower with her. Steam drifted around him as the warm water pounded onto him. Willow's wet body pressed against his.

"I wanted you with me," she whispered.

He kissed her. Slowly. Deeply. Savored her. And when his mouth left hers… "Then that's where I'll always be."

Their gazes locked. He wished he could read the emotions in her stare. Wished that he could understand so many of Willow's mysteries.

But he considered himself to be a lucky bastard just to have her in his arms.

There was a bench in his shower. He put her on that bench. Spread her legs. Opened her wide to him, and then he crouched between her splayed legs. Willow needed pleasure. With him, he always wanted her to know pleasure. He put his mouth on her. He kissed her. He stroked her. He worked her with his tongue until she was arching up against him and crying out her release.

And then, well, then he was just getting started.

***

"I don't like this," Sawyer Cage said later as he gazed down at the small cabin that lay nestled in the middle of the woods. The helicopter's blades made a *whoop-whoop-whoop* sound overhead as the bird hovered in the sky. Beside him, West Harper leaned forward, staring down at their target.

"Are you picking up anything?" West barked into his headset. He was the one steering the chopper. "Anything at all?"

Sawyer spared a quick glance over at their final team member. Flynn Haddox had his eyes on the cabin, and his body had tensed.

"We're still pretty far away," Sawyer muttered. But…

Flynn, are you picking up a damn thing? Sawyer asked, using the mental link that the Lazarus subjects had developed.

Flynn shook his head and his gaze didn't leave the cabin. *Not a thing. Could be that the chopper is too loud. But if Wyman was inside, I think we'd be seeing his guards. My bet is they probably all cleared out right after he made the call.*

There *was* a landing pad out there. The cabin was small, appeared low-tech, normal, but then there was the very distinct landing pad nestled about thirty yards away. Since the place was in the middle of nowhere, Wyman would have needed a mode of transportation to get himself in and out of that cabin, fast.

While we were hauling ass to get here, Wyman could have been flying away, Flynn added. His hard features showed his worry. The guy's brown hair was cut almost brutally short, and a line of dark shadow covered his clenched jaw.

"We should land," West barked, his words carrying into the headsets they all wore. "Check out the cabin. Even if Wyman is long gone, he might have left some clues behind. No way am I going back to Jay without something to report."

Wyman doesn't leave evidence behind. Flynn's terse reply shot through Sawyer's head.

He knew his buddy was right. Wyman wasn't a mistake making kind of man.

He knew Jay would track the call. Sawyer sent his thoughts out as he considered the situation. He could feel the bird starting to descend. *With Jay's tech, no way could Wyman expect that call not to be traced. I mean, shit, maybe Wyman had the signal bouncing around, but eventually, he knew Jay would find him. It was just a matter of how long the trace would take.* A matter of when, not if.

Only it hadn't taken long at all. It had just taken moments for Jay to get the location. Maybe they'd gotten there sooner than Wyman had anticipated.

I don't like this. Flynn let out a rough sigh. Then he spoke out loud, "Something is wrong."

Yes, something was very wrong, and Sawyer wasn't ready to land, not just yet. "Pull up," he barked at West. "Pull us the hell up and then let's figure this out. We should sweep over the woods again. Make sure we aren't missing anything."

But West gave a negative jerk of his head. "If Wyman's out there, he's heard our bird. No way would he miss the chopper. That's probably why he picked this place. So he could hear a threat coming from miles away. This is our chance. I'm not going to let Jay down."

This *was* their chance. It was also Wyman's chance. Sawyer knew how the guy operated. He'd gotten a firsthand glimpse at the way Wyman's mind worked. Wyman would eliminate anyone in his way, no hesitations.

"He knew we would come," Flynn mused. "And he isn't going to leave some kind of prize sitting inside that empty cabin for us."

No, he wouldn't. "Pull up," Sawyer ordered flatly. "*Now.*"

Wyman had known they would come, all right. Because he'd *wanted* them to come? Only maybe the wily bastard had thought Jay would come to the scene, too. After all, Jay was the one baiting the bastard. Jay was the one in the spotlight. Jay was the one with all the fancy tech.

Maybe Wyman had thought Jay would be the one leading the hunt, and if that were the case…

"I see something down there," Flynn shouted. "Oh, hell—"

Wyman has set a trap for us.

The cabin exploded.

CHAPTER EIGHT

An alarm was beeping. A slow, steady sound. Jay hadn't been sleeping. How the fuck was he supposed to sleep? He'd left Willow upstairs, naked, in his bed. *She'd* been sleeping. He'd slipped downstairs to wait, hoping for word from West.

Instead of a call from his brother, he'd just gotten an alarm blast on his computer. He sat in front of the double monitors, his fingers flying over the keyboard. He pulled up exterior shots of his grounds, searching for the guards, but they weren't at their posts.

They're not at their fucking posts.

And the alarm had just shut off. Only *he* hadn't been the one to deactivate the alarm.

He stiffened, right before his office was plunged into total darkness.

Jay knew someone had just cut the power to his home. He also knew that his generator would have power flowing back on within fifteen seconds. Jay yanked open his top desk drawer, counting as he did so. He found the weapon inside, he yanked it up, and he spun around.

Ten, nine, eight…

He heard the creak of his study door sliding open.

"I've got a gun on you, you sonofabitch," Jay growled.

Seven, six, five…

He eased from his chair, slipped to the side. "Did you think I wouldn't expect you to show up here? Why do you think I stayed behind? Because I don't trust your ass."

Two, one…

The lights flickered back on. And Jay found himself staring across the room at none other than Wyman Wright.

Except…the guy looked different.

Thinner. And his hair had been dyed a muddy brown. He wore contacts that turned his eyes green. The man looked as if he'd had a nose job, and his jaw shape was a little different, too. Rounder. If Jay hadn't studied the bastard so thoroughly, if he hadn't made Wyman Wright into his damn obsession, he might not have even recognized the fellow at first glance—

"Put the gun down, you fool," Wyman snapped. The voice—the voice was the exact same. "We both know you aren't a killer."

"You don't know anything about me." Jay didn't lower the gun. "Who else is in the house?"

When he'd grabbed the gun from the top drawer, he'd also taken the liberty of triggering the alarm he had wired in that drawer. An alarm that would send a message to guards who *weren't* at that location, but a secondary team that would be arriving within five minutes. He'd tried to have plenty of back-up plans in place, just in case.

"I didn't bring any men in with me." Wyman's hands were at his sides. He didn't look armed, but Jay was willing to bet the guy had a gun and probably a couple of knives on him.

"You just left them outside?" Jay snarled at Wyman, his body still tense. "If they've hurt the security guards I had on patrol—"

Wyman shrugged. "Your guards are unconscious, not dead. And my men are making sure they stay that way." He exhaled. "I get annoyed when people point guns at me."

"And I get pissed when a shady asshole breaks into my home and knocks out my guards, so I guess we're even, huh?"

Wyman's gaze went glacial. "We are a very long way from even."

Jay knew he just had to keep the guy there for five minutes. *Five minutes.* "You look pretty good for a dead man."

Wyman just glared at him.

Jay smiled. "She brought you out, didn't she? I figured she would. Willow was different from the others, I knew it right away."

"Willow is special." Wyman's jaw hardened. "Very special."

Yes, she fucking is. And you won't ever hurt her again.

Wyman glanced over his shoulder. "She's upstairs, isn't she?"

Jay stalked closer to the bastard. "You aren't taking her."

Slowly, Wyman's gaze swung back to him. "You honestly think you can stop me?" His smile was as ice cold as his eyes. "I could have five super soldiers standing outside your front door. You—well, you don't have *any* super soldiers at your beck and call, do you? Because you sent them out to hunt me down." Now Wyman laughed. "Amateur move. You should have brought them all here, to keep *you* safe. Instead, you fell for my trap like the fool you really are." His mocking stare swept over Jay. "You always thought you were so smart. I outwitted you at every turn. Now your soldiers are gone, probably fucking burning, and I *will* take Willow away."

The hell he would. "I'm going to put a bullet in your heart." His words were low and lethal because what Wyman had just said…

Your soldiers are gone, probably fucking burning.

No, *no.*

"What did you do?" Jay lunged for him and Wyman didn't even try to retreat. The SOB just stood there with a smirk on his face, so certain of his power, so certain he had the upper hand.

"It's not what I did," Wyman murmured. "It's what you did. You sent your *friends* straight into danger. It's a good thing they can come back from death, isn't it?"

But West couldn't. His brother *couldn't.* His brother wasn't a super soldier.

Jay put the gun right against Wyman's heart. "Whatever you did, whatever you *think* you're doing, call it off. Right the hell now. Because if my brother has so much as a scratch on him—"

"Ah…the Delta Force operative? I mean, *former* Delta Force." Wyman's expression didn't change. "Always thought he would make a great addition to my program."

"You fucking—" Jay's hand trembled on the gun. This was it. He'd kill the bastard. Right now. He'd taken him out, he'd—

"You think she'd forgive you for killing the only family she has?"

Jay blinked. What?

"Will you forgive her, if I kill the only family *you've* got?"

"What are you talking about? You're nothing to Willow." Nothing but her tormentor. The man who'd destroyed her life.

Wyman's jaw hardened. "I watched from a remote video feed. *This time,* I made sure the explosion didn't go off with the chopper too close. I made sure your only family survived. That means you owe me."

"No, it means you're a twisted SOB who likes to play God, that's what it means. It means you think that no one can stop you, but you're dead wrong." Fury hardened every word. "You go after my family? *Mine?* You break into my home and threaten Willow? Threaten me? No, that's not how this shit works." Jay smiled, and he knew the smile would show his rage. His reckless fury. "I'm not afraid to pull this trigger. You think you know me? You don't know a damn thing. I didn't drag your ass out of the shadows so we could make a new deal. I did it so that I could end you."

Wyman's eyelashes flickered.

"You think I don't have the PD in my pocket? You've got men outside, big freaking deal. My second team is coming in fast and coming in hot. So soon it will just be you. All by yourself with no back-up in sight. Then you'll be a dead man, and my friends at the PD will only be too happy to buy my story about a break-in." He laughed. "Thanks for changing your appearance. Now no one will connect the dots, Wyman."

Fear flashed—just for one perfect instant—in Wyman's gaze. But then the emotion vanished. "You really think you can shoot me in front of her?"

Her? *Willow?*

Instantly, his gaze whipped away from Wyman's face, and he saw Willow, standing in the study's entranceway, her body perfectly still. How long had she been there? How much had she heard?

"If you shoot me right now, Willow will see you for exactly what you *truly* are. What you've always been."

Jay had to unclench his back teeth. "You hurt Willow. You tortured her. She'll be glad you're gone."

"That's one version of reality." Wyman's reply was smooth. "Not the right version, but one." He paused, then he raised his voice as he said, "Willow, did I ever hurt you?"

"*Don't* talk to her," Jay snarled at him. In response to his words, Jay saw Willow flinch. Shit. *Shit.* "Baby, go back upstairs."

Wyman started in surprise. "What? What did you call her?"

"You don't need to see this, Willow. The nightmare is over. He won't hurt you or anyone else ever again." Jay fought to keep his voice calm. *He won't hurt you. He won't hurt West. He won't hurt anyone close to me.* "Just go upstairs and forget him. Our plan worked. We lured him out, and I'll take care of him."

Wyman was still staring straight at Jay, but when he spoke, Wyman said, "Willow, this was *your* plan?"

There was an odd edge to his words. Almost…pride? No, impossible. That didn't make sense.

Willow didn't speak. She seemed stunned, rooted to the spot. Jay wanted to go to her, to pull her into his arms, but when you had a cobra in front of you, seconds away from striking, you didn't look away. You didn't move.

You attacked first.

"I had a bad dream." Willow's voice. The first words she'd spoken. "I think…I think he was going to hurt me." Her words were too low, almost child-like. Not his normal Willow at all. She wore one of Jay's old t-shirts, and it covered her from shoulder to mid-thigh.

At her words, the rage inside of Jay flared even hotter. "Wyman, you *won't* hurt her—"

"It wasn't me, you bastard!" Wyman shouted back. "*I* never hurt her! I saved her! I picked up the pieces—I'm the one who found her broken body. *I saved her!* I protected her! Just like I'll always protect her."

The guy's voice—his face, his eyes—everything about him was suddenly blazing, and for just a moment, Jay almost believed him.

Almost.

But then, Jay wasn't an idiot.

Fool me once, shame on you.

Fool me twice…

Jay wasn't about to buy Wyman's lies again.

"He…found me." Willow's voice again, even softer than before. "You said he wouldn't find me, but he did."

She wasn't making sense. They'd planned for Wyman to take the bait, but, shit, maybe she meant that Wyman shouldn't have gotten in the house. "I'll take care of him," Jay swore grimly. "I'll—"

"I'm sorry, Willow," Wyman said, cutting through Jay's words. Only Wyman's voice was different. Almost gentle. Sad. "I thought I'd protected you. He was smarter than I anticipated. More determined. And he's hunting you again. That's why you need to come with me, right now. We need to get out of here tonight. I'll make you disappear again. He won't *ever* find you. I swear it. You'll vanish, and you'll be safe."

The hell that was happening. "Willow isn't leaving." Jay shook his head. "Are you just insane, Wyman? You're done. Either I'm putting a bullet in your heart," the option he preferred, "or *my* secondary team will be bursting in here any moment. We'll lock you up. And then you'll be answering every question that Sawyer Cage and the others have for you. You'll tell us how many super soldiers are out there. Where they are. What you've done—"

"It's over." Wyman's voice was flat. "Willow…*it's time to bloom.*"

What the fuck was that shit? Why was—

Willow attacked Jay. She burst forward and drove her body against him. They flew back, and the gun discharged, thundering in Jay's ears. He landed on the floor, and Willow grabbed his hand. She twisted his wrist, and the gun flew from his fingers. She drew back her left hand, her fist swinging toward his face.

Then she stopped.

Jay stared up at her. He wasn't fighting her. He *couldn't* fight her. Not Willow. There was no way he'd raise his hand against her. And he didn't understand what was happening. Why it was happening. Willow wasn't on Wyman's side.

"Finish him, Willow," Wyman ordered. "We don't have time to waste. Find out his fears. See them. *End him.* Then we're getting the hell out of here."

Wyman sounded as if he were controlling her. As if…as if he'd turned on some kind of weapon inside of her.

No, Willow is the weapon. It was more like…

Jay stared into Willow's eyes. And he saw no trace of the lover he'd known. It was like he was staring at a blank canvas. His Willow was gone.

How? Why? His mind raced.

Her fist was still balled, still just inches from his face.

"It's time to bloom," Wyman threw out his words again.

Her breath came faster. Rougher.

And Jay knew what had happened. The bastard was activating Willow. Hypnotizing her. Controlling her. Getting into *her* head.

But she was fighting Wyman. If she hadn't been, Jay knew her fist wouldn't be inches away. She would have already driven her hand into his face.

"Force his fears onto him! Knock the bastard out—and then we are *leaving!*" Wyman was shouting now.

"No." The one word burst from between Jay's gritted teeth. He wasn't going to fight Willow. He would never hurt her. But she wasn't leaving. Wyman wasn't taking her. "If you go with him, he'll hurt you, Willow. He'll lock you up again."

"I'm protecting her!" Wyman roared.

Jay ignored the bastard. His eyes were on Willow. Only her. "You want to see my fears? Do it, baby. I know exactly what I fear. You can come into my head, any damn time, because I'm not going to hide myself from you. See what I fear. See what scares me the most."

She blinked. Once. Twice. And a little of the cold blankness left her gaze.

"I can tell you what I fear," Jay continued, his voice low now, soothing, because he wanted to soothe her. He wanted to protect her. Always. "I fear losing you. I fear that bastard taking you away. Locking you up. But if he does, know this,

Willow. I'll find you. I won't give up. I won't leave you locked up. You can trust me. You can count one *me*."

"No, Willow, you can't!" Wyman fired back. "He's the one putting you in danger. I've been protecting you. Always protecting you. He's using you for his own ends. You can't trust him, you can't ever trust him!"

Outside, Jay heard the squeal of tires. The shriek of brakes. His men had arrived, the back-up team. "You've lost, Wyman," Jay said, but he was staring up at Willow.

Her fisted hand had lowered, but she still straddled him. Her left hand was at her side, and her right still gripped his wrist. Willow wasn't shoving his fears at him. She wasn't fighting him. She was struggling to find her way *back* to him. To push back the compulsion that Wyman had used on her.

"No, I don't lose." Wyman cleared his throat. "Willow, move away from him."

Her head swung toward Wyman. And Jay's gaze followed hers. Wyman stood just a few feet away, and he had Jay's gun gripped in his hand. Wyman aimed the gun at Jay.

"You're the biggest threat to her." A muscle flexed in Wyman's jaw. "So you're going to be eliminated. I always protect Willow." He exhaled slowly. "Get off him, Willow. Come stand beside me."

She didn't move.

"Bloom, Willow. Bloom!" Wyman yelled.

Her body shuddered.

"Willow, dammit, I don't want to shoot you!" Wyman's face flashed with what looked like torment. "But you'll come back." His fingers were shaking around the gun. "I made it so that you'll always come back. I just—I'm sorry, Willow. I have to do this. You should have just *moved away from –* "

He was going to shoot Willow. She might die again. She'd hurt, she'd bleed, and she'd go wherever the hell it was that she went when she died.

No. Jay surged up, shoving Willow back. "*No!*" Jay bellowed. He twisted his body, trying to protect her, even as he heard the blast of the gun. He tumbled Willow back onto the floor. He covered her with his body. Glared at her. "You *stay* down. You aren't dying again!"

He heard footsteps rushing away. Freaking Wyman trying to escape. Jay surged to his feet.

Willow's gaze was still glassy and cold, her body too tense. She looked confused and scared, and he wanted to protect her—

The best way to protect her is by stopping Wyman.

"I'll be back, baby, I swear." He chased after the bastard. "Wyman!" Jay shouted. "There's nowhere to run!"

The jerk fired the gun again. The bullet sank into the frame of the door, sending chunks of wood flying at Jay. He ducked, and Wyman's steps thudded again.

Sonofa—

"Freeze!"

The shout had come from the front of Jay's house. He scrambled toward the entranceway, and he saw that Wyman had wrenched open the front door. The guy stood there, his weapon in front of him, pointing it at whoever was waiting outside.

"I've had a really shitty night," came West's voice. "Nearly got blown out of a chopper. Since I figure that's your doing, you don't want to piss me off anymore. Drop your gun."

Wyman wasn't going to drop the gun. Jay knew it. The bastard was the type to go down in a blaze of glory, and if he could, he'd take out as many others as possible in that blaze.

And he'll take out my brother to hurt me.

Jay didn't hesitate. He surged forward, and he slammed into Wyman. They tumbled through the front entrance, and they hit the ground even as the gun fired one more time. For a moment after that thundering blast, there was silence.

Then Jay became aware of the drumming of his own heartbeat, pounding far too fast in his ears. He flipped Wyman over. "Okay, you asshole—"

Blood. A whole lot of it. The porch lights shone down on Wyman, and Jay could see the blood that was covering the man's stomach.

That last thunder of the gun –

Hell. The bullet had gone into Wyman.

"Get an ambulance!" Jay bellowed. He put his hands over Wyman's wound. The blood pumped between his fingers.

Wyman groaned. "You...you want me...dead..."

"Yeah, I do," Jay agreed immediately. "But I also want to know how many others you've experimented on. You're answering for your crimes. You got me? You're—"

The guy's eyes rolled back into his head.

West crashed to his knees at Jay's side. Flynn and Sawyer were there, too. Voices rose and fell behind Jay, but he didn't look back. He kept his focus on Wyman Wright.

The boogeyman. The big, bad ruler of D.C. Only the guy was bleeding out in front of him. Dammit.

"We need him alive," Sawyer gritted.

Jay just pushed down harder on Wyman's gut.

"He's the only one who knows how many test subjects are out there. Fuck." Frustration boiled in Flynn's voice. "He could have labs running right now. We need the bastard *alive!*"

"Then you'd better get an ambulance here fast," Jay bit off. "Because unlike you two, he's not going to come back once his heart stops."

A sharp gasp had his gaze flying up. Willow stood in the doorway, her body swaying a bit. Her eyes were wide, her face far too pale. She stared down at Wyman in horror. Then her shocked gaze rose to lock on Jay's face. "What did…" Her voice was barely above a whisper. "What did you do?"

Wyman's blood was all over his fingers. The guy was gasping out, barely breathing, and Jay knew the man's death would be on him. Literally on his hands. "Willow,"

A wild shriek erupted from her. She lunged toward him, her scream echoing in his ears.

Before she could reach him, Flynn grabbed her. He locked his arms around her stomach and hauled her back, having to use his own super strength in order to hold her in check.

"He can't die!" Willow yelled. "He can't!" Tears slid down her cheeks.

"What in the holy hell is happening here?" Sawyer muttered.

Jay never let up on the pressure. "He used some kind of trigger word on her, hypnotism or mind control or some freaking thing. Wyman got *in* her head."

She head-butted Flynn. Screamed. Nearly lunged free.

God, it hurt to say, but he had to do it. "Take her downstairs to containment," Jay had to force out the words from between clenched teeth. "Don't so much as fucking bruise her," he warned grimly. He'd made sure all of his properties had containment rooms. Rooms that he had specifically designed for the Lazarus test subjects. Some of those subjects weren't threats—some were like Flynn and Sawyer. Totally in control.

But others—like Bryce King—they were unhinged. Dangerous to humans. Psychotic. And they had to be secured.

Right then, Willow was fighting like a woman driven mad. Sawyer had to lunge up and grab her when she nearly knocked Flynn out.

Flynn and Sawyer carried her back inside as she screamed. Her screams were like knives cutting into Jay's soul. *I'm so sorry, Willow.* He'd said he wouldn't lock her up again. And he'd just been the bastard to give the order.

He looked over his shoulder. Saw the men who were there, tense, waiting. West was in front of them, his hand on his gun. A gun that had been up and aimed—

At Willow?

"Don't even think it, man." Jay gave a hard shake of his head. "She's going to be fine. She just needs—" Jay broke off because he didn't know what she needed. But he'd figure it out. He'd give it to her. "Just make sure all of your men understand the situation." Code words—what he really meant...*Make sure your men know that what happened here will never be discussed—or there will be hell to pay.*

"P-protect..."

Shit, Wyman was talking? He'd thought the guy had passed out.

"P-protect..."

"You think I'm going to protect you?" Jay demanded. "Hell, no. But I am going to keep you alive. You've got a lot to answer for—"

"Willow...Protect..."

Jay leaned closer because it was hard for him to hear Wyman's words. "Of course, I'm going to protect Willow. Why do you think I had her taken inside? *You* are the one who hurt her, you screwed with her mind, you—"

"Mine..."

A growl broke from Jay. "The hell you say! Willow isn't your creation, she's—"

"Daughter..."

The last word was barely a whisper. If Jay hadn't been so close to Wyman, he didn't think he would have heard it. But he fucking did hear it, and his whole world seemed to stop spinning.

Wyman Wright's eyes sagged closed. The bastard was barely breathing.

"No!" Jay shook his head. "You're lying!" Had to be a lie. A trick. Wyman was trying to get into *his* head, that was all. "You're lying!" Jay shouted even as he kept working on Wyman's body. Trying to help the bastard. Trying to get him to *breathe*. To live.

"Talk to me, you sonofabitch!" Jay yelled. "Talk, *fight!*" Because the guy wasn't dying. No way. Jay couldn't let him die.

Daughter.

CHAPTER NINE

"He can't die." Jay's words were flat as he stared at Dr. Elizabeth Parker. Elizabeth…his friend, former lover, and the woman who'd created the Lazarus formula. The woman who hated Wyman Wright just as much as he did.

No, probably more. Because Wyman had *killed* Elizabeth's lover and put Sawyer in Project Lazarus.

"You have to keep him alive, Beth."

They were in a private hospital. He'd taken over the whole floor. Money could be handy—money could buy nearly anything in this world. Right then, it was buying him a place to hide Wyman Wright and a mini-army of guards to keep the floor secure.

"He'll need transfusions," Elizabeth said. She was wearing green scrubs and a face mask dangled around her neck. "I checked before I came to talk with you. The wound is bad, not going to lie, but I think he'll pull through."

"He *has* to pull through."

Her eyes gleamed. "I understand how important it is to find the others, okay? I get this, I don't—"

"You have Willow's DNA."

Her lips parted. "Uh, yes, I have the DNA for her, Flynn, and Sawyer. Why do you—"

"Wyman said he was her father."

She stepped back. "What?"

"Wyman Wright." Jay glanced over his shoulder. No one else was there. "Bastard said he was Willow's father."

Elizabeth shook her head. "I didn't know that Wyman had any children."

"The guy's life is shrouded in mystery. He's got enemies all over the globe. Makes sense that if he *did* have kids, he'd keep them secret." Wiley bastard. "Or could be he was just jerking me around. We all know how much he likes his mind games."

Elizabeth pulled in a deep breath. "What if it is the truth? What are you going to do?"

Cross that damn bridge when he got there. "Priority one is keeping him alive."

She gave a brisk nod.

"We make sure he keeps living. We make sure he stays in *our* custody. Then we find out about Willow."

He heard the double doors swing open behind him. Jay looked back and saw Sawyer marching toward him.

"Status," Sawyer prompted.

"In surgery. And I'm heading in to monitor right now." Elizabeth squared her shoulders.

"I'll be here," Sawyer vowed. "I'm not leaving until I talk to that bastard." Rage vibrated in each word. Sawyer was justified in feeling his fury. His hate.

Plenty of people in the world hated Wyman Wright.

Plenty of people wanted to hurt him.

Is that why he kept his daughter's existence secret?

Elizabeth hurried away. Jay expected Sawyer to immediately rush after Elizabeth and push into the operating room, but instead, Sawyer asked him, "What in the hell happened with Willow?"

Jay straightened his shoulders. "Wyman happened to her."

"She was out of control." Sawyer's face was tense as he grabbed Jay's arm. "I tried to reach her mind, tried to use our link, but there was nothing but chaos inside."

"I'm going to her." He shrugged out of Sawyer's hold. He'd already been away from Willow too long.

But before he could get to the doors, Sawyer was in his path. Sawyer's eyes had narrowed. His body was tight with tension. "I need to know why Willow attacked."

Jay didn't have time for this interrogation. *He* needed Willow. He had to get to her. "The guy used some kind of trigger word. One minute, Willow was normal." Well, that wasn't exactly the truth. She'd seemed different, almost scared, when Jay first saw her in the study's doorway. "He said something about needing her to bloom, and then she was attacking me." His chin notched into the air. "But she stopped herself, you understand me? He was trying to control her, he wanted her to force my fears into my head and immobilize me, but she didn't. She fought him. Fought whatever mind control shit he did to her."

Sawyer shook his head. "Didn't look like she was fighting him when I was there. The woman was in a killing rage."

It hadn't just been rage fueling her. When he'd looked at Willow in that moment, he'd seen grief in her eyes. Grief and…betrayal?

Because I'd nearly killed her father? Did Willow know the truth? Somewhere, deep inside? Was it possible? Or maybe just seeing Wyman Wright had stirred memories for her. It happened that way with some Lazarus subjects. They could connect with certain individuals from their pasts. The stronger the emotional tie, the more likely the subject was to pull forth memories.

Sawyer was the perfect example of that scenario. He'd remembered nothing about his past, not until Elizabeth had come back into his life. As soon as he'd seen her, a primitive awareness had flared to life within him. After that, the guy had been determined to claim Elizabeth, determined to reconnect with the one person who mattered to him.

"We don't know how many men and women might be working for Wyman." Those at the scene had fled as fast as they could when they realized Wyman had been taken out. Jay had let them go, because his priority had been Wyman. And it wasn't like he could just lock up all those bastards. "We need to keep our guards up. Be ready for anything."

"Always am," Sawyer murmured.

"I'm going back to Willow." He nodded once, curtly, "I can trust that you'll make sure Wyman doesn't leave? And that nobody from his team comes to save his sorry ass?"

"No one will be getting in," Sawyer assured him. "Count on it."

Right.

Jay headed forward, reached for the door.

"I know you think she needs saving."

He stilled at Sawyer's low words.

"I thought the same thing. Flynn did, too. She's one of us, after all. She's been hurt. Damaged. But, hell, at one point, I thought Bryce King was one of us, too."

Jay swallowed.

"We all know how that turned out," Sawyer added darkly.

Yes, they did. Bryce had been a sadistic killer, and he'd formed an obsession with Flynn's lover, Dr. Cecelia Gregory. Cecelia had originally been hired by Wyman Wright. Her job had been to help the test subjects transition to their new realities. She hadn't been told the full truth about Project Lazarus. Cecelia hadn't realized that she was literally working with the dead, not until it was too late.

And Bryce King already had her in his sights.

"You should get Cecelia to talk with Willow." Sawyer's voice was low. "And, damn, I hate to say it, but you shouldn't let Willow out of containment until we get Cecelia's take on this shit."

Jay turned on his heel, once more facing Sawyer. "You're saying I should just keep Willow locked up? *You* are telling me this shit?" Sawyer had been locked away, too, once upon a time. He knew what hell it was.

But Sawyer nodded. "I don't like it, but I also don't like the fact that I couldn't touch Willow's mind. It was like she was gone, and someone else was in her place. Willow is very, very powerful. And when she wants to use her psychic strengths, she can completely disable anyone near her. She's a threat that can't be underestimated. We need Cecelia's take on this, and we need it now."

"Willow hates being locked away." He already regretted his order of containment. But when Wyman had been bleeding out, when Willow had lunged forward and had been fighting Flynn…*I just wanted to get her to a safe spot. An area where she'd be protected. No threat to anyone.* Sonofabitch. *He'd* done this.

Sawyer's face was grim. "I can get Cecelia to meet you at your house. Let her talk to Willow. Let her figure out this trigger stuff. If Wyman somehow turned on Willow's mind to follow his commands, then Cecelia can figure out a way to turn off what he did. She's the best shrink out there. That's the whole reason Wyman hired her. She can help your girl."

"Willow isn't mine." His hands had fisted.

Sawyer just gave a rough laugh. "Try telling that BS to someone who *isn't* a human lie detector." He inclined his head. "Get to her, and I'll make sure nothing happens here."

Jay didn't waste any additional time. He'd already been away from Willow for too long.

***

She was in prison again.

Willow sat on the bed. It was a big, comfortable, four-poster bed. A large TV was positioned on a nearby table. A heavy dresser was to the right. A small bathroom, complete with shower and toilet, waited to the left.

It looked like a typical bedroom. Except for the giant mirror that made up the wall directly across from her. A one-way mirror. People could see her from the other side of that mirror. She wasn't supposed to be able to see them.

But then, she wasn't supposed to be able to do a lot of things.

The walls were reinforced. So strong that even someone like her couldn't break out of the room. Not that she was trying to break out. Not right then. She was just trying to figure out what the hell had happened.

Bits and pieces were in her mind. She shoved her palms against her pounding temples. She'd been in Jay's study. Standing in the doorway. That stupid dream—memory?—had come to her again, and she'd left his bedroom because she'd needed to find him. She'd just wanted to be close to him, as crazy as that seemed. But when she'd found him, Jay hadn't been alone. Another man had been in there with him. She hadn't seen his face, but his voice had been familiar and Jay had said—

Wyman.

Then she'd…she'd lost track of what happened after that. She remembered being on top of Jay, having her fist ready to strike him.

Had she hit Jay?

Her temples pounded harder.

She couldn't remember anything else about being in the study. But...but she'd also been on the porch of Jay's house. She'd seen him, crouched over Wyman. Wyman had been bleeding. So much blood. And when she'd seen that blood, Willow had sworn she'd felt something just *break* inside of herself. She'd been screaming. Screaming on the inside, screaming out loud, and a red haze of fury and fear had overtaken her. She'd attacked...

Attacked Jay?

Why? They'd been on the same side. They'd been lovers. She'd started to lower her guard with him. He'd treated her as if she were normal.

But normal women didn't get locked up like this.

And Jay—he'd been the one to order her containment. That was one memory she had that remained crystal clear. *"Take her to containment."* His order. His shouted words. His face had been so hard and angry.

Her shoulders hunched. She pulled her legs up toward her. She was still just wearing Jay's shirt and a pair of panties. The shirt smelled like him. Her legs were bare, and she wrapped her arms around her knees, rocking a little bit, the movement instinctive. Why couldn't she remember everything that had happened that night? And why, *why* did her heart hurt so much?

She kept seeing Wyman. Bleeding.

And her heart *hurt.*

"Willow."

Her head whipped up. She stared straight at the mirror. Narrowed her eyes. Saw beyond the glass.

"Willow, I'm coming into the room." Jay's voice. Not cold, not like it had been before. But tired. Sad?

She rocked forward a bit more, but didn't get off the bed.

"Don't attack, Willow." His low order.

She'd attacked before. Tears stung her eyes. He'd made love to her, and she'd attacked him right after that. Talk about being a freak.

He must hate her.

Or fear her.

Both, probably.

Her head lowered, pressing against her knees. She didn't want to look at her reflection in the glass. She didn't want to look at him. She didn't want to see his disgust or his fear. "Go away." Her words were hoarse.

Instead of leaving, she heard the soft tread of his steps approaching. The keypad outside of the containment room beeped, and the door opened a moment later. She held her breath as he entered. His steps were hesitant, and Jay walked forward just a bit before he stopped.

"Willow..." Her name seemed to sigh from him.

A lump rose in her throat, but she swallowed it down. She should look at him. But she was afraid of what she'd see.

"Wyman is alive, Willow."

The pain in her chest actually got worse.

"He's in surgery. He's going to need a lot of blood."

She still didn't look at him.

"I didn't mean to shoot him. Hell, I wasn't even holding the gun when it fired. I tackled him. *He* had the gun. It went off. The bullet hit Wyman in the stomach when we fell. When you saw me, I was trying to keep him alive. I wasn't trying to kill him."

She heard Jay step closer.

"I *wasn't* trying to kill him. Dammit, Willow, will you *please* look at me?"

Her head lifted as she pulled in another deep breath.

Jay flinched when he saw her face, and her heart just stopped. *He hates me. He fears me. He –*

"Baby, you're crying." He rushed across the room. Climbed into the bed with her and yanked her into his arms. "I'm sorry." He kissed her cheek. "I just said containment because things were so out of control. He did something to you.

You weren't responding. I didn't want you fighting with the others. I couldn't have you hurt. Couldn't let you hurt them." He kissed her again. "I'm so fucking sorry. We're going to figure this out. I'm going to make this right. I'm going to make you—"

He broke off, but she knew what he'd been about to say. *I'm going to make you right.* "I don't feel right." Her temples wouldn't stop throbbing. The dull ache nagged at her. She lifted her fingers and pushed against her temples. "I don't know what happened." Her voice was so low. "Did I…hurt you?"

His fingers slid up. Moved to her temples even as her hands fell. He began to gently massage her, moving his fingers in soothing circles, and her breath whispered from her. "No, baby, you didn't hurt me. The guy wanted you to shove my fears at me and immobilize me, but you didn't. He was trying to control you, but you didn't give in to him. You stopped."

She had?

His fingers kept sliding in those soothing circles. Warm, strong fingers. He massaged her in silence as the moments slipped by. Some of the tension eased from her body, and Willow felt her shoulders sag as she seemed to sink into him.

"Tell me what you know about him," Jay urged her.

Her heart ached. That strange burn again. "He was…Wyman. I recognized his voice."

"The guy changed his appearance, got a nose job, did something different with his jaw. Dyed his hair, lost weight, but, yeah, that was definitely Wyman. He came out of his hiding spot for you, just like we thought he would."

A shiver slid over her, and Willow burrowed even closer to Jay. "Because I was the control experiment." That was what she'd been described as before. She'd been kept in isolation, while the other Lazarus subjects had been together. At least, the subjects in Sawyer's lab had been together, anyway. They'd gone out on missions for the government. They'd been tested, studied.

She'd been locked away and seemingly forgotten.

"I think you're a whole lot more than that." A new note had entered his voice, but his fingers never stopped their careful massage. Her temples weren't hurting any longer, but she didn't tell him that. Willow didn't want him to stop. She liked having him that close. Liked pretending…

I just like pretending. Hadn't he once told her that everyone pretended?

"How did you feel when you saw him?" Jay pushed.

She bit her lower lip. "I was scared." That part she remembered. "I'd had another bad dream." And that was odd. "I-I don't have dreams like that. Not typically, but it was the same dream, coming back at me, and—"

"Are you sure it was a dream? Maybe it was a memory."

She licked the lip she'd just bitten, a quick, nervous swipe of her tongue. "That's what scared me. I was afraid it was a memory."

"Was Wyman in that dream—that memory?"

"No." She was definite on that. "Another man was. Someone who knew me. Someone who'd been looking for me." Willow swallowed. "I think we were lovers."

She felt his body tense.

"He said I belonged to him." The words felt wrong. Goosebumps had risen on her arms.

"You have a lover out there? Someone looking for you?" His voice was different. Harder. Colder. But he was still moving his fingers in that careful massage.

"I told him it was over." Her eyes closed. "But he said it wasn't. That we weren't done."

Silence.

"I was afraid of him." Her stark confession. "That's why I went downstairs. And I saw Wyman, and for just a second, I felt…" Now her words trailed away because this was the craziest part of all. For just a moment, she'd felt, "Safe."

"Safe because of Wyman?"

She knew that didn't make any sense. "Everything got so mixed up. I can't even remember what happened next, but I can see myself on top of you, with my fist pulled back."

Now she eased away from him. Moved to face him. "I'm so sorry." She was. "I don't know what happened. I don't know why—"

"I think he triggered you."

Her stomach twisted. "What?"

"I think he used some kind of mind control on you. He said something, and it was like a switch had been flipped inside of you. You fought his control, but for a moment, he was definitely in your head. Wyman told you to attack, and you flew at me." The words were quiet, oddly calm, and his gaze was steady. She looked for fury. Judgment. Disgust.

There was nothing. She couldn't detect any emotion at all in his gaze. *That* scared her.

"When you saw him bleeding on the porch, what happened then?"

Her lips trembled. A tear slid down her cheek. "I…hurt."

His face hardened. His eyes seemed to blaze. "Right." That one word. Clipped. Hard. "That's going to fucking change things."

What?

He slid from the bed. Stood nearby, and his hands were clenched at his sides.

She didn't know what to say or what to do. She didn't… "You can't trust me," Willow whispered. It was something he must have already realized. "I can't trust myself." A truth that hurt the most.

His eyes narrowed. He leaned over her, putting his hands on either side of her body, caging her there. "You can trust me," he rasped back at her. "Trust me to stay with you. To get you through this. I'm not going to give up."

A lump rose in her throat again. "Maybe you should."

"Fuck that. I'd never give up on you."

The ache in her heart finally eased. She stared at him, wishing she could see past the mask he was wearing. Wishing she could understand him. "Why?" The word tore from her. "Is it guilt?" Because he'd given Wyman the money for Project Lazarus? Willow shook her head. "I don't want guilt, I want—" Her lips clamped together.

"What do you want?"

She wanted what they'd had hours before. Two people, making love. Giving each other pleasure. No other worries. No other fears. Just him. Just her. Normal.

But Willow heard the soft tap of footsteps beyond her room. Someone was coming to watch her.

Her gaze darted over Jay's shoulder, going to the big mirror.

"Easy," he soothed. "It's Cecelia. She's coming to talk with you."

The shrink?

"He got into your mind, Willow. We have to find out how."

She didn't want this.

"Just talk to her, for me, okay? Just talk to her for a few minutes, and let's see what happens."

She stared up at him. "I need clothes."

He blinked. Glanced down at her body. "You're wearing my shirt."

His scent covered her. Maybe it had even made her feel better when she'd been alone in the containment room. "I want my clothes. And I want you to stay."

His head jerked up.

"Stay," Willow said again.

"Baby, I'll do whatever the hell you want."

***

Reva Gray wasn't sure what time it was. Didn't really care, either. She'd just left another club, the pounding beat of the music fueling her blood. She'd had more drinks than she could count, and she didn't plan on stopping anytime soon. So what if dawn came? Screw the day.

She'd already closed down two places that night. Good thing some clubs in the city partied until the sun came up.

She breezed past the bouncer at another bar. She always got entrance to any place she wanted.

A perk that came with her looks. So few people ever saw beneath her beauty.

Jay doesn't want me back. Her heels tapped too hard against the floor. She hadn't loved Jay, that was true, but she'd had plans for his money. And she'd *liked* him. He hadn't been a total prick. Maybe, with time, maybe she could have loved him.

If she'd believed in love.

Reva made her way to the bar. She didn't buy her own drinks. Hadn't in years. Wouldn't be starting any time soon. She drummed her fingers to the beat of the music, knowing that a helpful fellow would arrive any moment. Someone who'd be happy to get her drink.

And sure enough, a tall, handsome stranger appeared, as if on perfect cue.

"Buy you a drink?"

Her gaze swept over him. His sandy blond hair was carefully styled, brushed back from his forehead. His body was muscled, lean and hard. He wore an expensive suit—she could always tell the price of a suit by just one glance.

The guy was money, all right. Money and muscle, and he was just her type. "You may." Reva smiled at him. Maybe she'd forget Jay.

He'd sure forgotten her.

The fellow motioned for the bartender. Then her new guy glanced back at Reva. "I believe you and I have a…friend in common." The hesitation was brief, but obviously deliberate.

She shrugged her shoulders even as she put her hand on his chest. A flirtatious move. One she'd perfected long ago. "And who is that friend?"

"Jay Maverick."

Her eyelashes flickered.

"And when I say friend…" the man continued in his deep, dark as sin voice, "I mean asshole that I'm going to destroy."

Maybe she'd had too much to drink. Because at his words, Reva laughed.

He smiled. There was something about his smile…

Her laughter stilled.

A shiver slid over her.

"Want to help me?" he asked.

CHAPTER TEN

Willow had changed into jeans and a sweatshirt. She hadn't bothered with shoes, and she sat, her spine perfectly straight, on the edge of the bed.

Cecelia Gregory—*Dr.* Cecelia Gregory—had pulled a chair close to the bed. Like Willow, Cecelia was also wearing jeans. She'd taken off her coat to reveal a blue sweater, and she offered Willow a reassuring smile.

Willow didn't feel particularly reassured. They were still in the containment room—still in her cell, and Cecelia made her nervous.

Willow's gaze cut to the right. Jay was there. His shoulders were propped up against the wall, and his arms were crossed over his chest. His stare was on Cecelia.

"How are you feeling, Willow?" Cecelia asked carefully.

It wasn't Willow's first session with the shrink. She liked Cecelia. She was also uneasy around her. Because Cecelia could figure out how to get inside of everyone's mind. Willow could touch a person and manifest their fears. But Cecelia could simply ask her careful questions and strip a person's soul absolutely raw.

"Willow?" Cecelia prompted.

Willow pulled her gaze away from Jay. "Got to say," she murmured. "I'm not at my best."

"It's almost dawn." Cecelia gave her a quick smile. "And you've had a rather, um, eventful night."

"Maybe we should wait until later for this," Willow rushed to say. "If it's nearly dawn, then—"

"I'm not going to stay long. Flynn will be coming for me soon. But I needed to check in with you, after everything that happened."

Willow's chin notched up. "You mean you had to check in to make certain I wasn't going to flip out and attack everyone."

"Yes." Cecelia nodded. "I did."

The woman didn't pull her punches.

"You know I'm not going to lie to you, Willow. That's not what I do. There was an extreme incident tonight, and I was asked to talk with you because we need to do a threat assessment."

Willow wanted to look at Jay again. Because she wanted it so badly, she kept her eyes glued to Cecelia. "I didn't—Jay said I didn't make him see his fears."

"No." Cecelia's voice was gentle. "You didn't. You fought whatever compulsion or trigger Wyman gave to you."

Her hands dug into the bed covers. "If I fought it, then that means Wyman can't control me."

"You *did* lunge across the room. You went for Jay. But something stopped you before you could follow through on the attack." Cecelia tilted her head to study Willow. Her red hair trailed over her shoulder. "What do you think that was?"

"I don't remember everything clearly. I just remember bits and pieces."

"I've found that Lazarus test subjects maintain primitive responses and memories the best. Fear is very primitive. So is rage. Were you afraid in that room?"

"Yes."

"Were you angry?"

"Y-yes…"

"Can you remember what Wyman said to you?"

Willow shook her head.

"What do you remember then?"

"I remember being over Jay. Staring down at him."

"Good. That's good, Willow. Tell me…how did you *feel* right then?"

Jay was watching. She'd asked him to watch, to stay, but now… "Can he leave?"

She felt Jay's start of surprise.

"Forget it." She huffed out a breath. Maybe he should hear this. "I felt ashamed. He'd treated me like I was normal, and then I was going to hurt him. I was like some kind of attack dog, that's how I felt. Like I'd been given prey to target. And I looked down and it was Jay, and I *couldn't.*"

"Do you remember how you felt right then? At that exact moment when you realized you were about to hurt Jay?"

"Frozen." Inside and out. Unable to move. "I wanted to say something to him, I wanted to pull away, but I couldn't move at all." Helplessly, her gaze darted to Jay. She found his stare on her.

Another shiver slid over Willow, and she made herself glance back at Cecelia.

Only to realize that Cecelia had caught her telling look toward Jay. The shrink was far too observant to miss any detail, no matter how small.

"What happened next?" Cecelia prompted in her calm, steady voice.

"I heard a gunshot. It was like the sound woke me up. I ran toward it." Her breath came a little faster, her heart beat faster. "I found Jay crouched over Wyman. Blood was on Jay's hands." Her lips pressed together.

"And then...?" Cecelia prompted her.

"Then I attacked." Heat stung her cheeks.

"There was no trigger word from Wyman this time? You attacked on your own?"

"I was…something broke inside of me." The only way to describe it. "I was just left with fury. Fear." Her lashes swept over her cheeks. "I couldn't lose him."

"Jay? You couldn't lose Jay?"

No. Wyman. "He did something to me." She looked up. "To my mind. Whatever Wyman did, you have to undo. Get him out of my head."

"I'll try," Cecelia said. She nodded once, briskly, then said, "Jay, I need to talk with you outside." She rose to her feet. "I think you should just rest for a while, Willow. Get some sleep." She turned for the door.

Willow rose, too. "You mean I should rest, *in here*."

Jay was at the door. So was Cecelia. The shrink glanced over her shoulder, and her hazel gaze was sad. "Yes."

Because Cecelia thought that Willow was a threat. One who had to be *contained*. Willow's gaze swept over the room. All the comforts of home, only it was a prison. "Right. That's fine. Things will be different in the morning." The lie came easily.

Then Cecelia was gone. Jay lingered a moment more, his gaze on Willow. "Are you going to be okay?"

No. "Of course. I just need to sleep."

His jaw hardened.

"Go talk to Cecelia. I'll be here." Not like she could go anywhere else.

He still hesitated.

"I'm tired," Willow told him and that was the truth. "I want to get some sleep, okay? Just doing what the doctor ordered."

"If you need me..."

"I don't." *I do.*

She slid into the bed. Closed her eyes. A moment later, the door shut. She heard the pad of his steps as he left her.

He thought the room was sound-proofed. That he'd managed to create a secure holding place so that Lazarus subjects couldn't use their enhanced senses to see or hear what happened beyond that room.

He was wrong.

"We have a problem," Cecelia told him quietly. Willow heard the shrink's words perfectly. "If he's set some kind of trigger in her head, then Wyman could have done the same thing to other subjects. He could have ways to control them all."

"That's just the beginning of our damn problems," Jay threw back, his voice hard and grating. "Wyman said—the SOB said he's her father."

"What?"

But Willow had lunged upright in bed, her heart racing and her mind seeming to…splinter.

***

"You're not dying on me, baby. You're not."

Wyman Wright's voice. But his face was different. His nose was bigger, his jaw harder, and his thin hair was gray at the sides. Fear etched deep lines onto his face as his shaking hand touched her cheek. "I'm going to help you."

She wanted to talk, but couldn't. Her whole body felt funny. Cold.

Numb?

"I'll make you stronger, baby. I'll make it so that he can't ever hurt you again. I'll fix what I did. I'll bring you back, I swear it."

He could do so much, she knew that. But even he couldn't cheat death. And death was there. She could see it in the darkness around her. She wanted to tell him good-bye, but couldn't. All she could do was stare at his face as the darkness around them both grew stronger.

"No, Willow, you hold on! I need you to hold on just a little longer. There are steps to follow. Fucking preservation process—*it's going to work!* It worked on the others, and it will work on you."

She couldn't see him. Had her eyes closed? Or had the darkness gotten too strong?

"Baby!" His voice seemed to break. "I won't lose you. You'll come back..." His words roughened. "Even if I have to fight heaven and hell...they won't take you."

Then she could have sworn that she felt the fire of hell. Because she seemed to be burning—burning from the inside out. Her whole body hurt, and the pain wouldn't stop. *It wouldn't stop.* She was being torn apart. The woman she'd been, the life she'd had, it was ripped away from her. She could see her life tearing into pieces. She tried to grab the pieces, but they were burning. *She* was burning.

She opened her eyes—

Strapped to a table. In a white, sterile lab. Men and women in lab coats.

Willow screamed.

***

"Her father?" Cecelia's hazel eyes widened. "Bullshit."

"Yeah, well," Jay raked a hand over his jaw, feeling the rough edge of stubble, "I hope to hell that's the case, but I've got Elizabeth comparing their blood and DNA. If he *is* her father, that would explain a few things, like why I can't find a trace of Willow anywhere."

"Because he would have protected her. Probably her whole life." She rocked back on her heels. "As many enemies as he has…no way would Wyman want the world knowing he had a daughter. He would have kept her away from everyone. He would have—"

"He would have trained her," Jay said flatly. "Made sure that she knew how to protect herself from any threat. *That's* where she got her skills. Wyman. *If* what he's saying is true. We thought Willow had a military background like the other subjects, but Wyman treated her differently from the beginning. He kept her separated because she *was* different."

"He protected her."

Jay nodded. "And he only came out of hiding when he thought she was in danger." When she'd been shot. *Hold the fuck up.* His mind started spinning. If Wyman had been protecting her, then had all of that BS about Jay being a threat to Willow—had it been true?

No, no way, it—

Willow screamed.

He instantly whipped around, staring through the one-way glass. Willow wasn't supposed to be able to hear anything outside of her room, but he'd set up the space so that he could hear her. And her scream was absolutely gut-wrenching.

She was sitting upright in bed, her body twisting and turning, and her scream kept echoing.

He didn't hesitate. Jay ran back to her, throwing open the door and rushing toward the bed. "*Willow!*"

CHAPTER ELEVEN

He grabbed Willow, fear thick in his stomach, and Jay's fingers tightened around her shoulders. "Willow!"

She wasn't screaming anymore. Her eyes were wide open, she seemed to see *through* him, but then she blinked once, shuddered, and color came flooding back into her too pale cheeks.

"I died," Willow whispered.

"No, baby, you didn't, you were having a dream, you—"

"Wyman was there. He said he'd bring me back. That he'd make sure I couldn't ever be hurt again." She shuddered again. "And then I was burning. Everything about me—everything was being torn away."

He pulled her against his chest and held her, hating her pain. Hating the fact that this wasn't just some bad dream. It was her life.

"It hurt. I thought I was in hell. Then it all changed. I opened my eyes, and I was strapped to a table. I was in a lab."

And that was where she'd stayed. Locked up. A prisoner.

I made her a prisoner again.

"Screw this shit." He scooped her into his arms. Carried her toward the door. Cecelia was there and when she saw him coming, with Willow cradled in his arms, Cecelia gave a frantic shake of her head.

"What are you doing?" Cecelia gasped.

"What I should have done in the first place." His hold tightened on Willow. "She doesn't belong in some cell. She's not going to be locked up."

"Jay, you know what happened before, you know—"

"I know she didn't kill me. I know she won't. And I know there is no way I'm leaving her locked up." It hurt her. *He'd* hurt her. "Step aside, doctor."

Cecelia hesitated, but she moved to the side.

"Thank you." He pressed a kiss to Willow's head. "We're going upstairs, baby. I'll open the blinds, let the light in. Just the way you like." He kept talking to her as he made his way down the hallway, then up the stairs.

With every step he took, he could feel Cecelia watching him.

***

"I need to ask you a question."

West Harper stared into the gleaming amber liquid. Whiskey. Not really his drink of choice, but it had been one hell of a day. Or, rather, night. After nearly being blown to hell and back, he could use something to take the edge off.

Cecelia cleared her throat. "West? Did you hear me? I need to ask you something."

He downed the whiskey and turned toward her.

She nervously tucked a lock of red hair behind her ear. "It's about Jay."

"Figured as much." He waited. When it came to Jay's secrets, West wasn't exactly the sharing sort. He liked Cecelia, she was good at her job, but he wasn't going to betray his brother. Not for anyone.

"How long has he been in love with Willow?"

Not the question he'd anticipated. West gave a low laugh. "He isn't." Jay had never gotten serious about any woman. Sure, he loved women. In general. Loved them in all sorts of shapes and sizes, but to be *in* love with one particular woman? Not Jay's style. Jay didn't go for permanence. Not for commitment. His life was his tech. His inventions.

"Are you sure?" She stepped forward. "Because I'm afraid that Jay's emotions may be blinding him to a danger that he shouldn't ignore."

Now tension swept through West. "You'd better elaborate on that danger."

She glanced over her shoulder. "Willow is dangerous."

"*All* of the super soldiers are dangerous." He paused a beat. "Including your lover."

"Flynn wouldn't hurt me." Her instant response.

"Yeah, but he'd sure destroy anyone who tried to come at you, wouldn't he? And the guy wouldn't hesitate."

She nodded. "True." Cecelia's hands pressed to the front of her jeans. "I think the subjects need an anchor of sorts. Someone they can connect with. Someone to help them maintain their link to humanity."

"That what you are to Flynn? His humanity?"

She glanced away from him. Her gaze swept around the room—Jay's study. Some of the furniture was smashed. Broken glass littered the floor. "What if she hadn't stopped?"

Like that question hadn't already run through his head a dozen times. When Jay needed him, West hadn't been there. Hadn't been close enough to save his brother's life. The guards outside had been unconscious. Jay had been on his own. "He was armed."

"Do you think he'd ever shoot her?"

No, he didn't. "She's locked up for the time being," West said, making sure he sounded confident and in control. The lady obviously needed some reassurance. "We can figure things out—"

"He's not locking her up. I think he should. And you know I don't say something like that lightly. Until we can figure out how that trigger worked, until we can figure out exactly what happened in this room, Willow should be secured. But he won't lock her up. Jay just carried her back upstairs. Not a logical move for a man who lives his entire life based on logic."

No, it wasn't a fucking logical move. It was a suicidal one.

"I'll ask again...how long has he been in love with her?"

West didn't speak.

"I need your help, West. I'm trying to figure things out." She began to pace. "If I could have just seen what happened here. Willow's memories are spotty, and Jay is hell bent on protecting her. I need to know exactly what went down, I need—"

He walked to the bookshelf. Lifted one of the books. Not really a book. It was tech Jay himself had created, only the guy hadn't realized West had used that tech against him.

Not precisely using it against him. Using it to protect him.

He pulled out the small drive. "You want to see what happened? Then pull up a chair. Let's both take a real, up-close look."

Her lips parted. "What is that?"

It was him, spying on his brother. Him, crossing a line that he knew Jay wouldn't forgive. But sometimes, it wasn't about forgiveness. Sometimes, it was just about making sure those who mattered most kept their asses alive. "I'm his head of security. So whether he likes it or not, I'm keeping my brother safe." And under surveillance. "Let's just see what the hell went down."

***

Carefully, Jay lowered Willow onto his bed. He wanted to hold her, too tight and too hard, so he made himself step back. He headed toward the window, pulled open the blinds, and let the first streaks of sunlight trickle inside.

"You can sleep in here," he told her. "There's no confinement. We're going to work this out." If he said the words enough, maybe they'd be true. Maybe he could fix everything for her.

He wanted that.

Jay turned toward the door.

"Will you stay with me?" Her soft voice stopped him. "Just for a little while?"

He'd stay with her forever. That stark truth settled inside of him as he squared his shoulders. "Of course." He headed back toward the bed. He ditched his shoes and socks, but kept on his jeans and t-shirt. She slid over, and he climbed into the bed with her. "Do you want to change?" Jay asked her. "Do you want—"

"You."

He stilled. "Baby…"

"Will it ever be like it was before?" Willow's voice was so low. "When we made love and there was no holding back. No doubts. Will it ever be that way again? Or will you look at me and always wonder, is she going to snap? Is this going to be the moment when she loses it?"

"Stop." Anger hummed in his voice. "I don't wonder that."

"Maybe you should."

Jay shook his head. "I want you just the same. The same way I've wanted you since the beginning." He leaned over her, needing Willow to absolutely understand this. "I want you more than I've ever wanted anyone else. And I'd fucking walk through hell to have you."

He heard her breath catch.

"Want me to prove it?" He pressed his lips to hers. The kiss was hot, rough, his tongue dipping into her mouth and tasting her. Adrenaline still spiked through his body. Adrenaline. Fear. Rage.

The fear was the worst—the fear that he might lose her.

I won't.

"Prove it," she whispered, dared, as her fingers curled over his shoulders.

He knew this time would be different. Not slow and tender. No gentle caresses. His control was far too brittle for that. He stripped her, yanking off her clothes. Tossing them aside. Nearly shredding her panties.

He'd buy her more.

He jerked off his own shirt. Kicked out of his jeans. His hand went between her legs, and he pushed two fingers inside of her. She wasn't ready, not yet, and he needed her to be. He needed her *wild.*

He worked her clit. Kissed her breasts. Sucked her nipples. Used the edge of his teeth on her until she was moaning for him. Twisting beneath him.

Then he yanked on a condom. Drove into her. Deep and hard, and there was no stopping, not for either of them. This was basic. This was primitive. He needed her as much as he needed breath.

Her legs locked around him. Her body arched toward him. She came, and the contractions of her delicate inner muscles slid along the length of his cock, driving him over the edge so that he erupted into her. The climax twisted through him and seemed to obliterate everything else. She was all he knew.

All he wanted.

She was his.

He pulled her close. Tucked her into his body.

She was his. And he'd fight the world to keep her.

Her breathing slowly evened out. Her body went lax against him. Jay still didn't move, not yet. He found that he liked holding her.

I was burning. Her words slid through his mind.

His lips feathered over her temple. He'd make sure she never burned again. He kept holding her, needing to be close a moment longer, then he carefully slipped away.

Jay had work to do.

***

"See anything interesting?" Jay drawled.

West and Cecelia both flinched at his words. And then they looked guilty as hell. They were leaning over his computer. Both intent on watching the screen. He knew why, of course. Did his brother really think he didn't know everything that was in his own study?

"Where's Willow?" West asked as he cast a nervous glance behind Jay.

"Sleeping." He yanked his t-shirt over his head, then tugged it down to his waist. He'd put on his jeans before heading down the stairs. "She needs to rest." They all did. But first… "I'm guessing you two were watching the video?"

Red tinged Cecelia's cheeks.

"Video?" West repeated. "What video?"

Jay rolled his eyes. West's poker face sucked. "The video from the surveillance camera you put in here. Don't play games. I'm really not in the mood for them." He headed around the desk. Only West knew his password, and maybe it was time to change that situation. But for the moment…

Jay peered at the screen on the left. Saw the still image. West must have paused the playback when Jay entered the room. "Did you really think I didn't know you'd stuck the camera in here? I mean, come on, it was my tech."

"You didn't say anything," West muttered.

A shrug was Jay's answer. "How many times have you two already watched the video?"

"A few," came Cecelia's quick response. "And you're right. Wyman was using a trigger phrase for her. 'Time for you to bloom.'"

Jay rewound the video. Went back to the moment when Willow was standing in the doorway. "You had good placement for the camera." She looked lost. Afraid. He played the video, and when he did, he saw Willow's face completely change when Wyman gave the trigger phrase.

In nearly a blink of time, she was across the room. On top of Jay.

"You could have tried fighting, man," West groused.

"No, I couldn't. I wasn't going to hurt her." Silence. He looked up and found West's gaze on him. "What?"

"Just realizing I've missed a few things, that's all." West's lips twisted. "At least she stopped." He motioned to the image. "You can see her expression change, right here. Cecelia and I were trying to figure out what stopped her, if you whispered something to her, if you did something—"

"*She* did something." Jay rolled back his shoulders. "She broke through the guy's power. He wanted her to fight me, but she didn't. She had more control than he thought." Jay's hard stare swept both Cecelia and West. "And that's why we aren't locking her up. She stopped. She fought him."

"Uh, yeah, but are you forgetting the part where she later went batshit on the porch and tried to take everyone out?"

Jay's hand rose to rub against his chest. "If he's her father, then it makes sense."

West backed up a step. "Hold on, did you just say Wyman was her old man?"

Right. He hadn't exactly filled West in on that part, not yet.

Jay glanced toward the study door. He almost expected to see Willow standing there, her expression lost. Scared. But she wasn't there. She was in his bed. Safe.

Willow was *safe.*

So why did he have the feeling something bad was happening to her? He cleared his throat and turned toward his brother, "Let me tell you what I know."

***

Willow opened her eyes. Sunlight filled the room, and soft covers were pulled over her body. She turned in the bed, reaching out—and touching Jay.

He was beside her. Warm. Strong.

A smile curved her lips, and her gaze met his. She loved his eyes. Loved the way that he looked at her.

But then his gaze flickered. Pain flashed on his handsome face. Pain. Horror. Fear.

"Willow?"

And the bed covers...the white bed covers were turning red. She shoved them out of the way and saw that he was bleeding. Stab wounds covered his stomach and chest. She started screaming. Screaming because this couldn't be happening.

Then Willow realized that she was holding a bloody knife.

CHAPTER TWELVE

The bedroom door flew open.

Willow blinked, shook her head, and found herself staring at Cecelia. Flynn Haddox was right behind the shrink. Of course, Flynn was always close to Cecelia.

He loved her.

"I'm sorry," Willow whispered. "*Help him.*"

"Help who, Willow?" Cecelia asked her softly.

Willow's gaze swung down, back to Jay, only...Jay wasn't there. The covers were white again. Jay was gone, and she didn't have a knife in her hand.

I'm losing my mind.

"Willow?" Cecelia crept closer to her. "Tell me what's happening."

Her heart was about to jump out of her chest. "Jay."

"Jay went to the hospital." It was Flynn who answered. Flynn who'd just put his body protectively in front of Cecelia's. "He needed to question Wyman. He'll be back soon."

Willow wrapped the covers around her body. "Jay isn't dead?" Her voice was a hoarse whisper.

"No." Flynn frowned at her. "Why would you think that?"

Because she'd just seen him die. Right there, in the bed with her. Her gaze darted to the window. "Something is wrong."

"It's okay, Willow," Flynn assured her quickly. "Jay is just fine."

She shook her head. "Something is wrong with me." Her stare slid back to him. Flynn would understand. He was like her, after all. "My mind isn't working right. I keep having flashes, seeing things that aren't there."

"You had a nightmare." That was Cecelia. Sympathetic. Warm. "Everyone has those. Nightmares are normal."

But Flynn's gaze had hardened. He knew nightmares for Lazarus subjects weren't like bad dreams for regular people. *They* weren't like normal people.

"I think I'm going to hurt him," Willow confessed. She could still smell the coppery odor of the blood. Feel the knife. "And it wasn't a nightmare." It had been too real. She'd *seen* the blood. Seen Jay dying. She rose from the bed. Hurried into the bathroom and changed into fresh clothes. She didn't look at her reflection. Willow couldn't do it.

When she went back into the bedroom, Cecelia and Flynn were still there.

Flynn...hadn't she attacked him the night before? The memory was foggy. Distorted. "Maybe I was kept away from the others because I was the threat." Her arms wrapped around her stomach.

Cecelia padded closer to her, and Flynn was right beside his mate.

Mate. Such a primitive word. But that's what the test subjects were all about. Primitive responses. Primitive instincts. Willow certainly felt a powerful instinct right then—to flee. "I can't hurt Jay."

"Willow, we need to talk things through." Cecelia's voice was mild. Her shrink voice. "You know I said I'd help you, and I will. We can deal with what's happening—"

"I made love with Jay."

Cecelia cleared her throat. A faint smile curled her lips as she glanced at the bed. "Yes, I sort of figured that out—"

"I've had dreams of a man telling me that we belonged together. A man who said he wasn't letting me go." Her temples ached as she thought of him. "I couldn't see him. Not clearly. Was that someone from my past?"

"Willow—"

"Then I just had a vision of myself, killing Jay. We were in bed together, and I killed him."

Sympathy flashed on Cecelia's face. "You aren't going to kill him. Jay trusts you." That was the problem. Now her stare slid to Flynn's. He would understand. "Maybe he shouldn't." Her tongue swiped over her dry lips. "Don't chase me."

"I don't understand—" Cecelia began.

But Willow had already leapt for the window. She knew what was inside of herself. The twisting, yawning darkness. The raw emotions that had erupted when she'd become Jay's lover. She felt wrong inside. Too much rage. Too much confusion.

And the image she'd had...the terrible vision of Jay dying, she knew what it was—

Her worst fear. If she stayed with him, it would come true. Because she was the biggest threat to him.

Before she could get to the window, Flynn stepped into her path. He let out a long sigh. "You know I can't let you do this."

"Let?" Willow repeated carefully. Her hands flexed at her sides. "Last time I checked, Jay said I wasn't a prisoner here. You *all* said that."

"That was before..." Flynn's shoulders were straight, his hard gaze locked on her. "Before we realized Wyman had a trigger word for you, before his men swarmed this house."

Flynn doesn't trust me. Neither does Cecelia. "Step aside, Flynn." She wasn't staying. She *had* to leave.

"I want to know more about the first dream," Cecelia said suddenly. "The dream of the man who said you belonged to him."

What? Now?

"How did that make you feel when he said those words?"

Seriously—Cecelia was always focused on the *feelings*. "Absolutely terrified." Dead truth. Her stare never wavered from Flynn. "I don't want to hurt you. But I am leaving."

"Willow..." He growled her name.

Cecelia put her hand on his shoulder. "She's not a prisoner."

Flynn's head turned toward her. "You're gonna let her just go?"

"I know when a woman's running scared." She inclined her head toward Willow. "But you aren't going to find what you need by running, Willow."

She inched toward the window. Stared down below. "You don't know what I need."

"Of course, I do." Cecelia's words were crisp. "And when you're ready to hear what I have to say, come back."

She wasn't going to stop her? Really? "Jay is going to lose his shit," Flynn muttered.

Willow flinched. Yes, he was. He was going to freak out, but there was something inside of her, something screaming that she had to leave. Had to go.

Before it was too late, for Jay.

"Tell him that I'm sorry." She reached for the window.

"Don't jump out," Flynn snapped. "You're not busting out on some desperate escape. Go down the stairs. Use the front door."

She wanted to do that. Wanted to be normal but…

"She doesn't trust us," Cecelia said, and there was a faint shock in her words. "She doesn't trust any of us."

No, Willow didn't. She was afraid the others downstairs would try to lock her up. So she didn't hesitate any longer. She burst through the window. Flew through the air and touched down easily even as glass littered the ground around her.

Adrenaline drove her. Fear drove her. Darkness and rage. The emotions were so thick inside of her. Swirling. And she just had to run. Had to get away.

Before madness overtook her.

Then again, maybe it was already too late.

***

The machines droned in a steady beep, beep, beep as Jay stalked into the hospital room. Guards were stationed outside, and he wasn't particularly surprised to find Sawyer sitting in a chair near the bed, his sharp blue gaze on the patient.

Wyman freaking Wright.

"Guess who's going to live," Sawyer muttered without taking his attention off the man in that bed. "For the time being, anyway."

Yeah, Jay had gotten that particular bit of news from Elizabeth. It was the reason he was there and not with Willow.

Wyman's eyelids fluttered.

"Been drifting in and out of sleep," Sawyer added as he ran a tired hand over the back of his neck. "Elizabeth said she decreased the guy's pain meds so he should be coming around any moment."

Sure enough, he was. Jay paced closer to the bed. He crossed his arms over his chest, and he waited. He'd been waiting a very long time for his chance to question this guy.

"Any chance he's going to trigger you?" Jay asked quietly. *Need to be on the safe side.*

Sawyer grunted. "I'm guessing that's why you've got a gun under your jacket?"

So he'd noticed that. "Only a tranq," Jay replied easily as Wyman let out a groan. "Just in case."

"Don't get trigger happy on my ass," Sawyer tossed back at him.

Then don't attack me.

Wyman let out another groan. His head turned. His eyes focused on Sawyer. "N…no…" His head rolled on the pillow, now moving toward—

"Hello, sunshine," Jay said to the bastard, feeling a grin stretch his face. "Isn't it a great day to be alive?"

"Screw…off…" The words rasped from Wyman.

Jay just laughed. "Glad to see you're feeling good enough to be pissy."

Another ragged groan from Wyman was his answer.

Jay headed around the bed. Then he leaned over, making sure he was right in front of Wyman's face. "You're a liar." And it gave him such pleasure to say those words.

Wyman coughed. "Where…where is…Willow?"

"You don't need to worry about that. You aren't going to use her again. She won't be your weapon."

"*None* of us will be," Sawyer snarled. He'd stepped up to Jay's side.

For a moment, Jay simply stared down at the man in the bed. Wyman Wright was pale, sickly. His body seemed fragile. His eyes were weak, bleary. This wasn't the monster of D.C. The guy who'd once made the whole world tremble. This was a guy who was, "Done," Jay said flatly. "There isn't going to be some grand ending for you. I don't care how many people *owe* you. You'll give us the answers we need. You'll tell us how many more test subjects are out there. Where they are, why—

"Wil…low…"

Jay stiffened. "She isn't yours."

Wyman coughed. Shuddered. "You lied, Wyman." A cold smile stretched his face. "Willow isn't your daughter. I had Elizabeth check your story. You're no biological relative to Willow, and you—"

"Dumb…ass…" Wyman groused. "You…of all… people…should know…" The machines beeped louder, faster. "More to f-family…than b-blood…"

Jay's phone rang, vibrating in his pocket. He ignored the vibration. "Don't you *dare* bring my brother into this, you understand me? You ever threaten him again, and I'll *end* you. I'll—"

The machines were louder. His phone had stopped vibrating. "He's…not blood…" Wyman gasped out. "But…f-family…like s-she's…m-mine…"

His phone was ringing again. Since it was his private line, Jay yanked it out. West. Shit. He shoved the phone to his ear. "Not now, man," he said. "Not—"

"Thought you'd want to know," West growled right back. "Your girl just left. Flynn and Cecelia let her run."

"*What?*"

"She jumped through the upstairs window. *Jumped.* I'm following her but that woman is *fast* on foot. I'm on my motorcycle…" And Jay could hear the groan of the engine. "Didn't think you'd want to let her go."

No, he *never* did. "Don't lose her."

"Yeah, well, *damn.* I think your lady just stole some dude's truck, so this is gonna get tricky—"

"West?"

The call went dead, but he knew he could count on West, just as his brother could always count on him. He shoved the phone into his pocket.

"Wil…low?" Wyman had forced out her name again.

Jay leaned over the bed. "You say there's a threat to her."

"Y-you…"

"I'd die to keep her safe. I'm not the threat. If someone is out there, gunning for her, you tell me who that is. You tell me *right* now."

The machines were going crazy. The door flew open as Elizabeth rushed inside. "What are you doing? I told you *mild* questioning, mild! He can't handle this! Are you trying to kill him?"

"Who. Is. It?" Jay demanded.

"L-lover..." Wyman wheezed. "Willow's lover..."

Jay jerked back.

"Oh, shit," Sawyer muttered. "That is *not* what you wanted to hear, huh, man?"

***

She didn't know where she was running to. She'd stolen a truck, she felt guilty as all hell about that, and Willow drove through the streets of D.C. like a woman possessed. Her body was operating on pure instinct, and her instincts were screaming for her to *run.*

She just didn't know where she was supposed to go. At first, she'd just been running blindly, the image of Jay's bloody body tormenting her, over and over again. She'd needed to get away from that bedroom. She hadn't been able to breathe because her fear had been so strong.

Only now...

Her breath slid in and out. And Willow realized that she'd turned on the street that led to Push. It was the middle of the day, and the club was closed down. The place would be empty inside.

The perfect place to stop. To think. To get her mind in check again.

She parked the vehicle and ran around to the back of the club. She grabbed for the door handle. *Locked.* Of course, it would be locked. But…

Willow just yanked harder. The heavy lock broke, and she rushed inside. The club's interior was dark and still. At first, she was afraid an alarm might sound, but there was no terrible blaring. There was only silence.

Her shoulders lifted and fell as she heaved out heavy breaths of air. And then…

A footstep.

Her head whipped up. Someone *was* in the club. Someone coming toward her. Someone—

"Seriously?" Benjamin Larson growled as he held his gun aimed at her. "You're the one who just broke into my place? I am not in the mood for this shit."

She could rip the gun away from him. He was about fifteen feet away from her, but she could bound across that room so quickly.

"Don't even think it, sweetheart," he warned her with a knowing smile. "You got the drop on me before, but that was when I didn't know about the super soldier freaks out there."

She flinched.

"Sorry," he muttered. "How about…that was when I didn't know about your *enhancements*?"

"I'm not here to hurt you."

"No? Then why are you here?" He looked around. "Here…without your shadow?"

Her shadow?

"Jay," he snapped. "Where the hell is he?"

"I don't know."

Benjamin laughed. "Right." He didn't lower the gun. With his dark hair and dark eyes, the guy looked sinister. Dangerous—which he was. "Look, you're gorgeous as all hell, but you're deadly. And I'm not going to make the mistake of ever lowering my guard with you again."

She winced. You made a man face his worst fears once…and he never forgave you.

Jay forgave me.

A door creaked. The sound came from upstairs.

Someone else was there? "I didn't know you'd be here."

"Just tying up a business deal. One of Jay's *friends* will be taking over security for this place. A good thing considering that I just had a break-in." His eyes gleamed.

Footsteps slowly padded down the stairs.

"Okay, Willow." Benjamin's voice was nice and easy. "Since we have an audience coming our way, how about you and I play nicely?"

She *had* been playing nicely. The guy wasn't unconscious, was he?

A few moments later, the other man appeared. He was tall, broad-shouldered. He wore a faded jacket and loose jeans. His thick hair was shoved back from his forehead, and faint laugh lines slid away from his eyes. "Hey, Ben!" the guy called. "There a problem here?"

Benjamin had just tucked his weapon into the back of his jeans. "No problem." He had a broad smile on his face. "Got someone for you to meet, Lucas. This is Willow. She belongs to the other owner of Push."

Lucas stiffened, just a bit.

So did Willow. "I don't belong to anyone."

Benjamin gave a long and suffering sigh. "She's involved, man. With Jay Maverick. So I'm telling you now, the woman may look like the best sin you've ever seen, but you're gonna want to keep your hands very much *off* her. And your eyes, too. Because if Jay catches you drooling over his lady, no way will he allow our deal to go through."

The guy didn't look like he was drooling. But there was *something* odd about his stare. It was too hard. Too…intense.

"I never take what doesn't belong to me." He strode forward and offered her his hand.

Willow stared down at his hand. A wave of unease slid through her. "Do we…have we…I'm sorry…have we met?" She took his hand.

His fingers immediately closed around hers. "You tell me." His voice was low. Gruff. And for a second, his eyes blazed.

I think I know his voice. "I'm sorry." She hated the tremble in her voice. "But I was in an…accident a while back. I'm afraid that my memories aren't what they should be."

His gaze narrowed. Swept over her.

"If we've met," Willow continued carefully, "then I don't remember you."

Benjamin cleared his throat. "Right, um, let's talk about who you *do* remember. Jay. Does your good buddy Jay know you're here?"

"We haven't met," Lucas said smoothly as he continued to stare at Willow. His hand tightened around hers. "I'm sorry to hear about your accident."

She was aware of a strange unease sliding through her.

His voice roughened. His heartbeat kicked up. His hold is too tight.

He was lying to her.

Every single nerve in her body went on full alert. She stopped trembling and hesitating. Willow pulled her hand from the stranger's as her spine straightened. "Jay doesn't control my movements. No one does." She nodded briskly to Benjamin, then to Lucas.

Lucas. The name didn't mean anything to her, but she was picking up so much from the guy. His heartbeat was racing. His body was thick with tension. And his gaze was far too knowing as it swept over her.

"I want Lucas here to take over security for the club." Benjamin had moved a step closer to her. "I get that Jay likes for West to be in charge of his company's security, but Push is *mine.* I want to make sure this place stays secure, and I'm in charge of the day to day operations. I'm considering bringing on Lucas to handle all my clubs."

Lucas was still staring straight at her. Seeming to see into her.

Her own heart was beating too fast.

Jay.

His name slid through her mind. She'd run from his house because she was scared—scared of what she might do to him. But right then…

I want Jay.

"Jay and Lucas go way back," Benjamin was saying, and his words caused Willow to blink in surprise. This man before her—the man who she *knew* somehow, even if the memories were lost to her—he also knew her lover?

"Hell, my phone's ringing. Give me a minute, would you?" Benjamin said as he hurried away, pulling out his phone.

And just like that, he'd left her with Lucas.

Lucas tilted his head as he studied her.

She wanted to back up a step, and because she did, Willow didn't move. "How do you know Jay?"

"He's been doing contract work for the government—hell, feels like forever. Sometimes, the work he does requires extra, uh, protection, I guess you could say. I've stepped in when needed."

Right. "You know West, too?"

A slow nod. "I served with him, in a different life."

Okay, that was reassuring. Or at least, it *should* have been reassuring. Only she didn't feel reassured.

"West is a good man. You can always count on him in a battle." Lucas took a step closer to her. His voice lowered. "Can't say the same for Jay Maverick."

"What?"

"The man will do anything for money. He's obsessed with his inventions, with his tech. With running the fucking world." And now pity filled his eyes. "You should watch yourself with him. The guy isn't someone you can trust."

No, this man—he *wasn't* saying this to her. "You don't know me."

He just stared back at her.

Do you?

"I know another lady who thought Jay was going to give her the world. Reva isn't exactly living the high life these days," he murmured.

Reva.

"Even though Jay called her up last night, wanting to talk. She thinks they're going to have a chance again." He exhaled. "Guess she doesn't know about you."

Jay called her up last night. He hadn't done that. Had he? No, no way. Last night had been chaos. Hell. But…

But when she'd woken up, Jay had been downstairs. How long had he been there before Wyman arrived? Had Jay—*why* would he have called Reva?

"The guy's a player. And he only looks out for himself." Lucas ran a hand through his hair. "You should be careful with someone like him."

Because she wanted to retreat from this man, because he scared her, unnerved her, Willow stepped forward. "I can take care of myself."

His lips quirked. "Yeah, I bet you can."

Benjamin appeared again. "Our meeting is over for now, Lucas. Thanks for coming in." His voice was harder than before. His gaze glittered. "Willow, we need to talk upstairs."

Going into Push had obviously been a mistake. She didn't need to guess in order to figure out who'd been on the phone. Jay.

She hadn't used her enhanced hearing to listen in on Benjamin's call. She'd been too distracted—and focused—on Lucas.

But Willow was *sure* the caller had been Jay. He realized she was missing. He was hunting her. "I think I'm done talking." She nodded briskly before turning on her heel. Benjamin called after her, but Willow didn't stop. She hurried through the back door. Went back into the brisk cold and—

He was behind her. She heard the rush of his steps right before he reached out and spun her around to face him. "You in trouble?" Lucas asked, a faint furrow between his heavy brows.

So much trouble. "I don't like being touched."

He immediately pulled his hand back. "My mistake."

She exhaled slowly. "And I'm fine."

"You don't look fine." He leaned toward her. Didn't touch her. "You look like a woman who is running." His voice was low, just for her. "It's Maverick, isn't it? You've found out what he really is. Just like Reva did. And now you're running scared."

"Willow!"

She didn't turn at the call of her name. She'd heard the thud of approaching footsteps. Hardly surprising that West had joined the party, too.

Lucas swore. "West is a good man, but he's blind when it comes to his brother." He nodded. "I can help you."

Why? Why would that guy want to help her?

"I can be your friend, if you need one." His grin was rough. Fleeting.

"*Willow.*" Now a warning edge had entered West's voice. "Lucas. What in the hell is going on?"

Lucas tossed a wave at West. "Just making a new friend, that's all."

They weren't friends.

"Willow already has plenty of friends," West threw back. "Stop flirting with her. She's not on the market. And Willow, we need to go."

She wasn't ready to go anyplace. At least, not with West. He'd just take her back to Jay.

"The lady doesn't seem interested in leaving with you," Lucas murmured.

"Shit." Benjamin's disgusted voice had joined their group. "I'm not in the mood for some pissing match at *my* club. Let's all just calm the hell—"

The explosion came then, hitting with no warning. Fire that roared and boomed as the lower level of Push ignited. The force of the blast lifted Willow into the air. It tossed her back, and she could feel the heat burning over her skin. She heard yelling, a furious roar, and the crackle of flames.

Burning, burning…

***

Jay seemed to watch the scene in slow motion. He'd been running toward the back of

Push, he'd had Willow in his sights, and then the place had gone to hell. Literally.

Fire seemed to burst out of Push, grabbing and stretching greedily. There was a boom, a loud, terrible boom of sound, then glass was exploding. Flames raging. Jay saw Willow fly into the air. West and Benjamin were tossed by the impact. They all flew and hit the ground.

They didn't get up.

Fucking hell.

He ran to Willow. She was face down on the ground, and he grabbed her, flipping her over. "Willow?"

Blood dripped from a cut on her cheek. His hands flew over her, but she wasn't burned. Scratched, cut a bit from impact, but—

Her eyes opened. She stared at him, and horror filled her gaze. Horror?

"Willow?" Jay wanted to lift her into his arms and get the hell away from there. But he didn't. He didn't move at all.

"What in the hell?" Benjamin's sharp voice.

Jay's head whipped to the right. Benjamin was on his feet, glaring at the blaze. "That's my fucking club!" Benjamin surged toward the fire.

West tackled him. "Man, you don't run *into* a fire!"

Jay pulled Willow to her feet. She stared at the building, her gaze on the flames.

"West!" Jay shouted. "You okay?"

His brother gave a grim nod. "Just trying to keep this dumbass from getting himself torched." He rose, moving off Benjamin.

"I have to get in!" Benjamin yelled. "That's my place! I have to stop the fire!"

Another man appeared, a guy that Jay recognized. Lucas Tate. What in the hell was Lucas doing there?

Benjamin tried to make another run at the building, but this time, Lucas shoved Benjamin back. "Man, you need to stay away. The place could—"

And another explosion hit. This one stronger than before. The top of the building seemed to ignite. Flames weren't crackling. They were shrieking. The fire was roaring. Jay hauled Willow back, pulling her away from the flames.

Could a super soldier come back if she was burned alive? He wasn't going to find out. He didn't want her anywhere near that place.

"Was anyone else in there?" West demanded.

Black smoke billowed in the air.

Coughing, Benjamin shook his head.

They'd all moved back. The club—Push had ignited.

"This is why you need me," Lucas said flatly to Benjamin. "I told you that people are gunning for Maverick. And you're getting caught in the crossfire."

Jay stiffened. His eyes met the icy blue gaze of Lucas Tate.

"You don't want to get caught in the crossfire," Lucas said as he stared at Jay. "That's no place any sane man wants to be."

In the distance, sirens wailed.

***

"Are you okay?" Jay's voice was low and rough. Firefighters were battling the blaze. Nearby, Benjamin was still cursing and raging, and Willow—Willow sat in the back of an ambulance, her gaze on the hands she'd twisted in her lap.

"Of course, I'm fine," she assured him. "You know how much it takes to put me down."

Jay caught her hands in his. Cops had arrived. They'd grilled him. Grilled the others. The fire had been contained, luckily, so no other buildings had been taken out. No one had been seriously hurt. A very fortunate thing. "Why did you run?" Jay demanded.

She wasn't looking at him. Hadn't looked him in the eyes, not since that one moment when she'd stared at him in horror.

"You shouldn't be close to me," Willow whispered.

"Too damn bad. Close to you is exactly where I want to be." He squeezed her fingers.

"Talk to me. *Why did you run?*" That wasn't the question he wanted to ask. He wanted to know...*Why did you leave me?*

"If you know someone is bad for you, why would you stay close?"

His shoulders stiffened. Willow thought he was bad for her? "Willow..."

"Take me to see Wyman Wright."

Those weren't the words he'd expected. "Uh, Willow..."

"I want to see him. I want to talk with him. He knows about my past. He knows *me*. I want my chance to question him."

"Is that where you were going when you left the house? You were going after Wyman?" No, that didn't make any sense. "Then how'd you end up at Push?" Right before the place exploded.

"I wasn't going to Wyman." Now, her gaze did lift. She stared straight at him. "I was getting away from you."

Jay took that hit right in the heart. "I see." He let her hands go. Eased back. "With everything that's happening, did you really think it was safe for you to be on your own?"

"Wyman is in custody. The threat is over. You don't have to keep me close any longer."

I want you close.

"I'm not a prisoner, am I?"

"You weren't ever my prisoner, Willow." Is that what she'd thought? Fuck, he'd been trying to show her how he felt. And all along, she'd been—what?

Waiting for the moment to leave?

"You had West tail me to Push. You followed me, too. If every step I take is watched, then how am I not a prisoner?"

Her voice was flat. Cold.

"I can't live like this. I can't be a ticking time bomb." Her gaze darted to the open ambulance doors. "Waiting to explode."

He didn't know what the hell he should do.

"Take me to Wyman," Willow said. "Take me, or I'll just find him myself."

The ambulance attendant was heading back toward them. "You can't trust Wyman. He'll lie to you."

"I can tell when someone lies. I'm stronger than you think."

Now he had to laugh, but it was a rough, grating sound. "Baby, I never doubted you were strong." He jumped out of the ambulance, motioned for her to follow him. She came down quickly, her body brushing against his.

They were lovers. He'd had her in his bed, then she'd run.

Run to Push? He still didn't understand why she'd gone there.

"You want Wyman?" He locked his fingers with hers. "Fine. You deserve your shot at him. But if he tries to get in your head again…"

She glanced away from him. "He's a demon I have to face. You don't know, you don't understand what it was like—"

"Don't I? I kept you away from him last night because I wanted to protect you. The bastard said he was your father."

She jerked away.

"Mind games," Jay gritted out. "That's what he does. But if you want him to screw with your mind again, then fine. We'll go face off against the bastard." He pointed to his car. "Let's get the hell out of here."

He turned, marching for his vehicle, but Lucas stepped into his path. Lucas—the guy had soot streaking over his cheek. His shirt was torn, and his blue eyes were way too intense as he locked his stare on Jay. "Running from a crime scene?"

"Hardly running. More like a slow walk." Jay took the guy's measure. He'd worked with Lucas before. Found the man to be ruthless as hell and dangerous to the core. Normally, traits he liked.

What he didn't like was the way the guy's gaze kept darting to Willow.

"The cops know where to find me," Jay added. "I already answered their questions.

When the arson investigators get done, they can come and grill me again."

"It was a bomb," Lucas said quietly. "Actually, I think it was two bombs. Two bombs that were placed in *your* club."

Wyman.

"You still have that long list of enemies?" Lucas asked as his lips curved into a faint smile. "So many people gunning for you."

Beside Jay, Willow was silent.

"Maybe you need some extra protection," Lucas muttered. "You think about that?"

"West has my six," Jay responded flatly. "He's my security."

"Oh." Lucas blinked. Once more, his gaze swept to Willow. "And here I thought she was the new bodyguard. That's the story I heard on the news."

"Don't believe everything you hear." Blue and red lights swept the scene. A crowd had gathered. Cameras were rolling. It was *past* time for Jay to get the hell out of there.

But Lucas was still in his way. "Benjamin hired me. He wants me in charge of security for his clubs."

Jay glanced back at the wreckage that remained of Push. "Hate to break it to you, but you aren't off to that great of a start. I mean, weren't you *in* the club right before it exploded? You're all damn lucky you didn't get blown to hell." And just thinking about that—about Willow burning, dying—had his body tensing.

If Wyman did this…

"The place didn't blow," Lucas took a step toward him, "not until you arrived on the scene. Interesting timing, don't you think?"

"What?" Jay snapped right back. "What in the hell are you—"

"Just got through checking the security feeds from the cameras that were outside. The feed goes to Benjamin's phone. He likes to keep tabs on things, you know."

Yeah, he knew. Jay had set up that freaking feed for him.

"Less than thirty seconds after you came roaring to the scene, the place ignited. You parked your car, lingered, then jumped out—running to the *back* of the club. Interesting that you went that way."

He'd gone to the back because West had told him that Willow went in the back door.

"And boom…the place exploded. Right after you arrived."

He didn't like where this was going. "You got an accusation, Lucas? Then spit it out. Don't waste my time by bullshitting around."

Willow was silent.

Lucas rocked back on his heels. "Benjamin told me that you weren't real pleased to be his partner. That you only did it because you owed him a debt."

"I *always* pay my debts." He slanted a quick glance at Willow, but her face was unreadable.

"Easy enough to get out of this particular partnership…just let the place go up in flames."

He didn't have time for this crap. "Out of the way, Lucas." He didn't wait to see if the guy complied. He took Willow's hand and pulled her with him. He had places to go. Things to freaking do.

And he didn't need Lucas's lame-ass accusations slowing him down.

When Jay got to the car, West was already waiting. They didn't speak. They just hauled ass away from the scene.

***

"Figures he gets to waltz away from the scene," Benjamin muttered as he watched Jay drive away and leave the flames behind. "Meanwhile, I have every cop in the area giving me the side eye."

Lucas kept his gaze on the car. "That's money for you. Let's the guilty walk."

"Uh, yeah." Benjamin gave a rough bark of laughter. "He's not guilty. Just an asshole. No way did he torch this place."

Lucas turned toward him. "You shouldn't be so sure. You *saw* the video feed—"

"I also saw how close Willow was to the building. No way would Jay risk her. So if you want to find the bastard who did this, then start looking elsewhere." Benjamin's gaze hardened. "When we do find the piece of shit, I'll deal with him. No one hurts what's mine. No fucking one."

Yes, Lucas had heard the stories about Benjamin. The guy was rumored to be one of the most powerful crime bosses on the East Coast. You didn't fuck with him.

Or at least, you weren't supposed to.

But sometimes…sometimes, anyone could get burned. Especially if that person got caught in the crossfire.

CHAPTER THIRTEEN

"Got to say, it's a new one for a lover to run from me the minute my back is turned."

Willow could hear the rough edge in Jay's voice. They were the only occupants in the small elevator—an elevator in some private hospital on the edge of D.C. His arms were crossed over his chest, and his gaze was locked on her.

She straightened her shoulders. "I shouldn't...*we* shouldn't have become lovers. That was a mistake."

Wrong words. She could absolutely tell they were wrong. He stalked forward. His hands flew out. She tensed, thinking he was going to grab her, but instead, his fingers hit the control panel on the elevator.

The elevator immediately stopped.

"A mistake?" Jay repeated carefully. "The first time?"

She swallowed.

"The second?" Jay pushed.

"Make the elevator move."

"Maybe the third. Yes, that must have been the mistake time. The third—"

"Stop it," Willow gritted out.

His jaw clenched.

She turned, fumbled and pushed different buttons on that control panel, wanting them to move.

"I didn't think any of it was a mistake."

The elevator was moving. Thank God.

"I thought it was the best sex of my life. Every. Single. Time."

Her cheeks flamed. "What?" She whirled back toward him.

But his gaze was hooded. His expression carefully masked. "I thought we were just getting started," he murmured. "Didn't realize you were making plans to leave."

She *had* to leave. Didn't he get that? Yes, she wanted him. So badly she ached. She was just trying to do the right thing. "I'll hurt you."

The doors opened with a ding.

"Oh, sweetheart, you already have." He strode out of the elevator.

It took a moment for his words to sink in, and when they did, Willow surged after him. "Jay!" She grabbed his arm.

He stilled. So did the armed guards who were on the floor. Everyone tensed.

"Easy," Jay said, his voice carrying a note of command. "She's with me."

The guards seemed to relax, a bit.

"I didn't mean to hurt you," she whispered. Everything was so messed up.

"Then what did you think leaving would do?"

Protect you.

"Come on. Sawyer's waiting." His voice was brisk as he led her down the hallway. He'd called Sawyer on the way over. Gotten this meeting set up. She knew Sawyer would be in the room during her time with Wyman. She also knew exactly why.

In case Wyman tries to get in my head again, Sawyer is there. Because Sawyer equaled her strength. Maybe he even surpassed her power, she didn't know. He'd been the first super soldier created. She didn't exactly want to challenge him to a fight in order to find out who was stronger.

West had stayed downstairs. He'd wanted to check in with his security team.

They walked in silence down the hallway. The gleaming white floors threw her reflection back at her even as the scent of antiseptic stung her nose. They passed dozens of hospital rooms, but all of those rooms were empty. "Where are the other patients?" Willow asked.

"There aren't any other patients on this floor."

"You got the whole *floor* for him?"

"Having a shitload of money gives you perks like that." His jaw hardened. "But there are some things money can't buy." His gaze cut to her. "And you're one of those things."

She sucked in a deep breath. "You think that you want to be with me. But you don't know how bad things can get."

"And you don't know how good they can get." He stopped near another door. This one had two guards in front of it. He nodded toward them, and the guards opened the door. She started to enter, but Jay caught her shoulder. "He's not blood."

She blinked. "What?"

"He tried to spin me some BS story about being your father. He's going to tell you the same story. He wants you to think a connection exists between you two. He wants you to feel bound to him."

Your father. A wave of dizziness slid over her.

"Don't buy his bullshit. You told me that you can tell when a person is lying, well, see his lies, Willow. See him for the bastard that he is."

Then he was striding inside. She sucked in a deep breath and followed him into the hospital room. She saw Sawyer first, standing near the bed, his hands loose at his sides. He gave a quick nod when he saw her, and his gaze slid to the bed.

To the man in that bed.

Wyman Wright.

The man who'd turned her into a monster. The man who…

Looked small. Weak. His skin was far too pale, and she could see the line of blue veins running just beneath the surface. Dark circles marked his eyes, and there was a stack of machines positioned near his bed. Those machines kept beeping even as green lines ran across their screens.

"She…shouldn't be here." Wyman's voice.

But his voice was different then. It wasn't the strong, rough voice she'd heard when she'd been in the lab. The voice of the man who came to watch her. It wasn't even the same voice he'd used in Jay's study. Instead, Wyman's voice sounded weak. Rough. Scratchy.

"Get her…out," Wyman wheezed.

"Sorry, but the lady wants to stay." Jay had paced to the window. Now he turned back, crossed his arms over his chest, and rolled one shoulder in a shrug. "She thinks she deserves the chance to talk with you, and I've got to say that I agree."

"Get her…" If possible, Wyman's face became even paler. "Out. Too…d-dangerous."

"You think I'm dangerous?" Willow took a quick step forward. "Who should I blame for that? Who did this to me?" Anger boiled inside of her. "Oh, right. That would be you."

He flinched. "Danger…is *to*…y-you…" The machines beeped faster. His breath heaved in and out.

"I told Willow the story you spun." Jay's voice was cold. Grim. "About being her father. Figured she deserved to know that, too."

A growl spilled from Wyman. "Since when…did you…grow…grow a con-conscience?"

Jay simply shrugged again.

"You aren't my father." Willow was surprised by how strong her voice was. "You're the man who kept me locked away. You're the man who made me into—" She looked down at herself and was surprised to see that her hands had clenched. "I make people see their worst fears. I turn their nightmares into reality. I *hurt* people." Her words came faster and faster. "You made me into a monster. And you think I should call you *father* because of that twisted shit? You—"

"T-taught you how…throw ball…" A mist covered his eyes. But he blinked, and it was gone. "Took f-first step…into my arms." His chin notched up. "H-hell yes…I'm your f-father…"

Her chest hurt. A sharp pain right in her heart.

"He is *not* biologically related to you," Sawyer told her, his voice low. "And the guy is a master at the mind screw."

She knew that. But…

But Wyman was staring at her, and she could have sworn there was pain in his eyes. He was staring at her, and his heartbeat was fast, a tremble shook his body, and his voice was so unsteady.

Could be from lies. Could be from pain.

Could be from truth.

"If she's your daughter, blood or not, why the hell would you put her through this?" Jay's voice cut like a knife. "Trapping her in the lab, making her an experiment."

Her gaze flew to him.

He glared at Wyman with white-hot fury. "You don't do that to someone you love," Jay snarled.

"You do," Wyman argued back, his voice getting weaker. "If you c-can't bear…to let go…"

She found herself moving closer to Wyman. Wanting desperately to know if this was another lie. Wanting any crumb that she could get about her past.

"We couldn't find Willow in any database." Sawyer still kept his position near the bed. "Jay is the best there is at hacking. He searched every government file out there. No mention of Willow was ever found. No one who matched her, no one who fit her description even remotely."

Wyman's eyes were on Willow. "If people knew…about our connection…they'd try—try to hurt me, th-through you. I k-kept you safe."

"Kept her safe?" Jay demanded. "Or made her spend her entire life hiding from the world?"

The machines beeped faster. "Y-you were trained." A smile came and went on Wyman's face. "So s-strong. M-made sure. Y-you could always p-protect y-yourself." But his eyelids flickered. "W-we d-don't s-see some threats…"

Now Jay stepped forward. His feet padded across the floor. "What threat? What happened to Willow? You said you couldn't let her go. That means—she was hurt, wasn't she?" Now rage was definitely cracking in his words. "Who hurt her?"

Wyman's breath wheezed in and out. "The ones…closest…h-hurt the most."

She didn't know what that meant. Not exactly, but… "I've seen a man." She licked lips gone dry. "He tells me that we belong together. But something is wrong. I don't—I think I'm afraid of him."

Beside her, she felt Jay tense.

Wyman's eyes closed. For a moment, she thought the guy had just—what? Gone to sleep? Shut her out?

But he gave a long sigh. With his eyes still closed, he said, "I t-tried to p-protect you…" Each word sounded like a struggle. "I m-made the m-monster."

Now she was the one to stiffen. Willow took a quick step back, as if she'd just been hit. He'd called her a monster. The man who'd just said he was her father. *Monster.* But she'd known that, hadn't she? She'd known—

Warm, strong hands caught her shoulders. Jay turned her toward him. She found herself staring into his eyes. "You are perfect," he said.

Her chest burned.

"You're not some fucking monster. You never will be. You're listening to a megalomaniac who tried to create his own army of super soldiers. Don't let anything the prick says get beneath your skin, you understand me?"

But it was Wyman who spoke. "N-not…my W-Willow…"

Jay whirled toward the bed. "She isn't yours."

Wyman struggled to sit up in the bed. As Willow watched him, the coppery scent of blood reached her, and then she saw a red bloom appear on the white bed covers. Instinctively, she rushed toward him. "Don't! You're hurting yourself!"

Wyman caught her hand. Held tight in a grip of surprising strength. *"He's the m-monster…I m-made…"* He pulled her hand toward his face. "S-so sorry…"

The door flew open. "What's happening now?" Elizabeth cried out.

Wyman was shuddering and bleeding, and Willow found that she was holding him as tightly as he held her.

"S-see my f-fear…" Wyman whispered. His grip was loosening. Hers wasn't. "See…"

And she did. She wasn't even sure if she tried to see it or if it just happened. But the hospital room vanished. The bed vanished. Jay and Sawyer and Elizabeth all vanished.

She was suddenly in a motel room. One with threadbare carpet. With cracks that cut across the ceiling. The salty scent of an ocean drifted to her.

She was staring up at that ceiling because she was lying on the threadbare carpet. Willow felt herself struggling to breathe. She lifted her hands and could see the blood on them. Her blood.

Her body was so cold.

Wood cracked. Her head managed to turn and she saw the thin motel room door come flying open. Wyman stood in the doorway. A different Wyman. Strong. Wearing a dark suit, but with his eyes blazing. He saw her on the floor, and all of the color drained from his face. "Willow!"

Then he was rushing toward her. Falling to his knees at her side. His hands reached out, not to hold her, but to press against her wounds. She had so many wounds. There were other men behind him. One guy in glasses. Armed soldiers.

His guards. He always traveled with guards. The only time he was without them—that was when they slipped away. Just her and Wyman.

She wanted to slip away. To go back, maybe to the little cabin they'd sometimes stay in when they wanted a holiday together. No one else around, no one to see, no one to know who they were.

"I'm going to kill him," Wyman promised her. His words were so angry and cold, and she knew he was speaking the truth. He didn't lie. At least, not to her. He'd once promised never to lie to her.

"I made him," Wyman continued darkly, "and I'll end him."

She wanted to talk, wanted to tell him so much, but Willow couldn't speak. And everything seemed to be getting darker.

"No!" Grief tore through the anger that had been in Wyman's words. "Don't you do it, baby! Don't!" And suddenly, he wasn't pressing on her wounds. He'd yanked her up against him. He was holding her so tightly, rocking her back and forth, and she could have sworn that she felt wetness on her cheek.

His tears?

"I can't lose you!" He held her tighter. "You're the only good thing in my life. The only thing I did right. I *won't* lose you, baby! You're too young. You've got too much living left." He was still rocking her. She wished she could hug him back. "You're going to get married. Going to have a family. Going to have those big Christmases like you always wanted. You're going to walk on the beach. God, baby, you love the beach. You're going to hike and eat your chocolate and laugh and you're going to—*Willow?"*

Her body felt strange. Hollow.

Empty?

He shook her. "Willow? Willow, look at me!"

He was all that she could see. There was terror on his face—and his face was crumbling. Tears were in his eyes, and he was shouting, swearing that she'd live.

"I'll make you live, baby! This isn't the end for you. I swear it!"

But she was dying, and he was breaking apart before her. She wanted to hug him, to tell him that everything was going to be all right, but it wasn't.

She wasn't.

CHAPTER FOURTEEN

"Willow!"

Jay's sharp voice had her snapping back to the present. To him. His arms were around her, and he'd yanked her away from the bed. Elizabeth had lunged toward Wyman, and she was shouting orders to others who'd entered the room—a man and a woman, both wearing green scrubs.

"Willow, are you okay?" Jay asked her.

No, she wasn't okay. Because Wyman's worst fear—it was her death. And everything about that scene had rung true to her. People *couldn't* fake their worst fears when she touched them. Wyman's nightmare was her death.

He'd cared about her. He'd *cried* for her. And he'd sworn to do anything to keep her living.

Willow swallowed the lump in her throat. He *had* done anything. He'd brought her back from the dead.

"We have to stop the bleeding!" Elizabeth barked. "He needs to get back into surgery. Dr. Brannon, he needs help, right away!"

They started to wheel the bed out of the room. Willow surged away from Jay and grabbed Wyman's hand. His head turned. His gaze seemed so weak, but he tried to smile at her. "B-brought y-you back..."

"Wyman..."

"D-didn't know...about all s-side effects...n-not then...just m-memory loss."

"This man needs to be in the OR!" The guy in green scrubs snapped. "Now!"

"Learned...others...t-too late...that's why I-I kept you in l-lab...trying to h-help...p-protect..."

She squeezed his hand. Made herself step back. There was so much blood.

"H-he's c-coming..." Wyman whispered. "S-sorry..."

And then he was gone. He'd been wheeled out of the room, and she was just standing there, her hands twisting in front of her. The image of her own death was still in her head.

"Are you okay?" Sawyer's voice. Sawyer had moved to a position in front of her. "You went absolutely white when you were touching him. You started shuddering, and I thought you were having a seizure. You didn't stop, not until Jay pulled you away from Wyman."

She glanced at Jay. He was watching her with an unreadable stare. Forcing herself to breathe, nice and slow, Willow tried to gather her thoughts. "Did you think he was lying?"

Sawyer's senses were so sharp, surely he would have picked up any tell-tale sign of deception from Wyman.

Sawyer shook his head. "No. I think he was telling the truth."

Jay swore.

"So do I," Willow confessed. "I saw what he feared, and it was me. Me, dying."

Jay swore, low and viciously.

"I died," Willow continued. "I was stabbed." Her hands slid over her stomach, as if searching for the wounds that should be there. "I was in some motel room, near the ocean. I'd been stabbed over and over, and left to die."

Jay surged toward her. "You aren't dead."

"Not anymore. Because Wyman brought me back. He couldn't let go." Her stare slid toward the door of the hospital room. He'd been taken back to surgery. But even as he'd been led away, he'd been warning her about danger. "If I wasn't the monster he made…" Another slow, deep breath. "Then who is?"

"My money is on the bastard who killed you." Jay gave a grim nod. "And I'm going to find him."

A shiver slid over her, and for just a moment, she could hear a man's voice in her head. *You belong to me.*

Her lover. Had her lover killed her? Was he the monster Wyman feared so much?

"I'm going to check with Elizabeth. See what the hell is happening." Sawyer rubbed a hand over his jaw. "The bastard tore himself open."

Because he'd wanted Willow to believe him.

She didn't speak again, not until Sawyer was gone. The machines were silent. The room suddenly seemed incredibly cold, but she could feel Jay's gaze on her. Watching. Waiting.

"I believe him, Jay. I believe what I saw. Fears can't lie." People could lie. Words could lie. Fear didn't. Fear was basic and primitive. Fear was people at their weakest. "Wyman was afraid for me. He didn't want me to die."

"So he put you in Lazarus. He kept you locked away in a lab and called that shit love."

She flinched. "I think that he did love me, in his way."

"And the bastard out there? The one Wyman called a monster?"

Bits and pieces were in her mind. Not the full picture. Just the whisper of fear. *Fear doesn't lie.* "I…I was hiding from him. He found me."

"Yeah, but was the bastard your enemy? Or Wyman's? Were you collateral damage in one of his wars? He made a monster, and the guy came gunning for the one person connected to Wyman on a personal level—is that what happened?"

She had goosebumps on her arms. "It's more."

A furrow appeared between his brows. "What?"

"I saw him. Had other flashes. He wanted me."

"You saw the sonofabitch killing you?"

She shook her head. "No. A man…found me. Said we belonged together." And the motel room had been the same. She shivered again.

He stepped closer to her.

"I think that I was afraid of him."

"A lover."

She couldn't be sure, not with so many memories gone, but… "I believe so."

Rage burned in his stare. "Wyman knows the guy's identity. If he hurt you, Wyman should have taken the SOB out."

"Maybe he couldn't." Not if he'd made a monster. And this was nagging at her. "Are we so sure that Lazarus was Wyman's first experiment?"

Shock covered Jay's face. "Fucking hell." He raked a hand through his hair. "Should have thought…of *course,* the guy didn't start with Lazarus. You don't go all in from the very beginning. I bet he's been doing work with soldiers for years. Making them stronger, better."

That was what she feared.

"He'll tell us," Jay vowed with certainty. "When he's out of surgery, the guy will tell us what we need to know. I saw the way he looked at you. *You* are his priority. He'll give me the bastard's name. We'll find him."

She rubbed her arms. "You think that he's the one who's been doing all this?"

"The shot at the club? The fire? Sure as hell could be. Right now, he's at the top of my list." He came even closer, but he didn't touch her. She wanted him to, but he didn't. "I know you want to run." His voice was low. Rumbling. "I know you want to head the hell away from me as fast as you can."

"It's not—"

"But I need you to stay. Until we figure out what's happening, until we know who he is…stay. Let me help you. Let the others help. You don't have to be alone in this world."

She'd been alone in that motel room. Alone on the floor. Bleeding out as she stared up at the cracks on the ceiling. Then Wyman had rushed to her side. Too late.

"I'll keep my hands off you, don't worry." His lips thinned. "But don't run again. Not yet, okay? Let's see what the hell is happening. We need to work together. To be part of a team."

Jay and Sawyer were a team. A team that included Flynn and Cecelia. And Elizabeth. And West. They were all working to find the rest of the Lazarus subjects. To see if those subjects were threats or if they were just people. People who needed help.

They'd found her. Or maybe she'd found them. But she'd never really felt like part of the team.

"I won't stop you if you want to run. I'm not here to cage you, Willow. That's not what I want." His gaze blazed at her.

"What do you want?" She hadn't meant to ask that question, had she?

He gave a grim laugh. "I think that's obvious."

"It's not."

"You, Willow. I want *you*." He rolled back his shoulders. "Having you once, twice, three times didn't cure me. It just made me need you more. *There is no cure*. But like I said, I can keep my hands off. Because this isn't about sex. It's not about me. It's about you."

He was doing that again. Putting her first when he shouldn't be. Trying to protect her when she was the threat to him. "I'm scared."

His hand lifted as if he'd touch her, but Jay seemed to catch himself. His hand froze in mid-air. "You aren't alone, Willow. You were *never* alone. Hell, apparently, you had the guy who ran the U.S. government pulling every string he had to keep you alive. Wyman might be a bastard, but I think he loves you. You were *never* alone," he said again. "And you don't have to be alone now."

She wanted to stay with him. And wanting that so much scared her even more. "We'll wait. Find out who the threat is."

Jay nodded.

"I'll stay." Her words were soft. He had no idea how much she wanted to stay. Didn't know how hard it had been to leave.

Will I ever be able to leave him again?

His hand had lowered. He was staring straight at her. "Maybe the next time you do decide to run, baby, why don't you think about running *to* me?"

"Jay..."

"I don't have super strength. I can't come back from the dead." His expression was determined. Dangerous. "But I'd fight like hell to keep you safe. When will you see that? This isn't about atonement for me. You're more. Willow..." He sighed out her name. "So much more."

And finally, some of the coldness that had settled inside of her eased. The image of the ceiling filled with cracks...of that threadbare carpeting...of all the blood—the image slowly faded.

Until all she saw was Jay.

Her lips parted. "Jay..."

The hospital room door swung open. "His wound reopened." Elizabeth hurried inside. "Don't know how this happened. I watched Dr. Brannon perform the surgery the first time." She shook her head, sending her dark hair sliding over her shoulders. "Wyman is being put under right now. They're going to take care of him, but it will be a while. And after the surgery, it's going to be hours before he can talk again."

"Did he just tear open some stitches?" Jay asked.

But Elizabeth shook her head again. "No. It's a lot worse." And her stare was grave. "The wound was bad, Jay. And Wyman wasn't exactly in the best condition before he got shot. His body…I'm sorry, Willow, but his body is frail because he has cancer. It seems he's been battling it for some time, and it's spread. I'd need to bring in a specialist, but Dr. Bannon already told me that he doesn't think Wyman has a lot of time left. Maybe a year at the most."

She felt her cheeks ice. "What?"

"I'm sorry," Elizabeth said again. "Sawyer told me what happened in here and I just…" She stepped forward. Put her arms around Willow. Hugged her. "I'm sorry," Elizabeth told her again.

Willow just stood there. The ice was spreading inside of her. "He's dying?"

Elizabeth eased back. Gave a quick nod.

She'd just found him. The man who was her past. The man who'd made her into what she was. And he was going to die?

"Not today," Elizabeth's face showed her sympathy. "He's not dying today. Dr. Bannon will get the bleeding stopped. Wyman will need some time to rest, but after that, you can come and talk with him again. You can learn everything you need to know."

Everything, but still lose the man who said he was her father? Not her biological father, though, Jay had told her that.

What had happened to her real parents?

"Go home," Elizabeth urged her. "Rest for the evening and tonight. The guards are here. They'll all stay here after the surgery. By the morning, Wyman should be stronger."

Okay, yes. There was no point in staying. Except that she wanted to see Wyman again. She wanted to talk to him. To remember.

Even if he'd been the one to take her memories away.

Elizabeth turned back for the door.

"Did you know about other experiments?" Jay questioned, stopping her.

Elizabeth's spine straightened. She glanced at him. "What?"

"Other than Lazarus, did you know about other experiments that Wyman was doing? Maybe running on soldiers?"

Elizabeth's dark gaze was troubled. "No, I was only working on Lazarus." She hesitated.

"But knowing Wyman, I do believe there could have been more."

"Yeah, that's what I thought." Jay was at Willow's side, but he still didn't touch her. "Call us if anything changes?"

"Absolutely." Elizabeth's promise was instantly given. Then she was gone. Willow was alone with Jay in the room. There was nothing for her there. No reason to stay but...

"He's dying?" Her voice seemed small.

"Not yet, he isn't," Jay said. "Not yet."

She pressed her lips together to stop the tremble.

***

Willow was hurting.

Jay sat across from her in the back of the limo, his gaze on her face. Her profile was turned toward him as she stared out of the window. She was right there. He could reach out and touch her, but she seemed to be a million miles away.

He could almost feel her pain. Her shoulders were stiff. Her chin up. But every now and then, her lower lip trembled. His hands were clenched in his lap so he wouldn't reach out and touch her. He'd promised not to touch. She'd run from him the last time he'd touched her.

He'd hold back. He *wouldn't* make the same mistakes again. He fucking wouldn't.

"How can I hurt inside, for a man who did this to me?"

His gut tightened. "People can do crazy things for love."

Her head turned toward him. He felt her stare like a physical touch. "You think he loves me? Wyman is the man you've called a bastard. A psychopath. You've said he wanted to build an army of super soldiers. That he *killed* innocent people."

"Yeah, and I'm not saying he's suddenly flown to sainthood." Never would happen. "But even people who are bad, well, they can love."

"Do you…do you think I could ever love?"

Now he knew he had to tread very, very carefully. "Don't see any reason why you can't."

"Lazarus subjects are supposed to be all about the dark emotions."

"You can't have dark without the light, baby. And are you going to sit there and tell me that you don't think Sawyer loves Elizabeth? Or that Flynn wouldn't gladly give *all* of his lives for Cecelia?"

Once more, she looked away.

More silence. The sun was setting. They lingered too long at the hospital, but he hadn't been up to forcing her to leave. Not until Willow was ready.

It had been one hell of a day. At least she was going back home with him. And at least he had a new target now. Willow might have been a ghost online, but the man who'd killed her, Jay *would* be finding him.

Then he'd destroy the bastard.

"Do you want to know my worst fear?"

Jay forced his hands to unclench. "I already know it." Keeping his voice gentle was an effort. "Being locked up. That's why—"

"I dreamed I hurt you. I killed you. There was so much blood, and there was nothing I could do."

Shocked, he could only stare at her.

"I don't want to hurt you. That's why I ran. I know I have something inside of me, something that can't always be controlled. And what if I can't stop? What if—what if something else or someone else triggers me? Wyman didn't even talk to us about that. What happens then? What happens if I go after you?"

"I'm not worried about that."

Her hand swiped over her cheek. "You should be!" Anger there, bursting through her words.

But there were tears on her cheeks. He knew she felt more than anger. It took all of his self-control not to move toward her. Not to pull her into his arms. "Do I look scared?"

Her gaze was on him. "You should be."

Jay shook his head.

"Why?" The word was torn from her. "Why do you still want me?"

"Because I'm not a fool. You're the sexiest woman I've ever seen." But it was a lot more than that. Desire wasn't just skin deep, not with her. Never with her.

"I want you." Her voice was low. "It doesn't stop. It's always there. Everything else is so out of control, but the need is still there." A stark pause. "Why?"

"Because lust is primitive. Basic. And while everything else might have been stripped away, Willow, primitive instincts remain. Your body trusts me, even if your mind—your heart—even if they don't."

"Fear is primitive, too."

Yes, it was.

Her long lashes swept down to conceal her gaze. "I'm afraid when I'm with you."

The last thing he wanted was for Willow to fear him.

"And I'm afraid when I'm not." Her lashes lifted. "I'm sick of being afraid."

Silence filled the car. Tension. When he spoke, his words were a low rumble. "Then tell the fear to fuck off, and take what you want."

Her tongue slid out to lick over her lower lip. Sexy as all hell. "I want you."

He wouldn't go to her. This had to be her move. Her moment. "I'm right here."

Red stained her cheeks. "In the car? The driver—"

"Told you before. He can't see or hear anything that's happening back here." Jay knew her emotions were savaged. After what had happened in that hospital, Willow had to be a wreck. And that was why he wasn't making this choice. If she wanted him, then she'd have to want him more than pain and fear. More than anything.

The way he wanted her.

She pulled in a deep breath. Then she slid off her shoes. She unhooked her pants. Pushed then down her hips while he watched and his dick jerked to quick, avid attention.

"Willow..."

"I don't want pain. Or fear. When I'm with you, I get more than that."

So she was using him. He should care. He didn't. He'd just seen the scrap of underwear that she was wearing.

Willow didn't take off her shirt, but she did move toward him. Her movements were hesitant but still sensual. Everything about the woman was sensual to him. Her panties were red, bright against her smooth skin. "This is wrong," Willow said. She reached for his hand. She touched him. Twined her fingers through his.

He forced a shrug. "Do I look like I care?"

"We shouldn't..." She pressed a kiss to his lips. Her tongue snaked into his mouth.

Oh, baby, we should. She slid onto his lap. Straddled him.

But he didn't touch her the way he wanted. Didn't take. Didn't make her moan and gasp. He waited for her head to lift. Waited for her gaze to meet his. "Tell me that you want me, Willow."

"I want you."

"Tell me you want my hands on you."

"I want...I want your hands on me."

Magic words.

His hands curled around her hips. His dick shoved toward the crotch of her panties. The silk and his trousers were all that separated him from touching heaven. Hot, sweet heaven.

Willow needed this. She wanted her oblivion. One day, she'd realize he'd give her everything she wanted. Every. Single. Thing.

His fingers moved between their bodies. Down, down, until he was caressing the silk that covered her sex. He stroked her through the panties at first, enjoying the way her hips arched. Loving the way she got wet for him. He could feel the moisture through the silk. But that wasn't quite enough.

Not for him.

He eased the panties to the side, moving so that his fingers could touch her. Bare flesh. And at first, he was gentle, trailing the tips of his fingers over her. She arched higher, gave a quick moan, and his touch grew harder. Stronger. Deeper. Two fingers slid into her. She rode his fingers, moving her hips quickly against him. His thumb pushed over her clit. Rubbed. Circled.

Her breath came faster.

The limo kept driving.

His dick was rock hard, surging against his zipper. His fingers were in her, and her sex squeezed him tight. Wetter, hotter, with every moment that passed. His fingers slid in and out of her, moving in a quick rhythm, thrusting in the way that he knew she liked.

"Not…enough…" Willow pressed a kiss to his neck. Her voice whispered into his ear, "Want *you* in me."

And there was the problem. He'd bring her to orgasm. He'd make her come again and again but… "Baby, I don't have protection with me."

Her hips pushed down harder on him. "I don't…*I don't care.*"

What? Oh, hell. Oh, hell, no, she hadn't just said—

"I want you, Jay. *All* of you."

Did she get it? There would be no going back, not from this. No saying things had been a mistake. No running away again.

"All of you," Willow said again.

And his control was gone. He yanked open his pants. His dick shoved toward her, and then he was driving his hips up, surging *into* her. Driving as deep as he could go. Flesh to flesh. Nothing between him and Willow. Nothing to stop him from taking what he thought of as *his.*

So he took. His hands clamped around her hips. He lifted her up, down. Felt her sex squeeze him so tight. She was licking his neck, lightly biting, driving him insane. He thrust harder. Deeper. His cock shoved up, going so deep into her. She surrounded him. Her scent, her body, *her.* His left hand slipped to her clit. Stroked ruthlessly as he drove into her. He wanted her to come first. Fast and hard. Wanted to feel the contractions all around him. "Baby…"

And she did. Her head tipped back. She gasped out his name even as he felt the contractions of her release all along his cock. He didn't hold back. His own release hit, slamming through Jay as he surged into her. He came inside of her, a hot blast that kept going and going. His hold was too tight. He should ease up.

He didn't.

He kept thrusting. Even as his orgasm ended, he was getting harder again, for her. He kept thrusting because she was moaning. Twisting and pushing against him. Fighting for another release, and he was going to make sure she got that release. She was slick and sensitive, and pushing her to the edge again was so easy. He thrust up, hard, gritting his teeth because nothing on earth felt as good as she did. Nothing was as hot. Nothing was as tight. Nothing was like this slice of heaven.

Nothing was like her.

She came again, calling out his name. He kissed her neck. Made sure to leave his mark on her. Was it wrong that he wanted to mark her? That he wanted to own her?

Seemed only fair. The woman owned him, body and soul.

His breath was heaving. So was hers. And it took him a minute to realize the car had stopped moving. She seemed to make the same realization, at the same time, because her head whipped up. Willow stared at him with wide eyes.

"Oh, God," she whispered as red stained her cheeks. "We're—"

"We're home," he said smoothly.

And her lips eased into a quick smile. The tension that had been on her face vanished.

He smiled back at her. Kissed her sweet lips one more time. He'd always love her taste. When they got inside, he'd taste her, everywhere. Every single inch of her.

He helped her right her clothes. He fixed himself. Then he was opening the door for her. The driver stood to the side, waiting, not saying a word because the guy wasn't a fool.

And he knew who paid his salary.

They were in front of the house. Behind the big gates, safely away from the guards. Jay took Willow's hand and led her up the steps. Her fingers were soft and warm against his. She leaned toward him as they neared the door.

"I think I can still feel you, inside." Her voice was a sensual temptation, one that swept over him as if she'd just stroked him with her hands.

He felt the impact, of course, going straight to his dick. Because inside of her was exactly where he wanted to be. It was—

She stiffened. "Someone else is here." Her gaze went to the front door.

"West is already inside." He knew his brother had headed back to the house before they had. "He's—"

"Not alone," Willow said. And her shoulders straightened. "I'd recognize that perfume anywhere." An edge had entered her voice.

Then the front door was opening. West stood there, his face unreadable. "We have a problem."

"Add it to the list," Jay muttered. So much for his time with Willow. So much for picking right back up where he'd left off…

Being balls deep in her.

"Jay."

He stiffened. The feminine cry of his name had come from behind West, and as the woman hurried forward, her perfume drifted to him, too.

He realized why Willow had called the scent familiar. It was.

Reva brushed past West. She went straight to Jay. Threw her arms around him. Held tight. "I thought I was too late." Her voice was muffled against him. "When I heard about the blaze at Push, I thought he'd gotten to you. I thought—"

She was pulled away from him. By Willow. Very deliberately moved.

"Don't," Willow advised the other woman with a killing glare. "Don't touch him again. Especially not when I'm standing right beside him."

Reva's mouth parted. Closed. She frowned in confusion. "But...Jay?"

West cleared his throat. "Let's get inside. And Jay, you're gonna want to hear what Reva has to say."

He wasn't so sure about that. Willow looked pissed. Possibly jealous? And if she didn't want the other woman there—

"He wants to kill you," Reva blurted. "H-he thought I'd help. That I'd be happy to join him in destroying you because of our break-up, but that's not who I am." She gave a sharp shake of her head. "I got away from him, and I've been trying to get hold of you all day. You don't answer your phone!" Her hands twisted in front of her.

This was definitely a conversation they were taking inside. Jay made sure Willow went in first, then he shut the door behind him.

West led the way to the den, and, once there, Reva paced behind the couch. "I thought he was kidding at first. I mean, he had to be kidding, right? And I think I even laughed."

Willow stood near Jay, her body alert, her gaze on Reva.

"Tell me who he is," Jay ordered grimly.

"I don't *know* who he is! He looked like money, walked like power, and had an air that said he was dangerous. Like, scary dangerous." She hurried to the bar. Poured herself some vodka and downed it in a blink. "Normally, I like that. Serious turn-on, but this time…" She shivered. Took another vodka shot. "Something was off about him. Way off."

Jay glanced at West. His brother inclined his head.

"Where did you meet the guy?" West asked.

"At Wander, the bar just a few streets over from Push. I'd gone in because I wasn't ready for the night to end. Not like anyone was waiting at home for me." Her hand tightened around the glass. "He walked right up to me. I thought I was going to have a good time. But he wanted something else. Something totally different." She spun to face Jay. "He wanted to destroy you."

West coughed into his hand. "Not the first time a business rival has wanted—"

"No." Reva's voice was sharp. "This isn't about business. This was personal. You think I can't tell the difference? He said he wanted to destroy Jay, and he meant those words. Not some business rivalry." Her eyes gleamed at Jay. "I think he wanted you dead."

Willow advanced on the other woman. "Describe the man."

"Jay's height. Muscular. Built. And he had money. I can always tell." Her cheeks puffed out and then she blew out a hard breath. "His eyes were intense. Like they were looking right through me. And I swear, it was like he really could see *straight* into me."

"Hair color, Reva." Impatience bit through West's words. "Eye color. Ethnicity. Physical characteristics, woman. Come on."

"Oh, um, dark hair, I think. Dark eyes. He had a...a scar on his chin. He's going to be back at Wander tonight. Two a.m. He thinks we're going to meet. That I'm going to bring you to him." She swallowed. "He offered me fifty grand to serve you up to him. And the guy actually believed I would do it."

Jay considered the matter for a moment.

"No." West shook his head. "Jay, absolutely not."

Absolutely the hell, yes. Because he knew who the stranger had to be. "You're about to make his fifty, Reva, and I'll give you fifty more."

The glass cracked in Reva's hand.

"Because you're taking me to the see this bastard. And I'll be the one to destroy *him*."

CHAPTER FIFTEEN

"I don't trust her." Willow wrapped her arms around her stomach as she stared out into the night. They were in Jay's room. The broken window had already been repaired, as if she'd never left him.

I was just trying to keep him safe. Only leaving hadn't worked so well. And now, she felt even closer to him than before. Willow swore that she could still *feel* Jay inside of her.

And Jay's ex-lover was right down the hallway.

He strode out of the bathroom, and she turned toward him, instantly aware of him with an intensity that was unnerving. He'd wrapped a towel around his hips. The guy's muscles flexed and shifted as he moved, and she tried not to let her gaze linger. She failed.

"Was she lying about her story?" Jay asked.

She wasn't as good at Sawyer and Flynn when it came to reading a person's lies. A point that was becoming glaringly obvious to her. "Her heart was racing the whole time. She was sweating. And nervous."

His head cocked. His hair was wet. Gleaming. She should have joined him in the shower. Should have picked up right where they'd left off in the car. Instead...

She'd hesitated. She'd become too nervous.

It's because I didn't expect to find his ex waiting for him. All cozy in his house.

"She didn't have to tell us about him." Jay rubbed his jaw. He was freshly shaven. He looked handsome. Powerful. Sexy. "Like I said before, Reva isn't who you expect her to be."

"She still wants you."

He laughed at that even as he strode closer. "Right. She wants me alive because I am *no* good dead to her."

But the man out there—*he* wanted Jay dead. "You think he's my ex."

Jay's hand came up and curled under her chin. "I think he's a problem that needs to be eliminated."

"I'm coming with you."

His jaw locked.

"I'm coming with you," Willow said again. Her words hadn't been a question. "This is my life. And in case you've forgotten, I'm the one with the super strength."

"And I'm the one with his own damn army of security guards. I can handle this. You don't need to be put at risk."

"I'm not exactly the standing-on-the-sidelines type, in case you missed that about me."

He leaned toward her. His lips skimmed over hers. "I haven't missed a single thing about you." The kiss was too short. Too fleeting.

Her sex seemed to clench. *Want him again.* She was starting to wonder if she'd always want him.

"If this man…if he's the one who did this to me, if he's the one who k-killed me," she couldn't help but stumble over that part, "Then I deserve to face him. I deserve to see who did this to me."

"He wants you." His pupils had expanded, making his eyes go dark and flat. "From what you and Wyman have said, it seems like he went fucking crazy, Willow. If he couldn't have you, then he wasn't going to let you walk away. And when you waltz in that place, when you get close to him again, what do you think will happen?"

Her mouth had gone dry. "I'll kick his ass."

His lips quirked. For a moment, his eyes seemed to lighten. Then the darkness returned. "His fantasy will be walking right toward him. He'll see you, and you'll be the only thing he wants. He'll do anything to have you."

"Is that why he wants to destroy you? Because he thinks that you have me?" She hadn't meant for her voice to become so husky. Had she?

"He wants me dead because I'm touching you." And he was. His fingers were sliding down her neck. A light touch. One that shouldn't have sent fire trailing over her skin, but it did. *He* did. "He wants me dead because the bastard knows that touching won't be enough for me." Down, down his hand went. Stopping over her heart. "I'll want to possess you completely. He can't have that."

Possession. "I'm not a thing. I don't belong to him or you."

Jay didn't move. His gaze was locked on her. "When I'm balls deep in you, Willow, I sure as hell feel like I belong to you."

Wait—what?

His hand fell away from her. He turned his back toward her. "You're right. It is your life. Your choices. And you have a right to face the sonofabitch who did this to you." She saw his hands fist at his sides. "But he won't touch you again. I'll bury him first."

Sometimes she forgot—sometimes, it was too easy to just look at Jay and see his controlled veneer. His intelligence. The tech billionaire. The charmer. The guy with the quick smile and good looks. But then he'd say something, he'd do something…a giveaway that spoke of his past. His time on the streets. The life he'd led long ago.

A life where he hadn't been quite civilized. A life where he'd been out of control.

"You'd do it," she said, realizing Jay wasn't just boasting.

"I'm not exactly the type to talk shit." His broad back was still to her. "I can make it so that no one ever finds his body. After what he's done to you, the guy doesn't get to walk away. You won't spend your life looking over your shoulder, wondering if he's coming for you. He'll end tonight."

"Jay, you can't just kill a man!"

He glanced back at her. "He killed you."

Her tongue slid over her lower lip.

"I can't believe Wyman hasn't taken out the bastard." Now Jay's eyes narrowed. "He calls you his daughter, but he let the man who murdered you walk? Doesn't make sense to me."

"He's…Wyman called him a monster." She crept closer to Jay. "He could be enhanced."

He inclined his head. The hard intensity never left his gaze. "That's what I fear. So I'll make sure my team is ready for him."

"What if he's like me?" The question slipped from her. "What if he just comes back from death?"

"Lazarus subjects don't come back from a bullet to the brain. Anyone can die. You just have to kill the person the right way."

He was ready to kill, for her. "I can fight my own battles." He didn't need to get blood on his hands.

But Jay just gave her a half-smile, one that didn't light his eyes. "One day, you'll get it. Your battles *are* mine." He motioned toward the shower. "Your turn in there."

She turned and took a step toward the bathroom. Stopped. "We aren't going to talk about it?"

"It?"

"You didn't use protection. I didn't want you to." She drew in a deep breath. "I know it wasn't responsible, and I'm sure we're safe. It's the wrong time of the month." Did those words sound as weak as they felt? "The risk of pregnancy is—"

"I'd love to get you pregnant."

She whirled back to him.

"So I'm not worried. Not the least bit. What I am trying to do, though, is keep my hands off you. In case you didn't notice, I have a bit of an issue." He turned fully toward her.

Um, that was more than a bit. His towel was tented. Extremely so. Her heartbeat sped up. "Reva is…beautiful."

"Yes."

He could have denied it. Her stare shot back up to his.

A mocking smile was on his lips. "Reva didn't do this shit."

Good to know. Her hands unclenched.

"Are you jealous, Willow? Because she's the past."

Willow believed that. She also—"Yes, I think I am jealous." She advanced toward him. *He wants me. Me.* "It's not good to make someone like me jealous."

A rumbling laugh escaped him. "Do I look worried?"

No, he looked sexy. He looked hot.

"Jealousy is supposed to be dangerous for Lazarus subjects," she reminded him. Not that he needed reminding. She didn't think he ever forgot anything.

He didn't move. Just watched her. Waited.

"It makes me feel…less." But she kept her spine straight. Her shoulders up. "Reva is beautiful, and she's normal. She doesn't make fears turn into reality. She doesn't get shot and wake up when she should be dead. She doesn't—"

He'd grabbed her and tumbled her onto the bed. Normally, she was the one who moved fast. This time, he'd been faster. "You are never less." Anger was there. In his voice. In his eyes. On his face. "Don't ever say it. Don't ever believe it. You are more than any other woman out there. Never fucking say less." Then he was kissing her.

Kissing her with the frantic need she wanted. The wild rush of lust. The consuming intensity that made her feel—

He wants me. Only me.

He tore off her clothes. Tossed them away. And she was glad. She wanted him wild for her. Wanted to know that this fierce desire he felt was just for her. Not for the lovers from his past. For her.

There wasn't foreplay. Wasn't some long seduction. He stripped her. He drove into her. Her legs locked around his hips, and they arched together. Driving for release. Sex to sex. Nothing between them. And it was even hotter than before. Because his gaze was on her. His fingers were locked with hers. His body was driving into her. Every downward thrust of his cock had him sliding over her sensitive clit. The orgasm was building, building, but she didn't want to come, not yet. She wanted to stay this way, to keep his focus so totally on her, to be linked with him. To *be* with him.

She wished she could be with him forever.

But Willow couldn't stop the release. It burst over her, through her, and she held him tight even as she felt the hot rush of his release inside of her. His hips kept thrusting. He kept coming, even as he was kissing her.

Her. The desire he felt was for her. Not the lovers he'd had before. Not any normal woman.

And even when the climax ended, he didn't withdraw from her. He was still heavy and erect in her, and he just lifted her up. Her legs curled around his hips as he carried her to the bathroom.

"Sweet Willow, you think this happens with just anyone?"

At first, she didn't understand.

Then he pushed into her, making her shiver.

"Only you, baby. Only you make me need this much."

They were in the shower. He'd yanked on the water. Steam drifted around them. He was still carrying her. Still *in* her.

His strength was such a turn-on.

So was his stamina.

He caged her against the wall. One hand was on her hip. The other had slapped against the tile behind her head. "You will *never* be less." His eyes glittered down at her. "Don't you get it yet?"

He withdrew, slid into her. The water beat down on them. Her hands were on his back. Her nails dug into his skin.

"Can't you…see?"

He withdrew, thrust. Her lips were parted as she tried to suck in desperate gulps of air.

"You think it's *always* this way?"

Withdraw, thrust. His long cock slid over her sensitive core.

"Only." Thrust. "You."

She was coming again. Willow couldn't stop it. She couldn't hold back. She couldn't—

His eyes stared into her soul. "Fucking." Thrust. Withdraw. "Love." Thrust. "You."

OhmyGod.

***

Willow was dressing. Putting on an outfit that he was sure would drive the men in Wander wild. Of course, the woman could wear a damn potato sack, and *he'd* still find her sexy.

But then again, Willow was his. He'd protect her, no matter what—or who—came at them.

Jay sat hunched at his computer, his fingers flying over the keys. He didn't believe in heading into any situation unprepared. The bastard thought he was going to take Willow? That he could destroy Jay?

"Think again," Jay muttered as his gaze flickered between his two monitors. A faint smile curved his lips.

No one would take Willow. She wouldn't live her life in fear.

He'd make sure of that.

***

The club was packed. Music and booze flowed freely. The women were dressed to perfection, and the men were ready to pounce.

"Where is the bastard?" Jay demanded. Reva was at his right side, shifting nervously from foot to foot. Willow stood to the left. No nervous movements came from her. Just stillness. Alertness. He knew she was aware of every single person in the place.

Watching. Hunting. That was his Willow.

Flynn Haddox was there, doing the same damn thing that she was. Only he was also blending. So was West. So were half a dozen of Jay's security team members.

"I don't see him," Reva said. She'd stepped up on her tip-toes. "I met him at the bar before. So I thought that's where he'd be."

Jay didn't like this scene. Too out of control. Too many bodies. Too many potential casualties. "If he's here, then he's seen me." Jay had no doubt about it. The guy's eyes would have been on him the minute he walked into the place.

Reva grabbed his arm. "There he is." Her voice was a hiss. She was staring across the room, her gaze on a tall, dark-haired man who wore a leather coat. The guy was staring at Reva, eyeing her like he'd just hit the jackpot. And he even lifted his beer, inclining it toward her.

Jay glanced at Willow. Her gaze was on the man, a furrow between her brows. "Anything, Willow?" Jay prompted, his voice quiet.

"He's no one to me." Her lips twisted. "But that's hardly a surprise."

The dark-haired guy put down his beer and began striding toward Reva. Toward Jay. His gaze swept to Willow. A faint smile curled his lips.

"We should go," Reva whispered. "Can't we lure him outside or something? This is making me nervous as all hell."

Jay wasn't nervous. He was pissed. The man was just striding forward, like he didn't have a care in the world. He was heading toward Jay, and Jay jerked his head, a signal for West and the others. They could close in. They would take this guy outside.

A body came flying at the dark-haired man. Lucas Tate. He tackled the guy. Started driving his fist into the fellow's face.

What the fuck?

Jay surged forward. So did West. Willow. Flynn.

The crowd was yelling. Some folks were shouting encouragement to Lucas. Some were rushing for the door.

Lucas rose, a gun gripped in his hands. He spun toward Jay. "He was going for his weapon."

The man on the floor was unconscious. His body slack.

"I saw it," Lucas growled. He still gripped the gun. "Thought one of your men would act, but no one did." Lucas fired a disgusted glance around him, then focused on Jay once more.

"You're so fucking lucky I was here tonight, man." His eyes gleamed.

Some women were screaming. Men were shouting, "Gun!" And general chaos was reigning.

Jay glanced at the man on the floor. A guy he'd never seen in his life. A guy Reva had identified for him. Willow stood at Jay's side. His fingers threaded with hers. "Yes, very lucky." Cops would be coming soon. No way to stop them. He was sure folks at Wander had already sounded the alarm. "Let's clear the scene, take this outside, shall we? Flynn, why don't you grab the body?"

Flynn yanked up the guy and tossed him over his shoulder, as if the unconscious man weighed nothing. Then they were making their way through the crowd, with Jay's security team clearing the way. Reva was hurrying with them. Lucas had tucked the gun into the waistband of his jeans.

Jay tightened his hold on Willow.

They exited the back of Wander and strode into a dark alley. His limo waited back there. As did several SUVs. His team.

"What are you going to do with the bastard?" Lucas demanded. "Can't believe he pulled the gun on you right the hell there. Must be the same prick who set Push on fire."

The fellow let out a groan. His eyes didn't open.

"I don't know him," Willow said. "I thought I'd feel *something*. I don't. Nothing at all."

Lucas's gaze was on her. "Why would you know him?" Suspicion cut lines near his mouth. "You working with him or something?"

"What? No, no, of course not—"

"Get him to containment," Jay ordered his men.

"I should get out of here," Reva said at the same moment. "I did my part. I gave him to you."

Willow's head turned. She gazed down at Reva. "Your heart is racing so fast."

"Yes, well, that happens when someone pulls a gun, and I get caught in shit that I don't want to be in." Reva shuddered. "How the hell do you know what my heart is doing, anyway? Know what? Forget it. I need a ride home. And by home—I mean *my place*." She pointed to West. "Take me home? Please?"

West hesitated.

The security team had just loaded the unconscious man in the back of an SUV.

Jay stared at the scene. "It's wrong."

"Maverick, the cops are coming," Lucas muttered. "Maybe take your kidnap victim and haul ass? You need to go, *now*."

Jay's gaze slid back to Lucas. "I never saw a gun."

"Yeah, well, you're not exactly trained to notice shit like that, are you?" Lucas threw right back. He took a quick step forward.

"I'm not," Jay agreed with a curt incline of his head. "But Flynn over there—he is. So is West. And as for Willow..." He brought her hand to his lips. Kissed her knuckles, but didn't take his gaze off Lucas. "Willow doesn't miss much."

Lucas tensed. His eyes narrowed. He rocked forward onto the balls of his feet.

"You were in demolitions, weren't you?" Jay mused, his gaze on Lucas.

"Um, I really want to leave now," Reva cried. "I don't want to be here when the cops arrive. And definitely not when you are *kidnapping* some poor guy!"

"Before I came here tonight, I thought I should take some time to do a little more research on the people who've been popping up lately. New visitors in my life, you could say." Again, Jay kissed Willow's knuckles.

Lucas's gaze went colder.

"You were one of those people I decided to research, Lucas. You *were* trained in demolitions. You were originally in a unit with West, but then you went off grid. Been doing a lot of private work since then, haven't you? Freelance?"

"What the fuck are you saying? If you've got a point—"

"I *want* to leave," Reva demanded. Her voice was close to shriek-level.

He was sure that she did want to leave, but that wasn't happening. "I accessed the security footage from this club." After he'd made love to Willow. She'd been changing, and he'd used that time to do a little hacking. Some skills never went out of style. It hadn't been that hard, especially since…"So easy—I designed their system. Oh, wait, bet you didn't know that."

Lucas's right hand was shoved into his pocket.

"When I accessed the footage, I saw Reva here the other night. But she wasn't with that poor jerk who just got shoved into the SUV." His gaze swept over Lucas. "She was with a blond guy who looked more like…you."

Flynn slapped a hand on Lucas's shoulder. He'd walked right up behind the guy, and Lucas hadn't even known it—because Jay had deliberately kept the fellow's attention on him.

"You're the one we came here to find," Jay explained with a cold smile. "And it's your ass we'll be dragging away before the cops arrive."

Reva wasn't speaking. Not anymore.

Lucas stared at him. Slowly shook his head. "You're fucking crazy, Maverick."

Jay just shrugged. "We'll see."

"I *don't* know him," Willow rasped. "I thought I'd feel something. I don't. It's like I'm staring at a stranger, and I just don't—"

A growl broke from Lucas. At the same moment, his right hand yanked out of his pocket. Jay expected a weapon. It wasn't. It looked as if the guy was holding a small, black phone. But—

Boom!

The SUV to the right ignited. The back of the vehicle flew into the air, then came crashing down as the SUV burst into a ball of flames.

The blast had Jay flying back. He turned his body as he flew, holding tight to Willow, trying to shield her. His body scraped across the pavement when he landed, but he jumped to his feet fast. His gaze went straight to the burning SUV.

Jay's men had been in that vehicle. The poor, unconscious SOB from Wander had been in there—

"You just weren't smart enough," Lucas snarled at him. "Two steps behind me, all the time."

And the back of Jay's limo exploded. The force sent him staggering back. He could hear someone screaming. Reva? It wasn't Willow. She'd run toward the limo faster than a blink. She'd yanked open the front door—and was dragging out the driver.

West was nowhere to be seen. The other guards were running. But Flynn—Flynn was driving his fist toward Lucas's face.

Lucas dodged the blow in a move that was too fast. He dodged, and then he punched out with his hand, driving his fist into Flynn's side. Flynn flew back. Flew back a good five feet before he hit the wall of Wander.

Definitely freaking enhanced.

Before Flynn could surge at the guy again, Lucas was firing his weapon. The bullets thudded into Flynn's body.

"Bastard!" Jay roared. He yanked out his own weapon. He hadn't come unarmed to this fight.

Lucas whirled toward him.

Jay fired. Once. Twice.

The bullets hit Lucas in the chest. He went down, his body twitching.

Jay took a step forward. *Need to shoot in the head, just in case.*

Reva grabbed him, her arms wrapping tightly around him. "I'm sorry!" Her eyes were wide, desperate. Fire blazed around them. "I didn't know—I thought—*ohmyGod,* he killed the men in that vehicle! He *killed* them, didn't he?"

Jay tried to pry Reva loose. She just held on tighter. He had one hand wrapped around his gun, and the other was trying to force her off him. "Willow!" Jay yelled. He could see her. She was on the ground, kneeling near the limo driver. The guy was bleeding a bit from a cut on his cheek, and his clothes were ripped, but otherwise, he looked okay.

"It was because of her!" Reva held him tighter. "He wanted her, and I just—"

Gunfire. A fast blast. Reva stiffened in his arms. She stared up at him. A tear leaked from her eye even as her body seemed to go limp. "I'm...sorry."

It took a moment for Jay to feel the pain. Reva was slumping and he tried to hold her upright, and that was when the pain burned through him. Pain in his side, tearing through him. Twisting.

He felt the blood on his hands. Reva's blood. She was bleeding and her body was slack, and he *hurt.*

Jay glanced up. He found Lucas staring at him. The bastard was on his feet, looking as if he'd never been shot.

"She was in the way," Lucas shouted. "This time, I won't miss."

He'd shot Reva. The bullet had torn through her body. Gone *into* Jay.

"No!" Willow's scream.

She flew at Lucas. Hit him even as he fired the next shot.

The burn hit Jay again. High on his shoulder, driving him back. The gun fell from his fingers.

He tried to hold Reva, tried to stay upright. "Willow!"

Lucas had her. Jay could see it. Lucas slammed Willow into the wall. "Get the fuck…" Jay staggered forward, still holding Reva, but she was a dead weight in his arms. "Away…from h-her!"

But instead of getting away, Lucas shoved the gun to Willow's head. Right to her temple. "I know what she is," Lucas bellowed. His stare was on Willow, not Jay. "And if you think I won't pull this trigger, you're wrong." He leaned forward. Pressed his forehead to hers. "Killed you once, baby. And I'll do it again."

Jay stilled. Reva wasn't making a sound. He could feel his own blood soaking his clothes.

Flynn was lying in a heap. Jay's guards had scattered. Those who were still alive, anyway. He couldn't see West. Didn't know where his brother was. *He has to be okay. He wasn't in the SUV or the limo. He wasn't.*

"We're going to walk away. You're going to stand right there and watch us." Lucas jerked Willow forward. Whipped her around in a lightning fast move so that she was against his chest, she faced Jay, and Lucas had one arm wrapped around her throat.

His other hand held a gun. And the gun was pressed hard to her temple.

"Willow was never yours," Lucas snarled at him. "She'll *never* be—"

"Really?" Jay shouted back at him. He wanted that gun away from Willow's temple. If it moved, just for a moment, Willow would have her chance. She could break free. "Could've fooled me. Especially when she was coming beneath me—"

Lucas roared. The gun flew away from Willow's temple. Aimed at Jay.

Run, Willow. Now is your chance. You can run—

"No!" Willow screamed.

The bullet was already firing. Jay didn't have the same reflexes that the super soldiers did. He couldn't dodge a fucking bullet. Couldn't jump to the side.

But he seemed to be watching the scene in slow motion.

Willow shoved at Lucas's hand. She didn't run. She fought him.

The bullet was coming at Jay. He turned, twisting even as his gaze stayed on Willow. He cradled Reva in his arms and—

The bullet hit him in the back.

Willow was screaming. He thought it was his name.

Run, Willow…

He hit the ground.

Fucking run.

CHAPTER SIXTEEN

The motel room's floor was covered by threadbare carpet. Willow glanced up, expecting to see thin cracks along the surface of the ceiling.

But there were no cracks above her, just yellowed paint.

"Sorry I had to dose you."

His voice. *Lucas.*

She sat up—slowly, clumsily—as she became aware of a deep lethargy that filled her body.

"When Maverick hit the ground, you started fighting me too much. The tranq was the best option."

Her hands were secured behind her back. She yanked, thinking she could just snap what felt like handcuffs—

"Yeah, that's not going to work. They're made of a special, reinforced metal. Designed to be Lazarus proof." Lucas sat in a wooden chair, just a few feet away from her. He'd flipped the chair around so that he straddled it, and his fingers draped over the back as he studied her.

"I'll give you two guesses as to who the SOB is who designed those cuffs."

She sat up, slowly. The lethargy seemed to weigh down her limbs. "Where...Jay..."

He laughed. "Right. Bingo. Jay. Jay Maverick designed the cuffs. Just like he designed all of the containment cells that held the Lazarus subjects. Just like he funneled a truck load of cash into the program." His laughter faded. His eyes gleamed. "He was behind it all, Willow. Every single moment. And you still let him touch you?"

Goosebumps were on her skin. "You..." Her tongue was thick in her mouth. "Shot Jay."

"A couple of times." He nodded. "Let's just hope he isn't enhanced and the jackass does us the courtesy of dying."

"No!"

His features hardened. "Willow, don't piss me off." He stood, kicking away the chair.

She struggled to stand, too, but her knees wouldn't hold her. She fell back to the floor.

He laughed. "So much for that Lazarus strength, huh? Doesn't do jack when you've got those drugs in your system." He crouched before her. "Didn't Wyman ever pump your veins full of the tranq? Didn't he experiment to see what it would do to *you*?"

Her lips clamped together.

"No, of course, he didn't. Because you were his precious daughter. He'd never hurt you. So the experiments were reserved for everyone else. He tested them, he hurt *them,* so he could keep his girl safe."

"I don't…know what you're talking about!"

Lucas snapped his fingers together. "Right. The amnesia. Unfortunate side effect. That's Wyman, though, he never talks about the side effects." He brought his hand to his lips and lifted his index finger. As if he were telling her a secret. "He only tells you the good parts. Like he tells you that you'll get stronger. That you'll be faster. That you'll be an even better soldier."

"You're…Lazarus?"

"Nah. I don't rise from the dead."

But he'd been shot. She'd seen—

He yanked open his shirt, sending buttons flying. "Bullet proof vest, sweetheart. If you remembered me, if you remembered *us,* you'd know I never go into any situation unprepared." He took off the vest, tossing it across the room. He rubbed his hands over his chest, and she saw the faint, red marks that had been left behind. The vest had saved his ass.

His hand lifted toward her.

Willow flinched.

"I'm not going to hurt you."

"You held a *gun* to my head," Willow gritted out.

"That was the only way I could get Maverick to back off. The guy is obsessed with you. Has been since the first time he saw you." He paused. "And you don't remember that first time. You think you met him after the lab. Oh, sweetheart, the guy has mind fucked you."

Jay isn't dead. I'll get back to him. I'll –

"He was *in* that North Carolina lab. Don't you get that? He was there. He would come to assess the progress of the test subjects. He'd watch them. He'd watch you. And the guy, soon he didn't just want to watch. He wanted *you.*"

"Stop it." He was lying. His heartbeat was slow and steady, his gaze never wavered, he wasn't sweating, but he was lying. He had to be lying.

"Wyman wasn't going to let you go. You're the only thing that old bastard cares about in this world. So since Wyman wouldn't turn you over, Jay took you."

"No!" Her temples were throbbing. Did he think she was a fool?

"He arranged for the explosions at the lab. He wanted the place destroyed so you could go free. Maverick planned to get you right away, but you slipped past him." His head sagged forward. "You slipped past both of us," he muttered.

"Shut up. I don't want to hear anymore." She needed her strength back. How long would the tranq be in her system?

His head snapped up. "You think I like this confession? You think I like admitting I worked with Maverick? He came to me. Got his brother West to do his dirty work, the way he always does. I agreed to light that lab up—only *after* I learned about you." And now he reached out his hand and trailed his fingers over her cheek.

She heaved away from him.

"I lost you once. I thought you were dead. When I found out about the lab, about Lazarus, God, I would have done anything to get you out of there." His mouth hardened. "Even make a deal with the devil himself—Jay Maverick."

Hate and fury twisted inside of her. "You didn't lose me. You *killed* me, you bastard!"

He blinked. Once, twice. "No."

"Yes! In a motel room—just like this one! You stabbed me, and I bled out. I was on the floor, and I was dying, and you left me because I said it was over and—"

He yanked Willow to her feet. His hands jerked up her shirt.

"No! Stop! No!" Willow screamed.

"If you were stabbed, where are the scars?" His hands were on her mid-riff. "You would have scars, sweetheart, don't you see that? Lazarus subjects can heal from just about anything, but you—if you were really stabbed by me before you were given the formula, you'd have *scars*."

Her breath heaved in and out.

"Wyman Wright did this." Rage ignited in his eyes. "He always did things to your head.

Didn't want you trusting anyone. Didn't want you leaving him. He *programmed* your mind, Willow. When you were in that lab, he created reality for you. He never wanted you to come back to me. He made false memories. He knew if I ever got close…you and I—we'd vanish. Because I can't, I *won't* lose you again."

"Stop." Her voice was too soft.

"He made memories in your head. I never hurt you. I wouldn't." His hands were still on her mid-riff. Warm. Strong.

Familiar.

Not Jay. He's not Jay!

Fear and fury were tangling inside of her, and they were growing worse with every moment that passed.

"You don't have full memories of the so-called attack, do you, my Willow? Because it didn't happen. You can't trust your mind. Wyman made that happen. He destroyed who you'd been. He took you from me." Pain flashed now, showing clearly on Lucas's face. "I love you so much. And you loved me. Wyman broke us apart."

"He…" *The memories are real.* They had to be real, didn't they? Her gaze fell. *Jay. I need Jay.*

"Willow. Willow, look at me."

Her angry gaze flew up, but he was staring at her tenderly. "It's going to be all right. We'll find our way back to each other."

No.

"Wyman did this to you. Maverick did this. They tried to take you away, but I didn't give up. I won't *ever* give up on you."

A tear slid down her cheek. "Did you kill Jay?"

"I sure as hell hope so."

***

"Get the fuck..." Jay growled, "out of my way."

But West just shook his head. "Get the fuck," he growled right back, "into that bed. And *stay there*. Your dumb ass was shot three times!"

And he'd been stitched up. The bullets hadn't hit anything vital, thank Christ. He was weak, he was on drugs, and he was *getting* out of that hospital. "I don't want to hurt you."

"Good. Then get into the bed—"

"But I will lay your ass out." Flat. "Willow needs me. I'm getting to her." Because that bastard Lucas had *taken* her. Jay had been lying on the ground, bleeding, and the guy had roared away with Willow. West had given chase, he'd shot at the vehicle, but Lucas had still escaped.

"He drugged her," West said.

Like that reminder was going to help? West had already told him that before—

"Drugging her means he wanted her alive. Willow is still *alive.* You have to heal. You get better and then—"

He shoved West.

West didn't shove back. "You're freaking hurt!" West yelled at him. "Are you trying to tear your stitches open? Are you trying—"

"I love her!" Jay roared at him. "*Everything* is tearing open right now! I'm losing my freaking mind. Willow is out there somewhere, with the piece of shit who *killed* her before. And you're telling me to get in bed? To sleep this crap off? No. No." He shook his head. "I'm finding Willow. Even if I have to rip apart this world to do it."

A knock sounded at the door. A second later, the door was swinging open. Sawyer coughed into his hand. "I, um, think you should hear a few things. Before you go ripping apart worlds and what not."

Did he look like he was in the mood for more bullshit?

"Wyman," Sawyer added. "He wants to talk to you." Without another word, Sawyer left the room.

Jay surged forward. Once more, West got in his path.

"I *know,* okay?" West snapped. "I know you love her. But I love your sorry ass. You're *my* family, and I'm not going to lose you. That bastard nearly took out a whole block with his explosives. He doesn't care about innocent casualties. I lost two men. *Two men.* He killed them, and I had to be the one to explain to their wives that they wouldn't ever be coming home." His jaw hardened. "I'm not going to step aside while you walk into a showdown with him. He took out a freaking super soldier. Tossed Flynn like it was nothing. You love her, and that's great. But I'll be damned if I let you die for her."

"West…"

"She can come back from the grave. You can't."

He felt like he was already in the grave. Knowing that Willow was out there with Lucas, that he could be hurting her was his living hell. "I said I'd keep her safe." His voice was rougher as his shoulders sagged. "I promised her that. She'd been hurt so much. I just—why couldn't I keep my promise to her?"

"Because we didn't know who we were up against." West nodded. "Time for Wyman to tell us *everything*. Then we'll figure this out. You always figure things out, man. Ever since we were kids. We can do this. But you're not doing it alone."

He wasn't alone. He'd never been alone, not since he'd gone into that foster home and seen a boy his age waiting for him. A boy in too-big clothes, a boy with rage in his eyes, and a boy who'd been his brother from then on.

Jay's hand locked around West's shoulder.

"Are you calm now?" West demanded.

"No." He wouldn't lie to West.

"Didn't think so." West measured him. "But you're not running out like a drunk cowboy."

"Not until we talk to Wyman." Then there would be no promises.

Wyman will know his weakness. Wyman always knows weaknesses.

And once Jay learned what would take down that bastard Lucas...*game the fuck on.*

***

"Deep inside, you must have known that Jay was a threat to you." Lucas was still in front of her. Her knees were weak, and his grip was the only thing that kept her upright. "I bet you had flashes, didn't you? I've heard the Lazarus subjects can sometimes see the danger coming. Did you see him attacking you? Lying to you? Did you see the threat coming?"

"I saw..." *Keep Lucas talking. Figure this out.* "I had a dream...where I killed him."

His shoulders relaxed. "Because you knew he was a threat."

Because she'd been the threat.

"You don't believe me." His breath exhaled on a rough sigh. "What did I expect? I mean, I knew it wasn't going to be easy. They took you from me. Tore away your memories. Brainwashed you when you tried to fight back." His gaze swept over her face. "Wyman never wanted us to be together. He knew I was going to take you away, and if I did, the bastard would never get his hands on you again."

"He…my father…"

"He *killed* your real father. Did he tell you that part? I bet he didn't. They were partners, back in the day, but Wyman killed your father on a mission. Friendly fire, if you believe that." His mocking laughter said he didn't. "And Wyman took you. Separated you from the rest of the world. You were never allowed any freedom. When I found you, hell, you were like Rapunzel. The princess who'd been locked away in a tower that he made."

"I'm no princess." And he was no prince.

Lucas pulled her closer. "I won't give up on you. We're together again. We're going to stay together. One day, you'll love me again."

"You going to keep me cuffed until then? Cuffs and tranqs—they don't exactly shout love." She could feel her strength coming back. Her voice wasn't as slurred or as weak. She just needed a little more time.

Lucas smiled at her. The smile chilled her to the core. "I have something better." He inhaled. "God, I missed your scent. I missed your body. I missed *you.*"

And he scared her. "What is your something better?"

"The Lazarus formula, of course."

That made no sense to her.

"Before I blew that lab—your prison—to hell and back, I helped myself to a few supplies. I've got the Lazarus serum. I'll give it to you, and it will be a reset."

"That's not how the formula works."

"That's how it *will* work. I'll give you the formula, you'll come back stronger, better, and your mind—all of those false memories that Maverick and Wyman tried to give you will be gone. You'll be a blank slate."

And the fear Willow felt got worse. Because if what he was saying was true…if he gave her that formula, and she woke up with no memories at all…

Will I believe him then? Will I believe a man who says he's my lover? That I love him? He could make up some story about her being in an accident, he could feed her any lie he wanted, and she'd—

Believe him?

"Now you're figuring it out." Lucas nodded, as if he approved. "You're realizing how vulnerable you've been all along. You *had* to buy the stories that Maverick and Wyman told you, but, sweetheart, they were lies. They were always lying. You were mine. I was yours. You *love* me. They kept us apart, but it won't happen any longer. We're together, and we're going to stay that way."

Why hadn't he already given her the formula? Why hadn't he given it to her when she'd been unconscious?

"There's just one small problem." His lips curved down. "I think that, for the formula to work, you're going to have to die first."

***

"You look like hell," Wyman muttered as he glared at Jay.

Jay glared right back. "Thanks, asshole. So do you." Wyman was paler than the sheets around him, black shadows lined his eyes, and twice as many machines were now surrounding the bastard as they had been before.

Wyman grunted. His eyes were slits. "You let him take Willow."

"I'll get her back," Jay promised.

"How?" Wyman shook his head. "He's stronger than you, faster, he's—"

"Not fucking smarter." Jay heaved forward. Walking was hard, standing was hard, but he ignored the pain. Nothing mattered but getting

Willow. "Tell me what I'm facing. If I don't go in blind, I can stop him. I can save her."

But Wyman was glaring at him with fury. "You were the threat. You brought her into the open." His breath choked out. "You made it so he found her, you—"

"It's all on me." Again, he lurched forward. "Fine. What the hell ever. Tell me what he is. Tell me how to stop him. Because I know you did something to him. You and your damn enhancements. He tossed Flynn like the super soldier was a rag doll."

Flynn coughed from his position near the window. "And I'm not exactly easy to toss."

Jay didn't look away from Wyman. "What did you do to Lucas Tate?"

"He volunteered." Wyman swallowed. A trembling hand swept over his jaw. "Early experiment, okay? Nothing like Lazarus. He can't come back from the dead. He's just..." He exhaled. Wheezed. "There was another doctor, okay? Before I met the ever so promising Elizabeth Parker."

A growl came from a watchful Sawyer.

Wyman didn't glance his way. "Dr. Gail found out that we could improve the human body in certain ways. Make muscles stronger. Reflexes sharper. Of course, I was interested to see this type of development in the field—"

"Let me guess," Sawyer cut in. "There were side effects."

Wyman's gaze fell to the bed. "Yes. Adrenaline was key in this experiment. Soldiers perform better when they have maximum levels of adrenaline in their systems, but too much of Dr. Gail's formula—too much adrenaline—led to *permanent effects.* Uncontrollable effects. The experiment had to be terminated."

"You mean the subjects had to be terminated," Jay fired back, reading between the lines.

Wyman sighed. "They killed without remorse. When a frenzy hit them, they went wild. Like the berserkers of the old days. Dr. Gail even called them her Norsemen. In a battle, the men instantly became better warriors. They didn't feel any pain inflicted on them, and their strength increased to stunning levels. But while their strength increased, their…their ability to distinguish between friend and foe—that vanished."

Flynn swore. "You already had one clusterfuck of an experiment, and you *still* went ahead with Lazarus after that?"

"My job was to create the perfect soldier. I was doing my job." Wyman's thin shoulders straightened. "And I learned from my mistakes. I kept the Lazarus subjects isolated so that they could be tested. I didn't let them into the general population, and I didn't—"

"You fucked up again," Sawyer snarled at him. "Then you tried to clean up your mess by killing us. Only this time, you'd made soldiers who *couldn't* be killed."

Wyman didn't speak.

Jay would *make* the guy talk. "Why didn't you kill Lucas?"

Wyman flinched at the name.

"He killed Willow." Jay was certain of this. "He killed the only person you claim to care about in this world. And knowing you, I just don't get it. Why wouldn't you have destroyed him right away? Torn the bastard apart?"

"You think I didn't try?" Wyman rasped. "You think I didn't send every man I had after him? That I didn't even send Lazarus subjects after him?"

"He's still breathing, so I don't know what the hell to think." He'd shot the bastard, and the guy had still come after him.

Wyman shook his head. "He's just a hard bastard to kill, okay? Best soldier I ever met." He jerked his head toward Sawyer. "Even better than you. With the Norse enhancement, the bastard could almost smell danger coming. He's killed everyone that I sent after him."

"But he *can* die," Jay pushed.

"If you can get close enough. That's the trick." Another wheeze. "Getting close."

"I hit him in the chest." Jay replayed the scene in his mind. Analyzed. Considered. "Bulletproof vest." Had to be. If the guy wasn't Lazarus, then he didn't get to magically rise again. He must have been wearing a vest. As Jay thought about the scene, he didn't remember seeing any blood on Lucas. "I'll be more careful next time. I'll just pretend he's Lazarus, and I'll shoot the guy in the head."

"Why is he so locked on Willow?" Flynn asked, finally stepping forward. "If he killed her before, why come after her again?" "Because he didn't mean to kill her." Wyman's Adam's apple bobbed. "He was in one of his rages. Freaking berserker rage. She wanted to get away from him. She didn't love him—she knew he was dangerous. But he wasn't letting go." His face hardened. "I'd hid her. Gave her a new place to stay. I thought she was safe, but he was obsessed. His mind was messed up. He couldn't let her go. And if she wasn't going to stay with him—"

"Then no one else was going to have her." Jay could taste rage. "Heard that twisted shit story before. Every abuser likes to sing the same song." And Willow was with that piece of trash right then. What was he doing to her?

I'm sorry, Willow. I'm going to find you. I'm coming. Wait for me.

"He tranqed her at the scene," Sawyer noted, voice emotionless. "That's what West told me."

Jay flinched.

"That's how he got her out of there. So the guy must have gotten access to some of the Lazarus material you used on us. A regular drug wouldn't have worked on Willow."

"More secrets?" Flynn all but shouted at Wyman. "Stop holding back!"

Damn straight. "This is Willow," Jay said. "She's—"

Everything.

"I think..." Wyman's voice was weaker. "I think Lucas is the one who destroyed the lab in North Carolina. Willow just got away before he could get to her."

"You think?" Jay's brows rose. "Or you know?"

One shoulder lifted. "I saw the video. It was him."

Secrets. Wyman, you are going to choke on them.

"He took...some vials. The tranqs. And...the Lazarus serum."

Jay's heartbeat drummed in his ears. "What is he going to do with the serum?" But a dark fear was growing in him.

"Use it on himself!" Flynn answered before Wyman could speak.

Wyman shook his head. His gaze was on Jay.

Jay's mind was spinning as he sorted through the possibilities. "If he was going to use it on himself, he would have done it by now."

"Are we sure he *hasn't?*" Sawyer pushed.

"How many vials of the formula did he take?" Jay tried to keep his voice steady.

"Just one," Wyman replied.

Because one was all he'd need. Hell. "He's going to use it on her."

Flynn grabbed his shoulder and spun Jay around. "Jump to freaking conclusions much? Why the hell would he want—"

"Because it wipes the memories away. I've read the research on the formula. I funded the program, remember? That means I had access to every single piece of research data. If he gives her the formula, then she's going to forget everything that's happened. She'll wake up again, memories of me gone. Memories of Wyman gone."

"I always feared…he'd try something like this. That he'd make her believe she wanted to be with him again." Wyman's breath seemed to rattle in his lungs. "When she woke in North Carolina, I was so happy, so damn happy to have my girl back, but she didn't know anyone. Didn't know who to trust."

The pieces were clicking in Jay's mind. He pulled from Flynn. Faced Wyman once more. "And that's why you put a trigger in her head. That bloom shit."

Grimly, Wyman nodded. "I needed something in her core, a way for her to understand that danger was near. I had the shrinks there work with her again and again." He stiffened as he stared at Jay's face. "You think I liked doing that? I was trying to protect her! Her memories were gone! I had to do something—*anything*—to try and keep her safe. I knew he could get to her. He'd spin stories about them loving each other. About her wanting to be with him. But he wouldn't tell her that he took a knife to my baby, and he stabbed her twenty times."

Jay's vision went absolutely black.

"So many wounds. So much blood." Wyman's eyes squeezed shut. "I saw plenty of men and women die in my life, but Willow—*she was my daughter.* I used every connection I had, everything *I owned* to get her back."

"She doesn't have scars," Jay said, his voice thick. Little more than a growl. "If your story is true—"

"If? *If?*" And for just a moment, Wyman didn't look so weak. His shoulders snapped up. His voice hardened. "I wasn't going to have her seeing the mess he'd made of her body. You have no idea just how many government projects I controlled. Getting her to live was step one. Healing her skin was step two, and trust me, the surgeries were one hell of a lot easier than step one." Red spots of color rose on his cheeks. "I made deals with every person I could find. When she got out of that lab, I worked with people I *hated* to find her. But she was my priority. Always has been. Nothing else can matter."

Sawyer cleared his throat. "Yes, um, this is very interesting, but I think you're all overlooking one important point."

Jay's gaze swung to him.

"The formula only works on the dead. Willow isn't dead, so the grand plan won't work. It won't—"

"He's going to kill her." Jay's voice was flat. Cold. Totally at odds with the hell-hot fury inside of him. "Then Lucas will give her the formula."

"He can't do that! For her to truly die, he'd need to put a bullet in her brain. Even with the serum, how does he know she'd come back from that? He doesn't have the medical training necessary to bring her back. He doesn't understand the preservation process!" Sawyer argued. "He can't—"

"Then he'll get someone who can." Shit. *Shit.*

Sawyer's eyes widened. "No."

Yes. There was only one person in the area who knew how to administer the Lazarus formula. Only one person who could bring Willow back.

Elizabeth Parker.

"He's not touching Elizabeth," Sawyer vowed. His face was mean, dangerous. His whole body actually seemed to expand with his fury.

Elizabeth was in the hospital. She was close by.

"Don't even think it." Now Sawyer was standing toe-to-toe with Jay. "You aren't using her as bait. That shit-show routine didn't work with Willow. And I'm not risking the woman I love."

They should be clear on one thing. "Elizabeth is my friend. I wouldn't put her in jeopardy." He held Sawyer's glittering gaze. "But I will do *everything* possible to protect the woman that I love."

Wyman sucked in a sharp breath. "Willow—"

His head turned. Jay inclined his head toward the man who'd been—still was—his enemy. "I'm getting her away from him." No matter what he had to do or who had to die.

CHAPTER SEVENTEEN

The needle shoved into Willow's neck. A hard jab, and then she felt ice snaking through her veins.

"Just have to keep you under control." Lucas leaned forward and brushed a kiss over her cheek. "But after you get the Lazarus formula, everything will be okay again. No more tranqs, no more road blocks. No more bastards in our way." Another kiss. "Just you and me. The way it always should have been."

Her legs gave way. But he caught her. Carried her to the bed. He put her down on the sagging mattress. Sat beside her. His hands caged her body, resting on either side of her as he leaned forward.

The ice had spread through her body. She wanted to punch him. Wanted to rage and attack, but she couldn't.

"That tranq could take down five elephants." He brushed her hair away from Willow's forehead. "It can take you down, too."

Her eyelids were trying to sag shut. She forced them open. Her cuffed hands were lodged behind her back.

He gazed at her tenderly. "I have missed you." His head cocked. "And you missed me. You love me, Willow. Always have."

No.

"Wyman introduced us, did you know that? He wanted someone strong for you. Someone who could protect you from all of the enemies that he had in the world." His eyes crinkled at the corners, as if he were remembering. Enjoying the memory. "The first time I saw you, I knew you were going to be mine."

Jay. She focused on him. Focused wildly and completely. *Jay.* Other Lazarus subjects could communicate telepathically, so maybe she could reach him. Maybe she could do more than just show fears to people. Maybe if she tried hard enough, she could get into Jay's head.

"You wanted me, too. God, I loved fucking you."

Jay. Jay, I need you.

"You don't remember what it was like, but you will, you'll remember—"

"Jay," she gasped out his name, forcing it past a thick tongue and lips that felt numb.

Lucas's smile slipped. The crinkles vanished near his eyes. "You fucked him."

Jay!

He grabbed her jaw, clamping down with fingers that bruised. "You'll forget him. Forget every second with him."

She didn't want to forget. She always wanted to remember him. He'd made her feel whole. Good. Special.

He'd made her…love.

I love you, Jay. I should have said something, but I was afraid. So afraid. She was tired of the fear, tired of—

"You bitch," Lucas snarled. "You *loved* him?"

Had she spoken out loud? Had she—

He yanked her head to the side, and the last thing she heard was the snap of bones.

***

"You really think he's going to come after Elizabeth?" Flynn demanded. They were in the hospital corridor. Sawyer had stormed away, probably to go and make sure that Elizabeth was safe.

Jay shook his head. "I think that's a strong freaking option, but I'm not going to wait around for him to show up." Because every second that passed, that was a second that Willow lost. "Where's Reva?" After he'd woken up from surgery, he'd learned that Reva had survived, too.

"Two rooms down. She's—"

He was already rushing away. Guards were in front of her room, but Jay hurried past them. He threw open the door and found Reva lying in bed. Her face was devoid of makeup. She looked younger and more fragile than he'd ever seen her.

And West was at her side.

What? The actual fuck? *This* is where his brother had gone?

West glanced up at him. "Tell him, Reva."

"I-I called him." Her breath stuttered out. She winced, as if in pain, and her hand flew to her side. "To let Lucas know that you were going to be at Wander, I called him. His number is on my phone—"

West threw the phone at him.

Hell, yes. Jay's fingers locked around the device.

"I'm figuring you can work your magic with that. You can find him." West nodded toward Jay. "You can get Willow back."

"Damn straight I can."

***

"Willow? *Willow?*" Lucas yanked back his hand. She wasn't moving. Wasn't breathing.

Her head lay limply, and he knew he'd killed her.

His breath sawed in and out of his lungs. His fingers shook.

She'll come back. She'll come back. It will be different this time.

He just had to wait. If he waited long enough, she'd come back.

His phone rang. He ignored the peals and vibration. Stared at Willow. "I was just so fucking mad," he whispered. "You don't love him. It's me. Always *me*." And to hear those words come from her beautiful lips…

She'd ripped him wide open.

The phone stopped ringing.

He had to get Elizabeth Parker. He'd snatch her. Kill the fools in his way. Then she'd help him administer the formula. When he was done with Elizabeth, he'd end her, too.

Then it would just be him and Willow. A fresh start. She'd never talk of loving anyone else. She'd belong to him, always.

His phone started ringing again. He grabbed the phone, ready to toss it against the wall. He'd given the number to Benjamin Larson, when he'd been trying to get close to that bastard, but no one else should—

Reva.

Her number was on the screen. Only Reva was dead. He'd killed her. Hadn't he? His finger swiped over the screen. "Who the hell—"

"Deal's…off," Reva gasped out.

"What are you talking about?" His gaze was on Willow. She still wasn't moving. How long would it take her to come back? She *would* come back.

"Not working w-with you..."

"Sweetheart, didn't you get a clue when I put a bullet in you? I'm not paying you a dime." How had she survived? She'd been a limp rag doll the last time he'd seen her. When she'd been in Jay Maverick's arms—

Jay. "Tell me he's dead," Lucas barked.

Silence.

"Tell me he's dead!" Now he was yelling and Lucas didn't care.

"He's not..." Her voice was lower. "He's...coming for you."

He threw the phone against the wall. It hit with a clatter. Impossible. He'd been careful when he left with Willow. No one had followed him. Jay *couldn't* track him down that fast.

He went to the bed, scooped up Willow. Just in case, he was getting them the hell out of there. Jay might triangulate the cell signal from the call Lucas had just taken and find them—eventually—but they would be long gone before then.

He slipped the cuffs off Willow's wrists. If anyone was in the parking lot, he'd just say that Willow had drank too much. That she was sleeping it off. The cuffs would attract attention. He didn't want attention.

He wanted to get away. To plan.

"We're going, Willow." He kissed her cheek even as he opened the door. She was in his arms. Cradled carefully. He edged outside, his gaze still on her. "He won't find you—"

"Guess again," Jay Maverick drawled. And the bastard was right there. Standing just a few feet away. "Your dumb ass was hiding less than ten minutes from the hospital. Of course, I found you. I had you long before Reva made the call. She was just the distraction while I got close. I hear getting close to you is the trick, you see."

No, no—

"I can do anything with tech. Things the government doesn't even know." Jay smiled. "I had you, and—"

Jay's gaze fell on Willow. He blanched.

Willow is his weakness.

"Too late," Lucas taunted him. "She's dead." Then he dropped Willow. Just let her fall.

Jay immediately surged forward, and that was the guy's mistake. Lucas yanked out the knife he kept strapped to his waist, and he drove it up and toward Jay. It sank deep even as Jay grunted.

"Jay?"

Willow's voice.

She was back, but staring up at them weakly. She tried to push herself up—

Lucas pulled out the knife. The blade was red with Jay's blood. "You're too weak," Lucas snapped at him. "No match for me. And you're dead—"

"Behind... you," Jay managed. "Distract..."

Lucas spun around. And he saw that Jay had just been the bait. The distraction. Sawyer Cage and Flynn Haddox were there. They'd come in the window, and he hadn't even heard them make a single sound because he'd been so focused on that bastard Jay. Now they were rushing toward him, and there wasn't time to retreat. They'd caught him. They were going to—

"Stop!"

Willow. Willow's weak order.

Everyone froze because Willow had risen to her feet. She trembled a bit, as if still struggling to recover, but she'd just put her body in front of Lucas. *She's protecting me from them.* He smiled at her because...She was his Willow. She loved him. Always had.

The two of them could win, as long as they were together.

"You belong to me," he whispered.

She stared into his eyes.

CHAPTER EIGHTEEN

"You belong to me." Lucas smiled at her. He held a bloody knife in his hand. A knife he'd just used on Jay.

Willow's body was heavy. She felt sluggish, but she was absolutely sure of one thing. "I belong to myself." And she grabbed him. She slammed his head into the doorframe as hard as she could. She heard the smack. The thud. She saw his eyes glaze, and then he was slumping to the floor.

The knife had fallen from his fingers. It was right there. She grabbed it. Held it clutched in her fingers. "You killed me, you bastard. And you think that's love?"

His breath came faster. He'd blinked, shaken his head, and he seemed about to rise—

She felt Sawyer and Flynn—actually *felt* them start to advance. "Stay back!" Willow yelled. Or tried to yell. Her voice was funny. Was that from dying? From the tranq he'd given her? She didn't know. Didn't care. Her hand tightened on the knife.

"Willow..."

Her head whipped up at that voice. *His* voice. Jay. He was standing near the door, still outside the motel room. His hand was at his side, and blood was flowing down his shirtfront. He stared at her with wide eyes, and he looked at her—

No one has ever looked at me like that.

Like she was everything. The only thing that mattered to him.

And she was about to kill. He was going to see her at her worst. Her darkest.

Lucas laughed. "He won't love you. You just figured that out, didn't you? You thought you had it all. But you don't get the good guy, Willow. You weren't made for him. You're dark and twisted, just like me. You love death and violence. *Just like me.* You were meant to be with me. You were meant—" He surged up toward her, rising in a too-fast heave, and she realized he'd snatched a gun from his boot.

She drove the knife into his chest. Straight into his heart. It sank deep. And then she twisted it. "We're done," Willow told him softly as she leaned toward him. "Because I say we're done."

His mouth was open. A gasp, a gurgle, spilled from him.

She yanked the knife back. And she watched as his body slid down the doorframe. He hit the floor as his hands flew to his chest, trying to stop the blood.

It wasn't going to stop.

"Damn," Sawyer whispered from behind her. "She's fierce."

She still held the knife. Willow made herself glance up at Jay. "H-he said—"

"Give me...the gun," Jay growled.

Willow shook her head. "What?"

"The gun he dropped—give—oh, hell..." He lunged for it, wincing as he leaned down. More blood soaked his shirt.

"Jay!"

He lifted the gun. For a minute, it seemed as if he were pointing the gun at her. But then she realized he was pointing at Lucas. At a Lucas who wasn't moving any longer. "He's dead," Willow said, voice stark. She'd killed him. Jay had seen her for exactly what she truly—

"He'll come back, baby. Or rather, he's not gone. Not yet. He's not Lazarus..." Each word seemed like a struggle from Jay. "But he's something else. And I'm making sure he won't come back—"

Right then, Lucas's eyes opened. He stared up at her with rage. Glared at Jay with fury.

"Didn't you hear the lady?" Jay gritted out. "You're done."

Then he fired. The bullet blasted into Lucas's head.

Willow didn't move. Her heart was racing too fast. She could hear shouts from outside. The other people in the motel seemed to be freaking the hell out. Not that she blamed them.

Her knees were shaking again.

"Super soldiers…my ass." Jay dropped the gun and frowned over at Sawyer and Flynn. "Didn't see you…saving the day…"

"You two had it covered," Sawyer said, but there was something about his voice…about the worried gaze that was on Jay…

"Jay?" Willow whispered.

He smiled at her. "Love you."

She started to smile, too. Because what she'd done hadn't mattered to him. And he'd *shot* Lucas, to make sure the bastard wouldn't come after her again. He'd fought for her, he'd—

Jay fell.

And Willow grabbed for him. Her hands flew over his body, and she heard herself yelling his name.

Just like that—in that one terrible flash—her worst fear came true.

Jay's blood. My hands in Jay's blood. A knife near us.

Her worst fear. Turned into reality.

"Don't leave me!" Willow begged him. "Please, Jay!"

But Jay wasn't answering her.

***

"The EMTs said they lost him twice on the way to the hospital."

Willow's shoulders hunched. Sawyer's voice was low, but she could hear him easily even though he stood ten feet away, talking with Elizabeth.

"They believed it was a miracle he made it here, but they weren't thinking he was going to last much longer."

Her body rocked forward, then back, and her gaze never left the operating room doors.

"He shouldn't have left the hospital." Elizabeth's angry response. "He'd been shot three times! Jay is smarter than this. He's—"

"He loves you."

Willow jerked. West had just stepped in front of her. She'd been so intent on listening to Elizabeth and Sawyer that she hadn't even noticed him, and West's words had stabbed right through her.

"Jay loves you, Willow. You know that, don't you?"

She could feel the tears on her cheeks.

"That's why he left the hospital when he should have been in bed. Why the fool let himself get stabbed, just so he could distract Lucas. Why he was willing to take any risk."

His words weren't helping her. They were just making her hurt worse.

"It's not about atoning. Not about any BS that someone else might tell you." He exhaled. His face appeared grim. "My brother loves you, and I want to know, just how do you feel about him?"

"He can't die." A hoarse whisper. "I can't lose him."

"And what would you do to keep him? Turn him into a Lazarus test subject? Take all his memories away, give him a life where he doesn't know anyone?" He paused a beat. "Where he doesn't remember you?"

She didn't care if Jay didn't remember her. As long as he lived. As long as he was there. As long as—

"Right," West drawled out the word. "That's what I thought. It's easy to blame others for the choices they made, when you're not walking in their shoes."

She didn't know what he was talking about. Jay—

"Your father didn't make the easy call. But that man—bastard that he is—he loves you. So maybe before *he* leaves this earth, you can take some time to tell him that you forgive him. And that you understand." His lips twisted. "But first, why don't you go back to the recovery room and see my brother? Because I know he wants to see you."

It took a few moments for his words to register. A few moments too long. Then she was surging forward. Grabbing his shirt in her hands. Fisting it. "Jay's awake? Jay's alive?"

"Yes to both." His smile softened his face. "And even though you didn't say the words, I could see the truth. Good to know you love my brother as much as he loves you."

She shoved him out of the way. Threw an apology over her shoulder.

Just heard his laughter in response.

Willow ran down the hallway, rushing past nurses and doctors. Everyone passed her in a blur, or maybe she was the blur who sped past them. Soon she was in recovery—she could see the thin curtain that separated her from Jay. She could feel him.

Her fingers curled around the curtain. Someone grabbed her shoulder, telling her that she shouldn't be there.

She ignored that someone.

She yanked aside the curtain.

Jay.

Jay was in that bed. Jay's eyes were closed. His head was turned toward her. The machines around him beeped steadily.

"Miss, you shouldn't be here," a woman told her sharply. The woman who'd grabbed her. "Only family can visit back here!"

Jay's eyes opened. They locked on her. And he smiled. "She is my family." His right hand extended toward Willow. "She's my home."

It was hard for her not to pounce on him right then and there.

The nurse backed away. Willow lurched forward. Her steps were uncertain and scared.

He kept his hand stretched out to her. Her shaking fingers reached for his. Their hands linked. Joined.

She couldn't even speak. A lump was in her throat, nearly choking her. He'd survived. He was alive. He was safe.

And he…

"Am I a super soldier?" Jay's lips lifted at the corners. "Tell me the truth. How awesome am I now?"

A tear slipped down her cheek.

"Willow?" His smile left. "I was…teasing. I know I'm—"

She threw her arms around him. Buried her face in his neck. "Don't ever die." *The EMTs said he died twice on the way to the hospital.*

"Willow—"

"Lucas told me lies. Tried to make me believe that you'd tricked me, but I knew he was lying the whole time. I could tell."

"Because of those super senses of yours."

"No." She forced her head to lift. She could taste the salt of her tears. "Because I love you. Because I trust you."

"Baby…" Emotion burned in his eyes. An emotion she wasn't afraid to recognize. Jay loved her, and she loved him, and everything was going to be okay.

"I should have said it sooner, but I was afraid. I don't want to hurt you. I never want to hurt you." Her words wouldn't stop tumbling out. "But I want to be with you. I want to have a life. You and me."

"And kids."

Her chest ached.

"I want kids with you, Willow. A boy with your eyes. A girl with your strength." His left hand lifted and stroked her cheek. "I want forever with you."

And he was looking at her with love. *Love.* Not possession. Not ownership. He was staring at her like she was some kind of gift, and Jay didn't get it. *He* was her gift. Her second chance.

The lover she wanted. The life she wanted. Jay was her everything. "Forever." Willow swallowed. "That sure sounds like a nice start."

He laughed. She loved the sound of his laugh. She loved the warmth of his skin. She loved the way he made her feel. Beautiful. Special.

Safe.

Most of all, though, Willow just loved him.

Her lips pressed to his.

EPILOGUE

Jay wheeled himself past the guards and into the quiet hospital room. The machines were humming, the curtains were open, letting sunlight pour into the room, and his nemesis was glaring at him.

"You're going to marry my daughter?" Wyman fired the opening shot.

Jay stopped at the edge of the bed. He couldn't quite get around without falling on his face, so he'd borrowed the chair for this little visit. "Hell, yes, I am. As soon as possible."

Wyman's head jerked. "Good. And you make sure, absolutely sure, that no one else ever finds out who she really is."

Jay held his stare. "Everyone wants you dead."

Wyman laughed. "Including you, right?"

"You're her father."

"Not blood…"

"Yeah, well, like you said, blood doesn't make family."

Wyman glanced toward the window. "Her dad was my best friend. The only one who could put up with my bullshit. He died, saving my sorry hide. Was I supposed to just turn his daughter away? Willow's mom passed in childbirth. I wasn't going to let strangers take her. I had to make sure she was always—"

"Protected," Jay finished. "She will be."

Wyman focused on him once more. "I was going to say loved."

"She will be." His gaze never faltered. "She is."

Wyman's shoulders relaxed. "And what happens to me? You gonna let the super soldiers tear me apart?"

The cancer was already doing that. The man was living on borrowed time. And the guy—yeah, he'd done terrible things. But he'd also done good things. Or at least, one good thing. *Willow.* "There's a special word I want you to focus on, *dad.*"

Wyman glowered.

"Atonement," Jay announced. "Know what that means?"

The glower grew worse.

"You're going to be joining *my* team. You're going to tell me about all of the test subjects out there. Lazarus. Norsemen. Whatever the hell else you've created. And in the time you've got left, you're going to show your daughter that you aren't just a monster. That there's something more inside of you. You're going to show her that. You're going to help give her memories back to her. You're going to give Willow everything she needs and *more*."

"Why the hell would I do that?"

"Why?" Jay repeated.

The hospital room door opened behind him with a soft squeak. The light scent of lavender reached him. *Willow*.

Wyman's gaze had slid over Jay's shoulders. It had gone to rest on Willow.

"That's why," Jay murmured. *She's my reason. And she's yours, too.*

Wyman gave a grim nod.

"Good." Jay turned his head and glanced back at Willow. The woman he loved. His damn life. He smiled at her. When she smiled back, he swore she lit up the whole room.

Willow came to his side. Her fingers twined with his. Fit his. Because she fit him. Willow was his perfect match in every way, and he'd prove himself to her, every single day. Jay squared his shoulders. Focused on the man who'd one day be his father-in-law. "Let's get started, Wyman. Just how many test subjects are out there?"

"You're not gonna like the answer," Wyman muttered.

"Never thought I would." Jay waited.

Then Wyman started talking...

Jay didn't let his expression alter, but, *shit*. They sure had one hell of a lot of work to do. It was a good thing he enjoyed a challenge.

He brought Willow's hand to his lips. Kissed her knuckles.

And he got ready to work.

The End

A NOTE FROM THE AUTHOR

I was very excited to write a female Lazarus heroine. I wanted to explore Willow's life, and I really tried to show her strength in this story. She's fought so hard for a second chance, and Willow deserved a good future.

The Lazarus stories have been so much fun to write. Would you like to see more? Do you have a favorite character who should get a story? Then tell me! I love to hear from readers. You can contact me at *info@cynthiaeden.com*

Thank you for reading RUN TO ME.

If you'd like to stay updated on my releases and sales, please join my newsletter list.

http://www.cynthiaeden.com/newsletter/

Again, thank you for reading RUN TO ME.

Best,
Cynthia Eden
www.cynthiaeden.com

ABOUT THE AUTHOR

Award-winning author Cynthia Eden writes dark tales of paranormal romance and romantic suspense. She is a New York Times, USA Today, Digital Book World, and IndieReader best-seller. Cynthia is also a three-time finalist for the RITA® award. Since she began writing full-time in 2005, Cynthia has written over eighty novels and novellas.

For More Information

- *www.cynthiaeden.com*
- *http://www.facebook.com/cynthiaedenfanpage*
- *http://www.twitter.com/cynthiaeden*

HER OTHER WORKS

Romantic Suspense

Lazarus Rising

- Never Let Go (Book One, Lazarus Rising)
- Keep Me Close (Book Two, Lazarus Rising)
- Stay With Me (Book Three, Lazarus Rising)
- Run To Me (Book Four, Lazarus Rising)
- Lie Close To Me
  - Coming in March of 2018

Dark Obsession Series

- Watch Me (Dark Obsession, Book 1)
- Want Me (Dark Obsession, Book 2)
- Need Me (Dark Obsession, Book 3)
- Beware Of Me (Dark Obsession, Book 4)
- Only For Me (Dark Obsession, Books 1 to 4)

Mine Series

- Mine To Take (Mine, Book 1)
- Mine To Keep (Mine, Book 2)
- Mine To Hold (Mine, Book 3)
- Mine To Crave (Mine, Book 4)
- Mine To Have (Mine, Book 5)
- Mine To Protect (Mine, Book 6)
- Mine Series Box Set Volume 1 (Mine, Books 1-3)
- Mine Series Box Set Volume 2 (Mine, Books 4-6)

Other Romantic Suspense

- First Taste of Darkness
- Sinful Secrets
- Until Death
- Christmas With A Spy

Paranormal Romance

Bad Things

- The Devil In Disguise (Bad Things, Book 1)
- On The Prowl (Bad Things, Book 2)
- Undead Or Alive (Bad Things, Book 3)
- Broken Angel (Bad Things, Book 4)
- Heart Of Stone (Bad Things, Book 5)
- Tempted By Fate (Bad Things, Book 6)
- Bad Things Volume One (Books 1 to 3)
- Bad Things Volume Two (Books 4 to 6)

- Bad Things Deluxe Box Set (Books 1 to 6)

Bite Series

- Forbidden Bite (Bite Book 1)
- Mating Bite (Bite Book 2)

Lazarus Rising

- Never Let Go (Book One, Lazarus Rising)
- Keep Me Close (Book Two, Lazarus Rising) - Available 10/24/2017

Blood and Moonlight Series

- Bite The Dust (Blood and Moonlight, Book 1)
- Better Off Undead (Blood and Moonlight, Book 2)
- Bitter Blood (Blood and Moonlight, Book 3)
- Blood and Moonlight (The Complete Series)

Purgatory Series

- The Wolf Within (Purgatory, Book 1)
- Marked By The Vampire (Purgatory, Book 2)
- Charming The Beast (Purgatory, Book 3)
- Deal with the Devil (Purgatory, Book 4)

- The Beasts Inside (Purgatory, Books 1 to 4)

Bound Series

- Bound By Blood (Bound Book 1)
- Bound In Darkness (Bound Book 2)
- Bound In Sin (Bound Book 3)
- Bound By The Night (Bound Book 4)
- Forever Bound (Bound, Books 1 to 4)
- Bound in Death (Bound Book 5)

Made in the USA
San Bernardino, CA
08 April 2018

Let's D

Written and photographed by Arthur Kingdon

Collins

I love to dive.

Some divers do it just for fun. Some study sea life. And some look for lost ships.

I take my camera when I dive. I've been to many coasts and seen many things, from big sharks to the smallest fish.

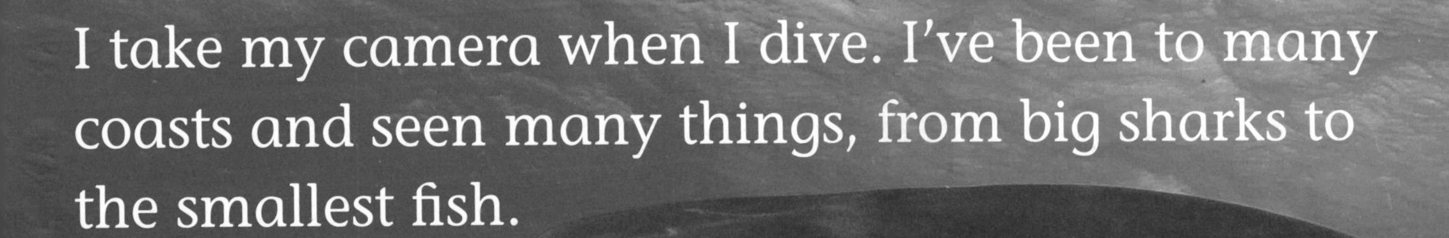

But some of my best dives are in the UK. Come and see life in the British seas.

Divers need a lot of kit.

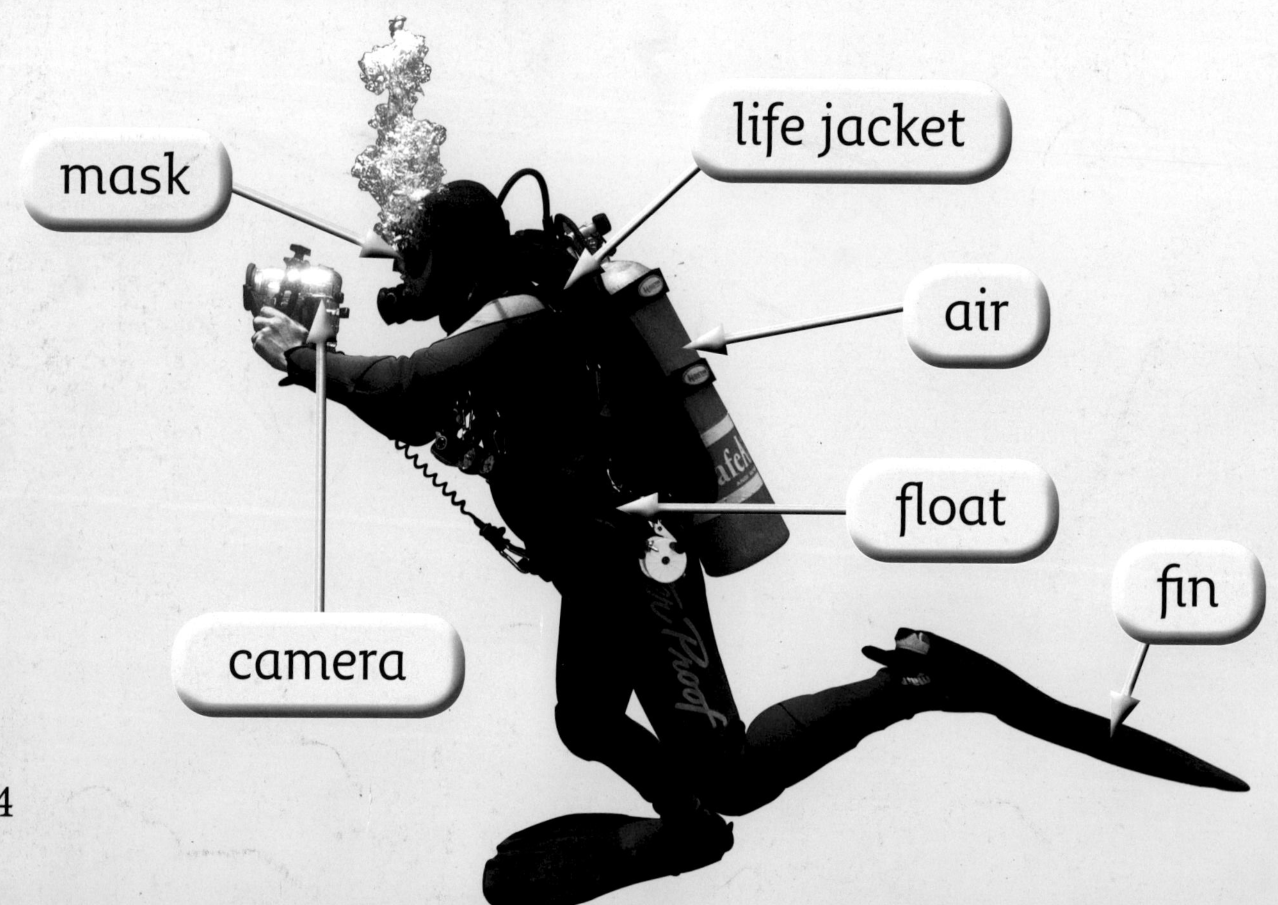

When I dive from a boat, my float shows the boat where I am.

The boat flies a flag to tell ships that there are divers in the sea.

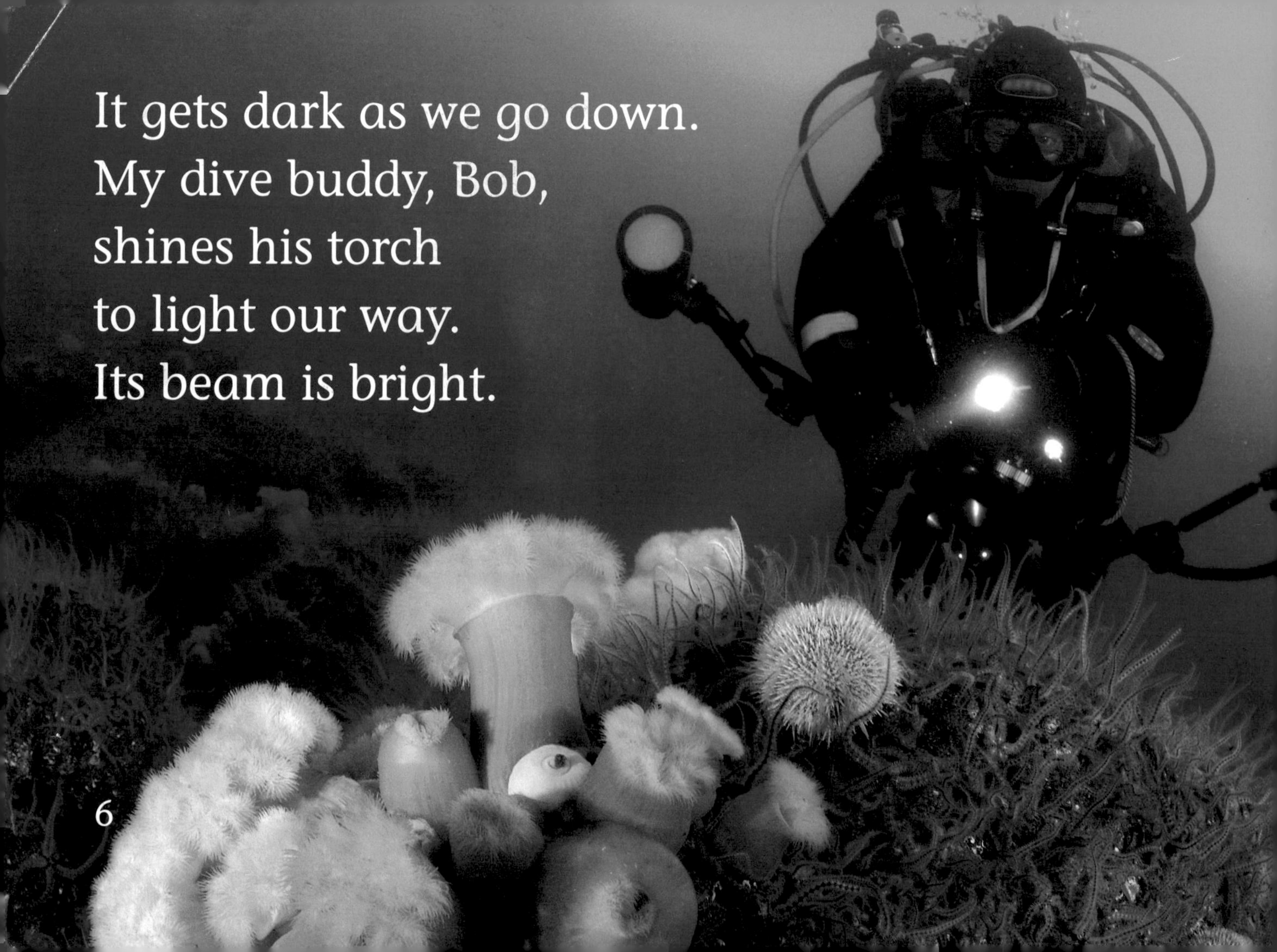

It gets dark as we go down.
My dive buddy, Bob,
shines his torch
to light our way.
Its beam is bright.

Some fish
are shy.
This pair stare
at us from a gap in
the rocks. Their strong
teeth can crunch up
crabs and shellfish.

The jellyfish floats and sways.
There are small fish
trailing behind it.
The fish feel
safe there.

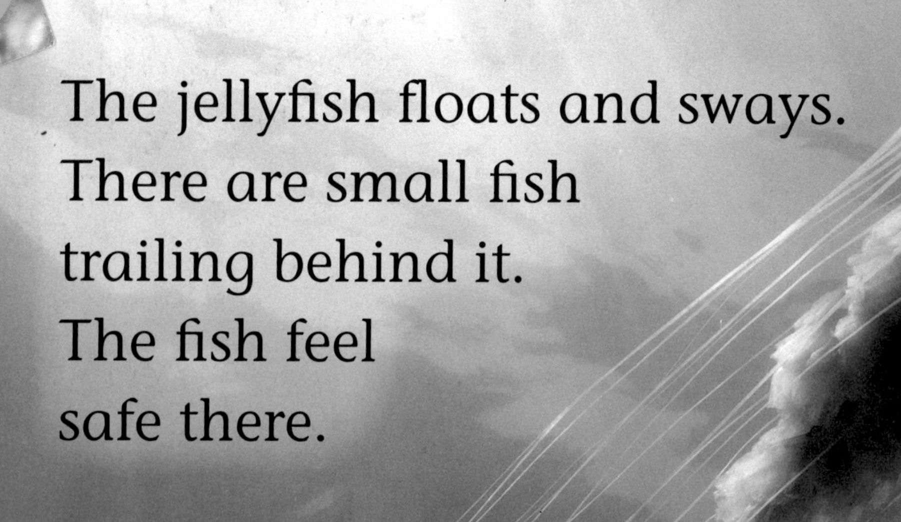

Look out! The jellyfish
has a nasty sting.

Meeting seals
is always fun.
This one is
just a pup.
She tries to
play a game
with us
by grabbing
my fins.

Cuttlefish are amazing. They can squirt jets of ink. This cuttlefish takes a long look at us before swimming away.

This fish is
a tompot blenny.
It lives inside
a broken pipe.
It's hard to
spot as it
blends in with
its home.

Each dive brings something new. I might get right up close. Or stay back to enjoy the sight of a shoal of fish swooping and darting.

lobster

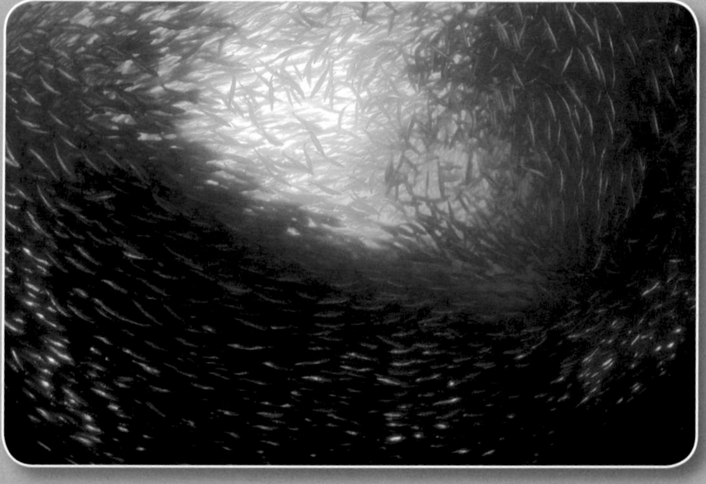

herring

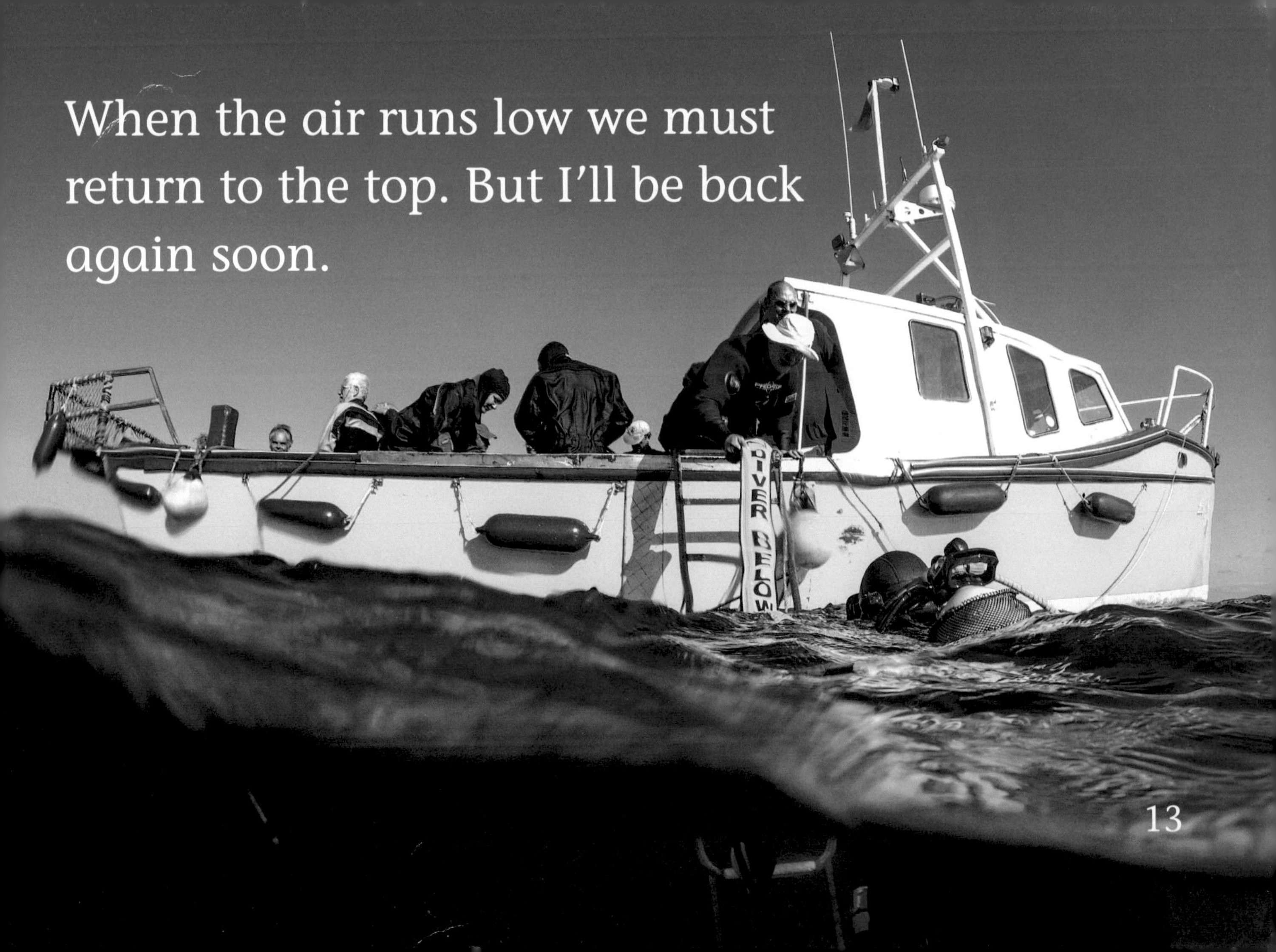

When the air runs low we must return to the top. But I'll be back again soon.

Sea life

jellyfish

cuttlefish

seal

tompot blenny

Index

Written by Clare Dowdall, PhD
Lecturer and Primary Literacy Consultant

Learning objectives: *(reading objectives correspond with Blue band; all other objectives correspond with Purple band)* apply phonic knowledge and skills as the prime approach to reading unfamiliar words that are not completely decodable; read more challenging texts which can be decoded using their acquired phonic knowledge and skills, along with automatic recognition of high frequency words; draw together ideas and information from across a whole text; explain organisational features of texts, including alphabetical order, layout, diagrams, captions, hyperlinks and bullet points; explain ideas and processes using imaginative and adventurous vocabulary and non-verbal gestures to support communication

Curriculum links: Science, Geography

Focus phonemes: i-e, ea, air, ow, igh, a-e, ay, ai, o-e, oy, oa

Fast words: some, there, their, jellyfish, seal, cuttlefish, blenny, lobster, herring

Resources: whiteboard, pencils, paper

Word count: 276

Getting started

- Discuss with the group what they think diving is and what people need to wear when they dive. Look at the front cover together. Ask children to suggest what it would be like to dive deep in the sea, and whether they would like to try it.
- Read the title and turn to the blurb. Explain that the apostrophe in *Let's* replaces a missing letter and that the title is an abbreviation of *Let Us Dive*.
- Read the blurb with the children and ask them to suggest what the diver will find when he dives in the sea. List each point on the whiteboard.

Reading and responding

- Turn to pp2–3. Model reading the text to the group, using phonics knowledge to decode words with long vowel sounds, e.g. *dive, sea*. Remind children of the split digraph patterns *i-e* and *a-e* and how to read them.
- Discuss who is recounting the information and help children to notice that this is a personal recount and an information book.